AT NIGHT ALL CATS ARE GREY
and other stories

AT NIGHT
ALL CATS ARE GREY

and other stories

by

PATRICK BOYLE

GROVE PRESS, INC., NEW YORK

To the memory of
BRENDAN BEHAN
for his help and encouragement

ACKNOWLEDGEMENTS

Some of the stories in this collection first appeared in the following: *Threshold, Evergreen Review, Kilkenny Magazine, Irish Times, New Writing, Sewanee Review,* and the *Dubliner. Meles Vulgaris* first appeared in the *Irish Times* and was included in *Winter's Tales* (Macmillan).

The author would also like to thank Frank Harvey, Una Troy, John Boyle and Benedict Kiely.

CONTENTS

Oh, Death Where Is Thy Sting-Aling-Aling?

PERHAPS if he had not delayed in the Glen Tavern on the way home he might have been in time. But there it was. Who could blame him for trying to wash away the taste of the Fair Day whiskey dished up by the pious publicans of the village to their country customers? Hadn't he been rinsing the same taste out of his mouth once a month for the past fifty years or more? Whatever about it, by the time he got within sight of the house it was to find every window lit up and a small group of neighbours already gathered round the door.

It came as no great shock to him for she had been ailing so long and been anointed so many times that they had all given up hope long since. Even so this sudden brutal invasion of the present by the future was an outrage to be resented. He straightened his shoulders, drew himself up to his full bantam stature and walked the last few yards of the laneway with caution, the drink dying in him with every step. By the time he reached the door he was able to shake the outstretched hands in sober silence and nod grave acknowledgement to the mumbled:

'Sorry-for-your-trouble.'

They moved awkwardly aside to let him pass as a woman's voice was heard to call:

'Here he is now, Annie.'

The rush of footsteps, the placid face ravished with grief, the low accusing voice: scattered his hastily-contrived excuses.

'Where were you, father? Where were you at all? Poor

11

Mother dying and you not to be found before 'twas too late.'

He put up a hand to silence her.

'When did it happen, Annie?' he asked.

'A good two hours ago,' she said. 'I was making a drop of tea for myself and I heard a noise in the room. It was only the mercy of Providence I peeped in. Michael had just time to go for the priest before she died. You should think shame of yourself,' she said.

His face crumpled up suddenly, lips quivering, eyes tightly shut, like a scolded child. She stepped forward and gave him a quick hug.

'Poor Father,' she said. 'Don't be taking it too much to heart. Sure even if you had been here it would have made no differ for she knew no one at the end.'

Turning, she started ahead of him up the stairs, saying over her shoulder:

'She went very quietly at the finish. The priest said he never saw an easier death.'

In the bedroom the women were nearly finished laying her out. One was threading the rosary beads through the clasped fingers, another brushing and arranging the white silky hair so that it fluffed out over the immaculate pillow slip, a third straightening the bedclothes. They stood back as the old man moved to the bed.

He blessed himself and knelt at the bedside, burying his face in his hands. He tried to pray but the simple phrases, worn smooth with use, refused to mesh. Obstinately he kept repeating: 'Hail Mary full of grace' but the rest of the prayer eluded him. He pressed his hands to his ears to shut out all sound and strove to project the words on the darkened screen of his closed eyelids. It was of no avail—only blobs of protean colour floated before his eyes. In his distress he shook his head in a violent gesture of rebuttal like a player desperately rattling the dice-box. Behind him the women glanced at each other significantly, one of them saying in a loud carrying whisper:

" Poor man, he'll not be long after her. He's taking it woeful bad. Far too attached to each other they were.'

At length the old man got to his feet. He stood gazing down with a bewildered expression at the unfamiliar austere countenance.

' She's very like herself, isn't she?' his daughter asked. ' Not a day over fifty she looks.'

He turned to face her.

' Aye,' he said. ' She's like herself all right.'

His puzzled gaze shifted from one to another of the pitying faces.

' Very young-looking surely,' he said.

Annie took him gently by the arm.

' There's a fire in the parlour,' she said. ' You might as well sit there till the crowd starts to come.'

The unfamiliar appearance of the parlour, with the chairs pushed back against the walls and the table stripped of its green plush bobbled cloth, jolted him into awareness.

' Where's Michael?' he asked abruptly.

' Gone down to the village,' she said. ' He's making arrangements about the funeral.'

' Is he seeing to the needs of the wake?'

She ran through the list in her own mind—sugar, tea, ham, butter, bread, cigarettes, snuff.

' He is, Father.'

' Where's he getting the drink from? He'd want to watch they don't give him the Fair Day brew.'

' We talked it over, Michael and myself, and we thought it best to have no drink at the wake. After the Parish Priest giving off about it from the altar.'

His face flushed up and his bushy eyebrows drew down **threateningly.**

13

'There's no one going to tell me what to do in my own house,' he said. 'The clergy can drink their fill at every Conference or Month's Mind and dare anyone criticise. But still they'll try and lay down the law for me and the likes of me.'

'Now, Father,' she said. 'You know fine well he was referring to the wake in Gartan. Where they fought half the night and the Guards had to be sent for.'

He lifted the poker and commenced prodding fretfully at the fire.

'We'll be thought a right mean crop of weeds. The talk of the parish,' he muttered, but his voice lacked conviction and he soon dropped the poker to relapse into apathy.

As the night wore on and the wake-house gradually filled, he came to life. But it was a purely clock-work life. As each new figure appeared at the parlour door he would get to his feet and, like a mechanical toy, travel the constricted path to the outstretched hand and the inevitable greeting:

'Sorry-for-your-trouble.'

It was a clock-work greeting, just as his automatic: ' 'Tis the will of God,' came from a similar uncoiling spring.

Punctiliously he fetched fresh fuel for the fire, brought in extra chairs, handed round the saucers of cigarettes and snuff at regular intervals to the mourners.

Every so often he would get up and go into the kitchen, traditionally the preserve of the men-folk. There he moved round the circle of chairs, shaking hands with the occupants, listening gravely to the expressions of sympathy and murmuring, like the responses in a litany:

' 'Tis the will of God. The road we all must travel.'

Or if some mourner, rendered speechless by drink, mouthed a dumb pity, he would nod his head and say:

'I understand, James. Thank you for your sympathy.'

At last the round of greetings completed, he would move out again, leaving behind him a wash of whispered comment:

'The poor man is taking it badly.'

'A very devoted couple they were.'

'He'll not survive her long.'

'Sure he must be near eighty, if he's a day.'

Out in the hallway he would wander over to the card-table where a neighbour-woman sat recording in a school exercise book the offerings of those who would be unable to attend the funeral. Over her shoulder he read the list of names and amounts, comparing them mentally with the offerings he himself had given over their dead relatives in the long years gone by. The mounting pile of notes and coin, indicating as it did, the solid standing and well-thought-of-ness of himself and his family, gave him a measure of comfort and satisfaction, winding up once more the clock-work mechanism that now sent him padding up the stairs, to stand outside the open door of the corpse-room, nodding silent greetings at the women so crowded around the big double bed that there was little space for newly-arrived mourners to kneel in prayer or in curiosity.

At the sight of his dazed expression the women would sway towards each other like heavy-headed flowers and whisper:

'He'll never get over it, poor fellow.'

'The shock will kill him surely.'

Back in the parlour despite the heated stuffy room, the constant hum of conversation, the drowsiness induced by the few drinks, now nothing but a dry-mouthed memory, he managed to appear attentive and alert until called by Annie at midnight for the customary prayers in the corpse-room. Kneeling at the head of the bed, he commenced giving out the rosary but so full of sleep was he that, at the first decade of the Sorrowful Mysteries, he continued yawning Hail Marys until, at the twelfth one, his son Michael, silenced him with a hasty Glory be to the Father.

The rosary finished, Annie shooed him off to bed with the excuse that: 'Someone has to be fit to rise the morrow.' She

herself stayed up till morning, serving tea in the kitchen to
relays of mourners, making the all-night vigil at the wake.

* * *

Next day the old man spent most of the morning in the corpse-
room only leaving it to avoid the few early callers at the wake-
house. He had no stomach left for the glib routine of sympathy. All he wanted was the chance to sit, alone and undis-
turbed, watching, studying, perhaps eventually accepting this
austere stranger who, like a cuckoo-bird, had ousted the gentle
familiar occupant of his bed.

In the still, stifling air, with door and window closed, the
two blessed candles burned clear and unwavering, their yellow
glow outshining the daylight banked up behind the drawn
blind. The tang of burning wax, the breathless air, the sleek
well-fed shadows cast by the candle flames, soothed him in the
same way as did an empty darkening church, lit only by the
red glow of the sanctuary lamp.

He pulled his chair in closer to the bed. The soft candle-
light dealt kindly with the remote severity of death, lending
the pallid features a fleeting illusion of life, as if somewhere in
that inert figure a tiny core of vitality still lurked, needing
only the coaxing of a stubborn love to burgeon once more into
growth. He was tempted to believe that under the waxen skin
a pulse of life still beat; that the urgent blood continued its
relentless merry-go-round; that perhaps his own shallow
breathing masked the sound of another fainter breathing.

On a sudden impulse he got to his feet and pulled up the
lowered blind. Garish daylight burst into the room, sending
the shadows scuttling, thinning to transparency the solid
candle-flames. The merciless sunshine flayed the figure in the
bed of every vestige of grace and dignity. The white hair
fluffed out on the pillow no longer shone with rich abundant

lustre: instead the dry scanty locks, skilfully though they were arranged, failed to conceal the dandruffed scalp. The skin had lost its borrowed glow and become dull as putty. Vulture-beaked by death, the nose sniffed in narrow-nostrilled disdain as if disgusted at its own hateful carrion reek. The thin lips, tidily closed, were cruel, intolerant, contemptuous. Hiding their malice under hooded lids, the eyes peered out, sly, unseen.

The smooth expanse of coverlet from the clasped hands to the up-jutting feet was so flat and taut that it seemed to cover nothing but the mattress. Surely, he thought, the long illness could not have wasted away her body till there was left of it only a sheet-flattened outline. The little figure huddled up hedgehog-like on her own side of the bed, with maybe just the two big eyes peeping over the sheet, so that she looked like some small wary creature—lizard or mouse perhaps— was far removed from this malevolent brown-shrouded court-card, slapped down contemptuously on the middle of the board by a greedy unfeeling gulpin of a Card-player.

Annie's horrified voice failed to rouse him.

'What in God's name are you doing with the blind up?'

Without waiting for an answer she rushed across to the window. When she turned round to face the once-more dark-ened room he was still standing over the bed, his face creased up in a puzzled frown. He looked so old, so lost, so tiny and shrivelled up with loneliness that the anger died in her.

'You'll have to stop fretting after her,' she said gently. 'It does no good. It's the last thing poor Mother—wish her rest —would have wanted.'

She took him by the hand and led him like a child from the room.

All afternoon he prowled moodily around the house unable to content himself anywhere for long. At length around tea-time he suggested to Annie that it might be as well to send to the village for supplies. Whilst she was making out the list of groceries required, the old man called Michael aside.

'Your sister is a right pooshey,' he said. 'The clergy have the living daylights frightened out of her. She thinks we'll be read off the altar if there's as much as the smell of a cork at the wake.'

'She's maybe right, Father.'

'Would you listen to that! You're every bit as bad as she is. Do you think they'll put horns on you?'

'I only meant to say . . .'

'Maybe you'd rather have us the laughing stock of the entire parish? If we aren't that already after last night. A house full of mourners and nothing to offer them but a sup of tea.'

'But, Father . . .'

'Pay attention to me now, boy. You'll call into the hotel when you're in the village, and you'll get half a dozen bottles of whiskey—the best they've got. You'll get a couple of cases of stout, making damned well sure it's not the Fair Day bottling. There'll be no porter posing as stout in this house if I can help it. And if you come back empty-handed, as God is my judge, I'll go down to the village myself and I mightn't be in too much of a hurry coming back.'

The old man waited impatiently for Michael's return. As if on purpose Annie kept waylaying him. Buttering me up, he thought, with a lot of old soft talk for fear I'd go on the booze. It would be the price of her if I did. Just the same he was careful not to annoy her and he was actually holding an animated talk with her about the respective merits of devotion to Our Lady of Lourdes or to Our Lady of Perpetual Succour when he heard the sound of the car stopping at the foot of the laneway. He broke off in mid-sentence.

'I better go and give a hand with the parcels,' he said,

making for the door. He hesitated long enough to see her go upstairs, then headed up the lane. He met Michael carrying a case of stout.

'She's upstairs.' he whispered. 'Get everything into the pantry before she comes down. And go quietly.'

Until all was stowed away he stayed fussing around, keeping a watchful eye on the stair-head. He was sitting innocently in the parlour when Annie put in an appearance.

'You won't give out the drink until after the rosary, Father?' she asked.

His eyebrows rose in astonishment.

'What drink?' he said.

'Now, Father, you surely didn't think the clatter of the bottles went unbeknownst?'

He jumped to his feet.

'And what harm is there if there is drink itself?' he said. 'We must try to keep our good name in the parish.'

'But you'll do as I asked?' she persisted. 'No drink till after the rosary?'

Too late she realised the trap she had sprung. Before she could change ground he had pounced.

'Are you putting me under rule of bail?' he demanded, hardly able to keep the relish out of his voice. 'Wouldn't you think the licensing laws are stiff enough without extending them to the very dwelling-houses?'

He drew a deep breath.

'I'll do as I see fit,' he hissed.

Stalking out of the room, he made straight for the pantry where he helped himself to a good jorum of whiskey. As he tossed it back he muttered to himself:

'The women, they're a total terror. They'd drive a man to drink.'

Once launched, however unwillingly, on an alcoholic course, he felt it his bounden duty to keep afloat. So the rest of the evening he spent, not in the parlour as on the previous night, but in the kitchen with the men-folk. Here, near the supply base, where the refilling of the saucers with cigarettes provided the opportunity of a quick drink he became mellow and talkative.

He spoke to everybody, moving to a fresh seat each time a chair became vacant, holding forth on the weather, the state of the crops, the uncertainty of the cattle trade, the latest stupidity of the Department men. More and more he forgot his duties as the head of a bereaved household. He would become so engrossed in a conversation with his neighbour that he would glare impatiently at a mourner who had ventured to interrupt with his condolences. A newcomer to the wake-house might stand a full five minutes at the kitchen door before his presence was noticed. By the time Annie arrived to announce the start of the rosary the old man's absorption in his own concerns was complete. As the company trooped upstairs to the corpse-room someone was heard to mutter:

' If you ask me, his lordship has a brave sup taken.'

The rosary over and the men back in the kitchen, the old man himself poured out the first round of drinks. Every person was given a glass of whiskey and an uncorked bottle of stout, the old man contenting himself with a stiff measure of whiskey in a willow-pattern cup.

The ritual for drinking never varied. The initial glass of whiskey was raised to eye level. Across its brim a long stare of silent sympathy was directed at the bereaved. Then with either a drawn-out: ' Wellllll ! ! !' signifying a meek submission to the Will of the Almighty, the acceptance of the Theory of Vanity and the pious acknowledgement that things will surely be worse before they are better or a crisp questioning: ' Well!' which meant: ' Down the hatch and God grant you a heavier hand with the next one,' the drink was tossed back.

Meanwhile, centre-piece of the puppet show, the old man

sat in silence gazing into his cup of malt which he swirled around chalice-like before tipping it up in a single raw ceremonial gulp.

The succeeding drinks, dished out by Michael, were more informal, some of the company settling down to a steady diet of stout, others sticking, like the old man, to the hard tack. As the night wore on and the drink began to take effect, he became loud and aggressive.

Coughing harshly to gain attention, he would sweep the company with an augur's eye until the silence was complete.

'It will come to all of us some time,' he would prophesy, wagging his empty cup in a hieratic gesture. 'The big fellow and the small. The wealthy rancher sitting on his rump and the peasant grubbing at his hungry acre. The priest and the shop-keeper. 'Tis ordained and laid down.'

'Michael!' he shouted.

'Yes, Father?'

The old man's outstretched arm circled the room in a stately traffic signal, an accusing finger pointing at the empty glasses.

Or he might say, his voice quavering with emotion:

'It's a cruel world, men. When you're happy and contented and harming no one, wouldn't you think you'd be left in peace for the wheen of years remaining? Oh, the old saying is right: "Never bless your lot or you'll live to sup sorrow with a spoon of grief." The Will of God is wicked hard to put up with sometimes.'

'Michael!'

Again the wide urbi-et-orbi sweeping gesture.

Once he broke the silence with a cryptic utterance:

'Give a man your coat and he'll take shirt and trousers forby.'

To all these statements the men chorused respectfully: 'You're quite right.'

'It's before us all.'

'You never said a truer word.'

Then the heads would swivel round again and the whisper go side-mouthed the round of the room:

'Sure the poor fellow's near mad with grief.'

'Fifty years married next month, they say.'

'Like Darby and Joan they were—it'll kill him surely.'

At length the old man began to show signs of extreme drunkenness. No longer did he act the part of expansive host. Instead he held out his empty cup.

'Wheeshky!' he demanded.

Michael attempted to fob him off with stout but he sent the bottle flying out of his hand.

'Swill!' he pronounced. 'Swill! A proper pig's drink. Wheeshky, I said.'

Provided with a cupful of watered-down sherry, he grasped it two-handed, lapping it up greedily like a calf at a bucket of milk. Placing the empty cup carefully on the table behind him, he wheeled around and glared aggressively at the circle of men from squinting, bloodshot eyes. He pushed himself to his feet, pendulating drunkenly, saliva drooling from his mouth, his arms dangling stupidly. From side to side his head moved constantly, his angry unseeing stare settling fortuitously on some unfortunate neighbour. He was for all the world like an old scraggy balding eagle crouched over its prey. This impression was strengthened by the faint ganderine hissing—the only sound that issued from his struggling lips.

The words broke through at last coming in carefully articulated sequence, like someone negotiating a river ford, jumping from stone to stone, pausing on each rock to gather strength for the next leap.

'All me days . . .' he proclaimed. 'I've been a farmer . . . a farmer, a swamper, a con-acre man . . .' There was a pause after this long difficult leap. He began again. 'I'm the son . . .

of a bare-footed reaper . . . that couldn't call . . . a rood of
land his own.' His knees started to buckle under him. He
commenced to topple forward to the ground, still in full cry.
' I've never said . . . a wrong word . . . or done a wrong turn
. . . to heathen or Christian . . . in all me living life.' By this
time he was on his hands and knees on the floor, his head
twisted upwards to face the astonished mourners. But he was
on the far bank of the river. Now each word came out with
the force of a sling shot. ' And . . . darr . . . any . . . man
say . . . otherwise.' A drunken witless Nebuchadnezzar, guzzled
with grass, the green drool hanging from his muzzle, bellowing defiance at his tormentors.

Michael rushed to his aid. Gripping him by the oxters he
pulled the old man to his feet but the rubbery legs would
not sustain the weight of the limp helpless body. The knees
gave way, the rump sagged, the entire carcase folded up like
a Chinese lantern. Even with the assistance of a neighbour.
it looked as if the old man would have his two arms pulled
from their sockets before he was dragged to bed. Eventually
he was hoisted on to Michael's shoulders and carried pick-a-
back up the stairs, with his toe-caps bumping noisily at every
step.

Behind them in the kitchen the jury were bringing in their
verdict:

' 'Twas the stuffy room did it.'

' He collapsed from the heat poor man.'

' Sure t'would smother a horse, never mind a Christian.'

' He'd be the better for a good night's rest, the crayther.'

It was left to Annie, bustling in with an armful of turf
for the fire, to pronounce judgment:

' Poor Father, Mother's death has knocked the heart out of
him altogether. I dunno will he ever get over it.'

* * *

At Night All Cats Are Grey

Sitting in the front seat of the chapel at the Requiem Mass next morning, the old man found it impossible to concentrate on any form of prayer or devotion. His thoughts kept whirling around like a moth spiralling a lamp.

Would the rain hold off till the burial was over? It would make a right hames of the graveyard if there came a downpour. Though God knows a wee sup of rain would lay the dust. It was thrown up so thick you couldn't count the funeral cars. But surely if there was one there was a hundred. Would Michael have ordered enough dinners at the hotel for all those coming a distance? A poor enough thing it would be if some of them had to travel back home on an empty stomach.

' Ooooooooohhhhhh-rate fratres,' intoned the priest, turning to face the congregation.

—He sounds well pleased with himself. And small wonder when he sees the crowd packing the church. He's mebbe figuring out in his own mind what the take will come to. It'll be a right haul anyway when they make the divide. (Two for himself and one for the curate, they say). It could very well turn out to be the biggest funeral ever held in the parish. Wasn't there twenty-seven odd pounds of offerings already lifted in the wake-house. Take care but it will top the hundred when it's all collected and added up. And why not? For a lifetime hadn't he himself paid offerings over every death in the parish? Hadn't he relations the length and breadth of the county?

The consecration bell sounded and he bowed his head on his hands. Through parted fingers he studied the trestled coffin, loaded with wreaths and Mass Cards.

—There was surely the guts of thirty, mebbe even forty cards in that heap. At ten shillings a time—and you'd get no priest to say a Mass for less—that was twenty good-looking pounds. No mean effort. And the wreaths. How many were there?

He commenced to count but stopped almost at once.

—The breastplate on the coffin! He had felt all along that something had been left undone. He was right. No one had checked the inscription on the breast-plate. For all they knew it could be the wrong plate altogether commemorating God-knows-who, died God-knows-when, aged God-knows-what.

Overcome by the burden of his worry and grief, he remained with bowed head and eyes tight-shut against the clamouring loneliness and self-pity threatening his resolution. Not till Mass was over was he able to regain control of himself.

When the sacristy door closed after the priest, he sat up with the rest of the congregation and watched whilst a table and chair were placed outside the altar rails. The Master took his seat and commenced the reading of the offerings gathered at the wake-house. Already familiar with the list, the old man sat unheeding and waited for the silence that betokened the end of the prologue. When it came, he rose to his feet, walked to the table and placed on it his contribution. As he returned to his seat he heard the Master announce:

'The family of the deceased—five pounds.'

There was a great shuffling of feet as the gathering moved out into the aisle and began to file past the table, in the van the relatives of the deceased. The Master called out:

'James Drohan, Creeve—one pound.'

'Charles Drohan, Glenbarren—one pound.'

'Edward Maher, Meenalargan—one pound . . .'

The relatives dealt with, the Master commenced to call out the donations of the general public. The old man sat up very straight, hand cupped to ear, listening attentively to the tally of the offerings.

'Michael Dempsey, Gartan—ten shillings.'

'John Wall, Meenalargan—ten shillings.'

'James Coffey, Largymore—five shillings . . .'

He tried to keep a running tot of the mounting collection

but soon lost count and gave himself up to the task of tracking down any unfamiliar name.

'Patrick Healy, Kilmeadon—five shillings.'

—Kilmeadon. That's to the north of the county. Very likely a friend of the wife's people.

'Vincent Corrigan, Feeney—two and sixpence.'

—If it's one of the Corrigans from beyond the Gweebarra it's little enough. Wasn't there ten shillings given over his father in Glen chapel not five years ago? And a like sum over his uncle that was killed in the quarry blast?

'Kevin Farrelly, Grange—five shillings.'

—Now who would that be? It must be that poor devil that was abroad in America when his people died. They say when he came home he couldn't resurrect the list of offerings and now he must pay at every funeral for fear he would offend somebody.

At last the offerings came to an end in a dribble of half-crowns. The Master commenced to count the take. The old man fixed his gaze on the tabernacle door, hurling his prayers against its bland gleaming surface but all the time his ears were assailed by the rustle and clink of notes and coin so that finally he gave up all attempts at prayer. Like the rest of the congregation he sat back waiting impatiently for the announcement of the total offerings. By this time the priest had returned from the sacristy. Kneeling on a prie-dieu, his nose propped on the knuckles of his clasped hands, his gaze trained in studious indifference on the snake-crushing foot of a gaudy plaster Patrick, he too waited the final tally.

At the last coin chink, he rose to his feet and took his stand at the altar rails where he remained until the Master handed him the pencilled total.

'On behalf of my curate and myself,' he began, laying the exercise book carefully on the marble rail and clasping his hands once more at chest level, 'I wish to thank you for the

generous offerings you have given today, the total amount
subscribed being . . .' he paused dramatically, ' one hundred
and twenty-three pounds five shillings.'

When the rustling had died down, he continued:

' Your generosity is a magnificent tribute to the many virtuous qualities of the deceased. Truly she could be described
in the homely language of our rugged country-side as a
" walking saint ". No one will ever know the extent of her
charity, for her good deeds were performed—as all good deeds
should—by stealth. She was a tireless worker and a ready
giver, whether her help was sought for parochial purposes, or
her aid enlisted in the wider sphere of the propagation of the
faith. Many a missionary father, toiling in the heat of the
African jungle, bringing the priceless gift of the true faith to
countless thousands, owes part of his education and training
in the priesthood to the assistance of this unselfish great-
hearted soul. She was constant in the performance of her
religious duties, her piety and devotion setting an example
for the parish. A zealous member of the Sacred Heart Sodality,
the Confraternity of the Children of Mary and the Altar
Society, her death will be a severe blow to these bodies. To
my certain knowledge, she never raised her voice in anger
nor said an unkind word . . .'

The old man sat with closed eyes, his bruised emotions
anointed and assuaged by the honeyed unction of the funeral
panegyric. What matter that he had so often anathematised
it as a scandalous hypocrisy, quoting acidly the local maxim:
' Big money, big talk!' On this occasion, he felt sure, the
priest meant every word he said. There was no mistaking the
ring of sincerity in his voice.

' . . . But all this devoted labour in the vineyard of Christ
would have been impossible without the fruitful background
of a truly Catholic family, consecrated to the love and service
of God and His holy Church. The sorrowing members of

this bereaved family I would therefore recommend to your charitable prayers.'

The priest paused and shook out a rosary.

' We will now say a decade of the holy rosary for the happy repose of the soul of the deceased. Oooouuuurrrr Father . . .'

The decade finished, the priest commenced the burial service, circling the coffin with swinging thurible, sprinkling it with holy water, murmuring soft Latin phrases that disguised their terrible prophetic content of misery and calamity. Beguiled with smoke of incense and sonorous incantation the old man knelt, head bowed on hands, his shallow breathing loud through his open mouth.

Still in the same numbed stupor he walked in the shuffling procession to the cemetery where, standing at the edge of the open grave, he watched dry-eyed the grave-diggers pay out the jerking coffin-bands till the strain ceased.

A gale was blowing in from the sea, a bitter south-west wind that had herded across a thousand miles of ocean a drove of sleek Atlantic rollers and now, land-bound, its vigour unabated seemed intent on ripping out the sedge-grass and hump-backed bushes that somehow managed to thrive on the barren stony soil of the western seaboard. It blew the comfortless alien words back into the priest's mouth and whirled away the sweet-scented smoke from the clanking thurible. It came in gusts, whistling and whining through the scrawny trees bordering the cemetery, chopping to bits and scattering wholesale the thud of clay on hollow wood: the scraping, raking, rattling of shovelled earth and stone, the tiny whimper of someone sobbing. It blew to the hungry nostrils of the departing priest the fragrance of the steak and kidney pie simmering on the kitchen range. It blew graveyard dust and spatters of rain over the huddled mourners, till they ran for shelter with streaming eyes and hunched shoulders. It only drew breath when the shovel-blades commenced the tidy tamping down of the mounded soil. But by this time there remained only a handful of relatives to shiver at the clipped finality of the smacking blades.

* * *

Annie did not know whether to be worried or relieved when her father allowed himself to be persuaded home as soon as the dinner in the hotel was over. Certainly it was a blessing that he had not made a public exhibition of himself as he had done the previous night, but she would have felt happier if he were not so obviously and so determinedly sober. His customary method of coping with trouble or misfortune was to get blind drunk, staying soaked in liquor until the cause of his unhappiness was as unimportant as a once-aching tooth. It was a cowardly way to face trouble, she had always thought, but in his case the system worked. That was its justification. At the end of his self-enforced purgatory he would emerge, a little ashamed perhaps, certainly very sick but able to face up once more to the demands of daily life.

This last cruel blow, however, seemed to have robbed him of his only defence against adversity—a headlong flight from reality. He sat now, crouched over the kitchen fire, eyelids drooping over rheumy eyes, cupped fingers clawing at his trouser legs—an old and feeble house-cat, whose tepid blood craved the heat of the smouldering turf. All evening she had tried to capture his interest, urging him out of his listless torpor.

' It's cleared up a nice day now,' she said. ' You should go as far as the Four Acres and take a look at the cattle. There's a few hours of daylight left.'

The old man did not stir.

' It'll be time enough the morrow,' he said.

' You told me you had it in mind to skull one of the heifer calves. Mebbe when Michael gets back . . .'

'Where's Michael?' he cut in.

'He's not back from the village yet,' she said.

He gripped the arms of the chair and made to rise.

'Better if I go down and see what's keeping him,' he said.

She looked down at him doubtfully.

'It's getting late,' she said. 'It'll be dark agin you get there. But whatever you think . . .'

She broke off, for he was once more slumped down in his chair staring dully into the heart of the fire.

He sat there in silence, until darkness set in. When Annie switched on the light he roused himself.

'I'll make for the bed, I think,' he said, yawning and stretching.

'You'd be doing the right thing, Father,' she said. 'You've had a long hard day of it.'

As he crossed the room she said, hesitantly:

'Michael said you could . . . sleep with him . . . tonight . . . if you . . .'

He turned and glared at her. He said:

"Where else d'you think I would sleep but in my own bed?'

She listened to his footsteps slowly mounting the stairs. The two days of the wake had taken the spring from his step, leaving him the shuffling gait of the truly vanquished. Upstairs the door clicked shut but almost at once re-opened.

'Annie!' he called.

She ran up the stairs, giving thanks to God that her father, stubborn and all as he was, had changed his mind about sleeping in the corpse-room.

At the open door she stopped. He was standing beside the bed, gazing down at the freshly-laundered pillows. Her hand flew to her mouth. My God! What had she been thinking of when she made the bed? Laying out two pillows side by side as if nothing had happened to make one of them superfluous.

He looked up.

'Did you call me, Father?' she asked.

'I hear the dog barking,' he said. 'Did you lock him up? You'll have him worrying the neighbours' sheep if you give him the habit of roaming after dark.'

'I did,' she said. 'But I'll go this minute and see if mebbe he has got out.'

Glad of the reprieve, she turned to go.

He went on as if she had not spoken:

'That was the last thing your poor mother—God be good to her—always did every night. Went out to the shed to make sure the dog was locked in securely. She had a shocking dread of rising trouble with the neighbours.'

He moved over to the window and stared out at the gathering night.

'A queer woman she was in many ways, your mother. If she got a notion into her head, not the devil himself could drive it out. Though, to do her justice, there was nearly always something to be said in their favour. These notions of hers.'

He paused and there was no sound but the gentle drumming of his knuckles on the window pane.

'But that figayrey she had,' he went on, 'about the blood leaving your head if you slept with it raised too high—that was one notion you'd find it hard to understand. A body, after all, spends the better part of his waking hours with his head as high as he can hold it. Unless he's a miserable hang-dog afeared to look you straight in the face.'

He paused again.

'She'd have had you sleeping with your head on the mattress, if she had had her way' he said.

'Still,' he said, in final judgment, 'she could be . . . could have been right.'

The jumbling of past and present scalded her eyes with tears.

'Would you like . . .' she began.

'Better see about the dog,' he interrupted, 'before it gets too dark.'

Back in the kitchen, after checking that the shed door was locked, she sat at the fire with an open book on her lap, seeing nothing on the printed page but the image of her father staring down at the empty bed. She wished she had had the strength of mind to insist on him sharing the bed with Michael instead of sleeping alone in his old room. Not that he would sleep much, she felt certain. He would lie, shivering and miserable between the cold crackling sheets, staring into the darkness, whilst the rising flood of loneliness broke over him, drowning him in waves of self-pity. Or else twitching and tossing in the big empty bed where once there had been warmth and company, the vacant pillow would at last bring home to him the full extent of his loss and, stricken with desolation, he would invoke divine comfort with prayer and pious ejaculation. She forced herself to wait a full twenty minutes before she crept upstairs and called softly through the closed door:

'Are you all right, Father?'

Getting no answer, she eased open the door. In the dim glow of the landing light she could see the huge bulk of the double bed but her own shadow, falling across the head of the bed, obscured all but the outlines of the tiny huddled-up figure. Crabways she edged across the floor until her shadow, like a theatre curtain, was drawn clear of the bed, disclosing its sleeping occupant.

He lay in the precise centre of the bed, knees drawn up to chin, cheek resting on outspread palm. His face, turned towards her, was curiously serene and childlike. He slept, too, with the complete abandonment of childhood, his breath coming in quick gentle sighs from the maw of the two fat heaped-up pillows into which his head was plunged.

As if sensing her presence, he came awake.

'What's wrong?' he asked, rubbing his eyes.

'I just looked in to see if you were all right,' she said.

He scowled up at her, his eyes squinting against the light.

'Are you gone clean demented?' he said. 'You had a right
to stay below in the kitchen instead of barging in here, disturbing a body's rest.'

Peevishly he slewed around, squirming deeper into the
mounded pillows and pulling the bed-clothes over his head.

She was closing the door when he called out to her, his
voice muffled by the blankets.

'And leave out me Wellingtons. The morrow'll be a day
for the bog, by the look of things.'

Go Away, Old Man, Go Away

A STING of heat was beginning to creep into the morning sun. Like a warm hand, it clamped down on the old man's scrawny neck as if it meant to push him down into the mounds of cut turf he was so busily spreading. It wormed its way through the layers of cardigans and undershirts, it scorched his meagre shrunken buttocks, it soaked through his boots so that his scalded feet chafed against the damp wrinkled socks. Sweat trickled down his face, smarting his eyes and salting his mouth, but he worked on steadily, rolling the heaped-up sods back through his straddled legs like a terrier rooting frantically at a burrow.

Stretched ahead of him to the bog-hole were rows of cut turf, lying in close-packed heaps just as they were heeled up by the barrowmen. The skin had barely formed on the spongy wet sods and often he had to ease them apart as though they were slabs of toffee. As he scrabbled and plucked and clawed, he kept up a continuous muttering grumble, punctuated by grunts of exertion.

His irritation was increased by the growling insistence of an empty stomach. Each time he stooped his guts would plunge madly around, whinnying like a horse fresh from the grass. Soon all minor grievances—his aching back, the heavy woollen drawers lacerating his fork, his scalded feet—all became blended into and seemed to increase the clamour of his empty belly. More and more frequently he paused, squatted down on his hunkers, glaring across the bog at the cottage on the roadside a few fields away. Once he saw someone come to the door and he straightened up, wiping his hands on his trousers while he waited for her to call him but she only took a look up the road and went in again.

The fowlman, he thought. I'll gamble a bob that's who she's keeping an eye out for. Damn the hait she cares if I die in my tracks with the hunger as long as she's there for the egg money. So help me God, I'd get more attention if I was a clocking hen. Dancing and jack-acting is all that one cares for. Oh, a nice stumer of a wife I let myself in for!

He started in, half-heartedly, to work again but soon gave it up.

'I'll not put up with it a day more,' he muttered.

He picked up his coat and started off up the deeply rutted track leading out of the bog.

By the time he reached the main road his temper had cooled and he began, as usual, looking for excuses for her. Maybe the fire had gone against her. Or she had to go for water. She was terrible sore on water, that one. Scrubbing at herself night, noon and morning. The smell of the soap trailing after her round the house till you'd nearly trip over it, it's that strong. He wrinkled his nose and sniffed. That time he had come on her, washing herself in the room. Standing there in her pelt with the pride and sleekness and grandeur shining out of her white skin like you'd see it in a blood mare. Admiring herself in the glass, no less. Posing and stroking and smirking at herself as if she were some class of a cat. My God, she could have been struck dead for less. And then rushing at him like a mad thing, spitting and cursing and slamming the door in his face. It had been that way from the start. Never letting him as much as put a hand next or near her. Cringing away from him in the bed as though he was a black stranger. He sighed. Well, it wouldn't last that way for ever. She would come round some time. He would just have to take her easy and thole a while longer.

He hesitated for a second on the porch, then cleared his throat and pushed in the door briskly.

'Are you aiming to starve me, girl?' he asked.

At Night All Cats Are Grey

There was no one there.

The kitchen floor was unswept; the table still littered with yesterday's dishes; the fire burned down to a few coals of turf. He unhooked the kettle swinging from the crane and shook it.

'Are you within there, woman?' he roared.

He heard the bed creak and the slow reluctant steps dragging along the floor. He shook the kettle again savagely.

'Motherajaysus, are ye still in yer bed?'

She came out of the room and stopped in the doorway, yawning and scratching her head—a fine strapping piece, bubbed and bottomed like a tinker woman, with oily jet-black hair, thick sensual lips and dark eyes, blurred and heavy with sleep. The dirty woollen-jumper, sweat-stained at the armpits, barely reached the rumpled partly-fastened skirt. Her bare legs were brown-blotched with the heat of the fire.

She yawned again and knuckled her eyes.

'I just threw myself on the bed a minute,' she said. 'Till the kettle would come to the boil.'

Speechless, he swung aloft the steaming kettle, as if he were exorcising her with a smoking thurible.

She stared at him, open-mouthed.

'What are you aiming to do with that thing?' She demanded.

She darted across the room.

'Give it here, man,' she said, trying to snatch the kettle from him.

He pushed her away roughly.

'Lookat here,' he said dramatically, tilting up the kettle over the hearth so that the few remaining drops went sizzling into the fire. 'Boiled to nothing.'

The sleep had gone out of her eyes: the listlessness from her body. Her sallow face was flushed and her thick lips pouted aggressively. But though her features were distorted with rage, there was about her a curious air of satisfaction as though the very volume of her emotion brought with it some measure of bodily fulfilment.

'Is it trying to quench the fire you are?' she asked.

'Quench be damned. Wouldn't a good spit smother it?'

'Maybe if you had the trouble of lighting it, you wouldn't be so quick—'

She broke off and, stooping, commenced heaping up the glowing embers with the tongs.

'Listen here, me young tit,' he said, addressing the swaying rump-filled skirt. 'It would fit you better if you stopped home at nights instead of roaming the country. You'll have the priest naming you yet from the altar.'

The strip of white flesh below her rucked-up jumper, winking at every movement, kept ogling him slyly.

'A man at my time of life slaving and sweating like a Turk while his wife goes trapeezing around the country to every bit of a dance or a card game that's held in the parish. Sure I must be the laughing stock of half Europe.'

His gaze travelled down to the creased hollows behind her knees.

'Letting a man off to his work without a bite to eat. Have you no shame in you?'

He moistened his flabby craving lips.

'The women . . . they're a terror . . . the same the world over . . . rising a mutiny wherever they be . . .'

He pushed out a tentative hand, but at once let it fall to his side and remained staring at her dumbly, his eyes sick and glazed with desire.

Across her shoulder she looked—taunting him with bold mocking eyes.

'Give over,' she said. 'It's the same ould tune—day in, day out. It's a wonder you took me at all, the way you go on.'

The old man struggled for speech.

'Ye-Ye-Ye-Ye're damned smart, aren't ye.'

Failing to think of any more crushing remark, he spat viciously into the heart of the fire and turned away. At the door he shouted back:

'And don't be the whole day getting me me bloody bit of breakfast.'

Outside, he squatted on the low window-sill—tired, hungry, emotionally deflated.

You common idiot, he told himself. Letting that one get the better of you with a few flirts of her backside and her stooping over the fire to give you a right view of her wherewithal. As if it wasn't sticking out like the side of a church at the best of times. Up half the night jack-acting and then basking the day long in her bed, snoring and grunting like a sow at the pigging. And across in the bog making slaughter of himself is no less a person than the boss of the house—the boss; how are you!—hugging his grinding puddings with sheer starvation. The impudent trollop, slooching around half-dressed, the bare ones scalded off her with the heat of the fire and the two elders swinging out of her like she was six months gone. God above, man, I don't know what you see in her.

The sun beat down on him, soaking him with listless warmth so that he sagged forward, his chin knuckle-propped, staring with drowsy cat-blinking eyes at the sweeping expanse of dun-coloured bog.

His eyes closed and the scraggy dewlap settled its folds deeper round his knuckled hands. From one nostril a green dangle of snot rattled out and in with each wheezing breath like the flickering tongue of a snake.

Her voice roused him.

'Did the fowl cart go by?'

He looked at her stupidly. Blobs of colour swayed and danced before his eyes. His legs and the back of his neck were stiff and sore.

'Henh?' he said, rinsing the foulness from his mouth with fresh-sucked spittle.

'I suppose you fell asleep and let him pass unbeknownst. Didn't you know I had three fat pullets ready waiting for him? He'll not be here again till next week.'

He noticed she had changed her clothes, put on stockings and brushed her hair.

'Aye, so,' he said.

'Well, can't you answer me anyway? Did you see e'er a sign of the fowlman?'

'Would that be why you were toveying yerself up instead of getting me me breakfast?'

'You'll get your breakfast time enough, never fret.'

'It's borne in on me that it's only when there's callers coming round the house that you take time to tidy yourself. Other times you're not so particular.'

She glowered down at him in sulky silence.

'If it's the fowlman or the post-boy or even a stinking ould tramp itself, you're into the room pulling and hauling at yourself. Wasting the day blethering to the likes of them but never a civil word for your own husband. Though God knows it's little enough to expect from you for the wheen of minutes you spend at home every day.'

'Is it staying at home at the fire I'd be? Listening to you nagging and backbiting? You'd scald the heart off of a saint with that bitter ould viper's tongue of yours. I'll go out of my mind if I have to listen to much more of it.'

He rasped his hand across his stubbly chin and gazed up at her with an air of patient resignation.

'That's right. That's right. I'm to blame for everything. It was me let the fire down. It was me kept you in your bed all morning. It's me hunts you out at night to the dances.'

He struck his knee with his fist.

'So-help-me-Jaysus, there was peace in this house till you

come into it. I'd a right to leave you stewing in misery where you were. A bit of a tin shanty with all the winds of the world whistling through the chinks and that so-called father of yours pasted to the bed, dragging his guts up and spitting them round the floor till you could bloody near skate on it. That's what I took you from. And let you never forget it, me girl.'

He knew as he finished that he had said too much.

Two quick steps brought her standing over him, her face mottled with rage.

'Throwing the like of that up in my teeth,' she said. 'I'm as well got as the most of them, if the truth were known. There was none of this talk when you were plastering over me to have you. Oh, you made promises then to no end! Telling me the fine easy life I'd have with all the money you'd saved. Well, it's easy to count what I've seen of it. If it weren't for the few ha'pence I get for the eggs I'd be in rags.'

She looked down contemptuously at him hunched up in misery on the window-sill.

'That your dirty money may choke you, you hungry old scaldcrow. I've a mind to pack my duds and clear out of here this minute.'

He heard her go inside and then the angry clatter of roughly handled dishes. After that—silence.

His heart missed a beat. Surely to God she was never in earnest. An awful desolation swept over him, leaving him sick and trembling.

He started to rise but stopped when he heard her voice. deep and husky, singing very low as if to herself:

> '*For an old man he is old*
> *And an old man he is grey.*'

He could picture her leaning across the table, head tilted back, eyes half-closed, a cool impudent smile on her face.

Go Away, Old Man, Go Away

> ' And an old man's nose is damp and cold
> Go away, old man, go away!'

Furtively he wiped the drop off his nose with the back of his hand. The venomous targe, he thought. There's no length she'll not go to bait me.

She was singing again. Louder and with a kind of a glad lilt to her voice.

> ' But a young man he is young
> And a young man he is gay
> And a young man's kiss will bruise your lips
> Come away, young man, come away!'

So that was it, by the Lord. That was how she spent her nights. Lurking in outhouses or sprawled her length at the back of a ditch or maybe under the dry arch of a bridge. With any one of a hundred young rams from the four quarters of the universe. Giving them what *he* should have been getting. The nights she'd slip out without a word and come back hours later with two glowing coals for eyes. Her cheeks flushed, her hair tossed. ' It's a grand windy night,' she'd maybe say and sit gazing into the fire with a queer twisted smile at the corner of her lips. Thinking back on the night's doings. Feeling the moist seeking lips and the groping hands roving her body. Hearing wild, whispered words and harsh breathing and maybe the sudden step on the road to put them cowering down with their hearts pounding. Seeing the whiteness of a face looming over her, strained and vicious.

And across the fire from her is sitting . . . himself. Blind to it all.

He closed his eyes to shut out the torturing vision but his relentless imagination kept on insinuating new and ever more humiliating possibilities.

How many? In God's name how many in the parish had

had her? Was there one at all he could look straight in the face and not be left wondering? Why, even that little brat she'd been on the look-out for all morning could have been . . .

He tried to thrust the thought away from him but it had taken root. Wasn't he nearly always out working when the cart called? Wouldn't he be down in the bog this minute only for she sleeping in? And wouldn't that little whelp be inside bargaining for the fowl with the whole house to himself?

The bitterness rose in his throat like a ball of puke.

It's too much, he thought. It's more than mortal man can stand.

He got to his feet and looked aimlessly about him. Something would have to be done. Things could not go on this way. Suddenly he started off towards the hen-house, muttering to himself:

' There'll be an end put to his capers.'

Unbarring the door he flung it open.

' Chook! Chook! Chook!' he called in a loud aggressive voice.

There was a flutter of startled wings and a raucous babble of excited cluckings.

He glanced over his shoulder apprehensively, then tried again, sinking his voice to a seductive whisper.

' Chooooook, chook, chook. Come on the little chookies.'

He rasped his fingers together enticingly.

They came scampering out, heads craned forward, wings tucked tight against bodies, as if they were skaters racing to reach him.

Grabbing the nearest bird by the neck, he squeezed tight with finger and thumb on its gullet. A few frantic wing flaps and he had hold of its legs, hauling on its neck like an archer bending a bow.

He flung the quivering body aside and called again.

'Chook. chook, chook. Oh, the poor wee chook-chooks.'

They stood around, eyeing him with a cagey stare, never budging an inch. Picking up a handful of gravel he shook it out on the ground.

Pushing, scrambling, they surged round him, pecking at the bare ground. This time he chose carefully—a fine fat pullet, larded with meat. He stooped down cautiously and picked it up, one hand pinioning the wings to the body, the other nipping the squawk rising in its thrapple. Holding it up before him, he watched the gaping beak and the frantic scampering legs.

'What hurry is on you, girl?' he said. 'You'll get to the pot soon enough.'

Its neck was hard to stretch and by the time he had finished the fowl had scattered. Only one remained, picking half-heartedly at a bedded stone.

It sidled away from him, neatly avoiding his clutch. Stooping, he followed it up, his hands outspread as if to impart a blessing but it slid from under them in little mincing spurts. At the gable end of the house he caught up with it and grabbed it by the legs. The accumulation of rage that had been festering in him all morning broke out at last.

'Ye little blirt,' he roared. 'I'll put manners on ye.'

He swung it up, flapping wings and squawing beak, and made pulp of it against the wall. He kept flailing away, although the bird's head was almost torn off. His face and hands were spattered with blood: the lime-washed wall red wealed. A fluffy nimbus floated over his head. In time with each welt, he ground out:

'I'll teach ye . . . to turn my house . . . into a bloody knocking shop.'

He heard her footsteps running around the house but paid no heed. It was the rough grip on his shoulder that brought him back to reality.

'What d'you think you're doing, man?' she demanded. 'Are you gone mad?'

He shook himself free and glared at her, the dead bird swinging from his hand, its head scraping the ground.

'Have you lost the use of your tongue?' she asked.

His lips moved noiselessly, seeking the right words—the bitter lacerating words. He held the limp body up, shaking it before her face.

'That'll be one less for your fancy man when he calls,' he said, throwing it down at her feet. 'And if you look beyond you'll see two more he'll be at the loss of.'

His hand was still up, thumbing over his shoulder, when she slapped his face.

The shock of the sudden blow left him dazed for a moment. He rubbed his tingling cheek, gazing at her stupidly. Then he let a roar out of him.

'Sowbitch!' he shouted and flogged the back of his fist across her mouth, feeling the rasp of his knuckles on her clenched teeth.

He stood over her, his arm drawn back threateningly.

'Ye low trollop,' he said. 'I've a right to hammer the living daylights out of ye.'

At the sight of the blood trickling from the corner of her mouth the anger died in him. They stood facing each other, so close that he could see a tiny reflected sun glittering at him from each of her eyes. There was a kind of blindness about her eyes, he thought, as though the sight in them was turned inwards. And her face too, with a queer unmindful look to it, like you'd see in the face of someone you're talking to and him listening all the time to the sound of music or great talk going on behind him.

The curious expression of her face and eyes, the glossy sheen of her freshly combed hair, the smell of scent and sweat and warm flesh sent a tepid ripple of desire through him.

'There's no rhyme or reason for a doggery the like of this,' he said. 'It's a fret to man . . . the way people gut other . . . for nothing.'

'Or next to nothing,' he added.

He put an awkward hand on her shoulder.

At once she swung in towards him, gripping him with savage arms, grinding her tensed body against him, clawing and tearing at his coat with frantic urgent fingers.

The intensity of her passion appalled him. This is awful, he thought. Outside my own house in the broad light of day.

I'm a done man if anyone sees me.

He made to push her off but his hands buried themselves in the softness of her breasts. The ache that had been coiling and twisting around inside him came back worse than ever. Crab-like his hands began exploring, finger after cautious clumsy finger, ready to shrink back at the slightest rebuff. As though calmed by his touch the convulsive shudderings died away and she lay against him inertly, breathing heavily with small pathetic gulps like a child sobbing itself to sleep. He felt the urge to comfort her—to dry her eyes and stroke her hair and say the crazy foolish things that had been shame-locked in his heart for all these years. His lacerated dignity, the turmoil of his thoughts, the pent-up torrent of his love that could be breached by the smallest, the most casual gesture of affection—all these things he pleaded through the pressure of his rough unskilful hands.

She sprang away from him, her eyes blazing, her blood-smeared face torn with hate and revulsion.

'Take your filthy hands offa me,' she screamed. 'At this age of your life to be pawing and groping at a woman! 'Tis of the grave you should be thinking, you doting old fool.'

She turned away and walked with a contemptuous swagger towards the house. Leaning against the doorjamb she watched him, her eyes spiteful: pitiless. Deliberately, in a low mocking voice, she commenced to sing:

> '*For an old man he is old*
> *And an old man he is grey*
> *And an old man's love is a thing of shame*
> *Go away, old man, go away!*'

For a few moments she stayed, her eyes fixed on his grimly squared shoulders and rigid stubborn back, expecting an answering jibe. When he did not rise to the bait, she turned and went in.

He stood as she had left him—stiffly erect, hands locked behind his back, his lined face expressionless but for the twitching lips.

From far across the bog a lone gull called. And called again; a tiny fretful wail as if mourning something irretrievably lost—the twinkling silver of breaking mackerel, a calm sea frosted with moonlight, the tall waves bowing their grizzled arrogant heads to the land.

The old man turned his head towards the sound, staring miserably, hopelessly, blindly ahead; the tears coursing unheeded down his ravaged face.

He heard her come to the door.

'Your breakfast's ready,' she called. And back over her shoulder as she wheeled round, 'Or maybe you've something more important to do.'

Her jibing laugh was merged in the tinkling of delf.

Again the gull mewled, a harsh discordant cackle, then rose on lazy sun-bleached wings. High overhead it flew, piping shrilly, its swaying searching neck outstretched, settling down at last in a freshly ploughed field to gorge its empty craw.

The Port Wine Stain

'Six weeks to half-sole a pair of shoes! It's a disgrace. But what can you expect? Half the day reading the Bible and the other half playing cards, little wonder he has no time for work.'

That was how my mother sized up Andy Foster, the cobbler. Though she had the grace to add:

'Of course there's no harm in an odd game of patience, Jim. When the housework's done. And a body should read a chapter of the Bible every night. But there's no sense going to extremes.'

She held up the shoes, examining them critically.

'You must hand it to him, though. He does a nice neat job. It's a pity the poor man's face is raddled with the port-wine stain.'

She put the shoes away in the cupboard and turned to face me.

'You should thank God every morning, Jim, with the first breath you draw that you can travel the roads by daylight instead of creeping out after dark like that poor disfigured creature.'

At school I learned that the port-wine stain was either a curse-mark laid by God on the cobbler as a punishment for his drunken dissolute past or else some awful disease he had contracted before coming to the village. Like leprosy, it was highly contagious and any contact with it might prove fatal. It was dangerous even to shout 'Scar-face' at the cobbler as he had once thrown a paring-knife at one of the older boys before the nick-name was properly out of his mouth.

Mother was indignant when I told her this. She said the curse-mark was nothing but an affliction from God and that those who provoked the cobbler would do well to remember the two and forty children torn to pieces by wild animals for jeering at Elisha's bald head.

When I was eventually entrusted with the job of collecting from the cobbler a pair of shoes left in weeks back to be soled and heeled, my mother, after warning me not to come back without them, said:

'Now don't be gaping at him, Jim. You'll only hurt the poor man's feelings. And remember, no mocking or jeering. God's hand will be swift and sore if you do.'

All the way to the village I could think of nothing but that final warning and the need to avert my eyes from the cobbler's gorgon gaze. By the time I reached the dark little shop I was in such a state of funk that I would hardly have dared venture in but for the reassuring figure of a policeman standing at the door of the nearby barracks.

Keeping my eyes firmly downcast, I stood at the counter and blurted out my message:

'Me-mother-wants-the-shoes-she-left-in-a-month-back.'

'Go away, boy. Can't you see I'm busy?' a deep voice growled.

I would have been contented enough to accept the dismissal but I knew a further effort was demanded.

'She-said-to-wait-till-they're-ready,' I muttered still addressing my boots.

'You're welcome,' the gruff voice replied. '*The patient man is better than the valiant.* Proverbs 16.'

I stuffed my hands in my pockets and prepared to wait.

The only sound was a steady rustling, so familiar and yet so out of place that at last I was forced to look up.

Mother was right. The big, grey-haired man seated at the work-bench was playing cards—seven-up patience.

At once I forgot my fears. Elbows on the counter I leant across, watching the fall of the cards. When the rustling

48

ceased and the silence began to drag, I could contain myself no longer.

'Mr Foster,' I said. 'You want to shift that red Queen. It's blocking up the play.'

The cobbler faced round to glare at me and I saw the port-wine stain for the first time.

It was dark red, almost plum-coloured, entirely covering the right side of his face. It started under his coarse grey hair and oozed down over his forehead till it engulfed one eye, closing the eyelid in a drowsy leer: it welled down the side of his nose, leaving the nostril puffed out almost to the corner of the mouth: it flowed over his ear, gorging it with thick dark blood so that it hung bloated and shapeless: it spread across his jaw to the centre of his chin, dragging down the heavy thickened lower lip in a grotesque pout that exposed the broken and discoloured teeth to the gums: it seemed to seep into the open mouth, perhaps as flecks of bloodied foam to be swallowed back in disgust—how else account for the restless flickering tongue that kept making tiny petulant noises as it clicked against his palate. The stain even invaded the unblemished side of his face, forming on his forehead and chin a ragged purple fringe like the indented coastline pictured on a school atlas.

Like molten lava, the stain had scorched all before it, leaving not a trace of beard, eyebrow or eyelashes—only a smooth expanse of taut glistening skin that must surely have the tacky feeling of raw liver. Appalled though I was at the thought of a face partly constructed of raw meat, I could not help thinking of the glory to be gained if I could boast in school of having discovered, through my courageous finger-prodding of the cobbler's cheek, that the curse-mark did not bounce back as ordinary skin should, but filled up again slowly like uncooked liver.

We stayed staring at each other while you could count ten,

the cobbler making no concession to the fear and disgust that must have shown on my face.

At last he spoke:

'I suppose your mother taught you how to play patience as well as give ould lip?'

'She did indeed, sir,' I replied. 'Three different kinds.'

The cobbler commenced to laugh. It was like a locomotive starting off—a succession of explosive puffs from the funnel, loud, startling, steam-laden: a burst of throaty coughing as the driving wheels skid in a false start; then the rhythmic wheezing chuckle from the steel belly as the engine gets under way.

At length he gathered himself together sufficiently to say:

'You're a prime boy, all right. Who would think a wee scaldy like you would be a master-man at the cards?'

He started chuckling again. I tried hard to keep a straight face but against the cobbler's laughter there was no defence. I broke into a fit of giggling that rapidly turned into hysteria. My shrill hoots and screeches so scourged the cobbler that he could do nothing but wheeze and splutter and cough. If the funeral bell had not started to ring we would have laughed ourselves sick.

When the funeral had passed the cobbler said:

'Come round here and show me these new-fangled versions you're bragging about.'

After that I called each day on my way home from school.

Andy was always glad to see me, putting away at once whatever he was doing, clearing a space on the workbench and producing with a flourish the pack of cards from the window-sill. My seat was on the cobbler's left, allowing him to conceal the port-wine stain but exposing me to the angry gaze of irritable customers complaining about the delay.

The cobbler had one answer for them all. A long look over

his shoulder at the frightening pile of unmended footwear heaped up in a corner of the room. A slow regretful shake of the head, signifying that the wanted shoes had still to work their way up from the very core of the mound. The few words of advice and comfort flung as casually as meal to chickens:

'*The impatient man shall work folly.* Come in again next week.'

Before the customer was well clear of the door he would be into the cards again.

Cassino we played, the only card-game—barring patience— that the cobbler knew. It was a rowdy brawling affair. Cries of protest and shouts of triumph were continuous. Cards were thumped on the work-bench or flourished derisively under an opponent's nose. Nagging or bullying were legitimate weapons for sapping morale.

If the cobbler was studying his hand, trying to work out a plan of campaign, I tried to distract him by a flow of grumbles and jeers.

'Get a move on, Andy, you're holding up the play. It'll be nightfall before we're through. What's holding you anyway? Are you thinking of passing off that nine of diamonds as Big Cassino when it gets too dark to see what we're doing? Or are you just trying to hatch out a clutch of aces?'

Let him start easing out a card from his hand and I forestalled him, waving one of my own high in the air and shouting truculently:

'Play it if you dare, Andy. I've the beat of it here.'

He would commence fumbling around, plucking at one card after another in an agony of indecision, until at last he slammed one down on the bench, saying:

'Make what you like of that, me young cock-sparrow.'

When, with shouts of glee, I swept his card up and maybe along with it a couple of aces and Little Cassino he would chuckle delightedly as if he got more fun out of losing than winning.

I was constantly devising new pin-pricks to put the cobbler off his game. On one occasion, impatient at the hold-up in the play, I laid down my cards, hooked my forefingers into the corners of my mouth and called softly:

'Hey, Andy!'

As the cobbler turned his head, I pulled at my mouth till it was slotted like a pillar box, thrust out my tongue and rolled my eyes madly round in their sockets.

Andy did not laugh. He gazed at me, mouth agape, tongue clicking furiously as it always did in moments of embarrassment.

I stared back at him aghast. So familiar had I become with the cobbler that the port-wine stain no longer registered on my consciousness. Now I discovered that the ugly bloated flesh of nose, lip and ear still filled me with disgust and repulsion. Yet in spite of the prospect of dire and instant punishment for trifling with a curse from God—a punishment maybe leaving on my face the angry print of a divine Hand—I felt the urge to discover, once and for all, the nature of the plum-coloured skin of the cobbler's cheek, so glossy, so unwrinkled, so utterly alien and inhuman. I was even toying with the thought of reaching out to put the matter to the final test when the cobbler's laugh broke out.

'Dear but you're the right villain,' he spluttered. 'Trying to put me off my play with your jack-acting.'

The laughter was so patently forced that, stricken with shame, I turned away muttering, 'Sorry, Andy,' as I gathered up my cards.

The cobbler's only other interest, as Mother had proclaimed was the Bible. It was the mine from which he quarried the quotations that clinched an argument or pointed up an absurdity, that clarified, instructed, reproved. My eagerness to win—

and win quickly—gave the cobbler many opportunities for criticism. He would clear his throat and growl:

' Substance got in haste shall be diminished.'

or:

' He that is greedy of gain troubleth his own house.'

There was no sting in these reproofs and I had a sneaking suspicion they were learned off by heart so that they could be produced at the appropriate time, like rabbits from a hat, as proof of a deep knowledge of Biblical lore.

But once when I repeated an item of scandal picked up in school, the cobbler rounded on me with chapter and verse:

' The words of a talebearer are as wounds and they go down into the innermost part of the belly. Proverbs 26, verse 22.'

His voice, harsh and full of anger, had me cringing in terror as if it was the growling voice of God himself.

Each day, at the end of the card session, the Bible was taken down from the shelf and the cobbler read from it a chapter picked out the previous night, explaining the illusions and obscurities that might mislead the unwary. Head flung back like a preacher, his glance barely grazing the page, he declaimed the passage, his deep rumbling voice moulding and polishing the words until meaning and glittering sound were one.

I listened enthralled to the tales of prophets, kings, soldiers, peasants: to deeds of splendour and treachery: to the epic of palaces, temples and monuments, doomed to destruction before ever a stone was laid. I shuddered cheerfully at the tally of death and disaster—death by famine, pestilence or the visitation of God: murder by stealth in the darkness of the night or in the broad light of day by the command of tyrants: the slaughter of a kinsman, the implacable butchery

53

of an enemy tribe, the decimation of a peaceful city. I learned that the ant is wiser than the wise: that the lizard lodges in the palaces of kings: that foxes, little foxes, can spoil a vineyard: that the golden calf was the symbol of a people's subjection to the ox—a people too stiff-necked and lazy to till the soil. This biblical lore, some of it as familiar as the toothache, the cobbler set forth in his rich velvety voice, savouring every syllable, so that the word was made flesh—vivid, exciting, immediate.

There was no knowing how our friendship might have turned out had I not one day, after fetching over the Bible, had the sudden notion of scrambling up on the workbench and sitting there, knees dangling, my breath fanning the disfigured cheek.

Poor Andy was mortified. He made a move to rise from his seat, changed his mind and sat on, shuffling his feet and shifting about uneasily. At length, to cover his embarrassment, he opened the Bible at random and commenced to read the first passage met his eye:

' *I am a man that hath seen affliction by the rod of his wrath*

' *He hath led me and brought me into darkness but not the light . . .*'

I paid no attention to this meaningless incantation. I was too preoccupied with the sudden chance of impressing those at school who expected more from my vaunted friendship with the cobbler than footling tales of card-playing and Bible-thumping. No use describing the drooping, lashless eyelid: the sagging lower lip, moist with spittle; the bulbous ear, frayed and pitted like an over-ripe mushroom; these disfigurements were known to all and sundry. Something more was required.

The cobbler read on:

'*My flesh and my skin hath made me old: he hath broken my bones . . .*'

This was my opportunity to boast of being granted, like Thomas the unbeliever, the privilege of touching the ravaged flesh of my friend. There was nothing to hinder me. The fear of divine vengeance, instant and appropriate, had lost its dreadful immediacy. No punishment awaited me except the remote possibility that my friendship with Andy might be endangered.

The cobbler's sombre voice rolled over me:

'*He hath set me in dark places, as they that be dead of old . . .*'

Perhaps if the blemished skin was really dead and sodden, as I suspected, Andy would not even feel the touch of a finger. Tentatively I pursed my lips, leaned over and blew smartly on the flawed cheek, half-expecting the answering twitch, like the twitching flanks of a fly-tormented beast. Unheedingly the cobbler continued to read but at last the growing bitterness in the deep rumbling voice forced me to listen to the words.

'*He hath enclosed my ways with hewn stone, he hath made my path crooked:*

'*He hath turned aside my ways and broken me to pieces: he hath made me desolate . . .*'

I had a vision of a ruined temple set in the midst of an arid desolate plain. Huge blocks of tumbled masonry and a ring of pillar stumps like worn-down fangs encircled a sunken courtyard, choking off all exit down the maze of crooked paths reeling senselessly into the distance—the tracks beaten down by drunken curse-marked pilgrims. In the centre of the

courtyard a shrivelled figure lay stretched in the burning
sun, its arms and legs broken and twisted by torture—lonely
and terror-stricken, too weakened by hunger and thirst to
make the effort needed to escape.

The cobbler's voice, hoarse with anguish, brought me back
to reality:

*' I am made a derision to all my people and their song all
the day—'*

He made an effort to continue, but gave up and remained
with head bent, staring down at the open page, his lips
moving soundlessly, his eyes moist with tears.

He was actually crying. It was grown-up undignified grief
but it would serve my purpose. For this was indeed my
chance. At long last I had the pretext for satisfying my
curiosity. I reached over and stroked his cheek.

' Poor Andy!' I murmured. ' Pood old Andy!'

Retribution came swift and startling. Before I could draw
back, I found myself grabbed, dragged off the work-bench and
held imprisoned, my head crushed against the cobbler's
shoulder.

In the hope that my punishment might be mitigated by
submission, I did not shout or struggle. Docilely I waited the
inevitable outburst of fury, prepared to recognise at last that
surely God is not mocked.

Suddenly, to my shocked surprise, the cobbler commenced
to shudder and moan like a sick animal. His breathing became
harsh and stertorous. There was a sound of grating teeth. It
seemed to be an onset of convulsions or epilepsy. Perhaps
something even more serious. Cautiously I tried to worm
myself free so that I could run for the doctor. But the more
I squirmed and wriggled the tighter became the cobbler's grip.

More alarming still, he was now muttering wildly to himself in rushing disconnected snatches of speech. Like a funeral

bell, I could hear the constant tolling of my name: 'Jim! Oh Jim!' the only sound I could identify in the unintelligible gabble. Death at the hands of a raving madman seemed the price that an offended God meant to exact for my transgression.

This thought started me struggling in earnest, tugging and pulling at the clamping hands. Just when I had nearly freed myself, the cobbler swung round and trapped me between constricting knees.

Dourly and in silence I fought on, flinging myself wildly from side to side, trying desperately to escape, whilst the cobbler with his free hands stroked my hair, patted my back and made soft soothing noises like you would to a frightened colt.

I felt there was something sinister about this attempt to quieten me. Just in time I looked up. The cobbler was bending over me, eyes closed, lips twitching rapidly in mute frantic appeal and I knew with a dreadful certainty that the hideous curse-marked face was about to be thrust against my own, seeking God knows what of pity and sympathy. He started to wheeze and whine like a brute beast. It was too much.

'Let go of me, Andy! Let me go!' I shouted.

The cobbler clapped one hand over my mouth.

'Hush, Jim,' he whispered, in a queer, hoarse, excited voice, leaning down till his warm breath fouled my cheek with spittle.

Frantic with fear and disgust, I tore away the stifling hand.

'Let me go, Heel-ball,' I screamed. 'Don't come near me with your rotten stinking poxy face.'

I felt the cobbler flinch and jerked myself free of his slackening grasp. At the door I stopped and looked back.

He was slumped in the chair, arms and legs sagging like a cheap worn-out cloth doll, saliva dribbling out of his mouth

instead of sawdust. He stared back at me slack-jawed, his
tongue clacking the time of day like an eight-day clock. The
hurt bewildered look on his face only served to goad me to
further insults:

'It's in the mad-house you should be. Carrying on like
that. Don't you know that thing is catching? Like the leprosy.'

I looked down at my rumpled clothes and my indignation
grew.

'You have my shirt tore,' I said. 'And there's a button off
my jacket.'

The cobbler's misery was piteous to watch.

'I . . . I . . . I'm sorry, Jim,' he mumbled. 'I thought when
you stroked . . . it was all a mistake . . . I thought because
you . . .'

His voice trailed into silence, although his mouth continued
to open and close as if he were swallowing back a bitter
unspoken cud of grief.

'Well, you thought wrong, whatever it was,' I said. I was
sick with loathing and hatred, as much for myself as for him,
and I meant to make him pay for his share in my humiliation.

'And what's more,' I went on, 'my stomach's turned looking at you chewing and slobbering over the cards. And I'm
fed up with your silly old Cassino, wherever you picked it up.
And I'm sick to death listening to your ould Bible blather—
it's worse than Sunday school, and that's no picnic. And I'm
never coming in here again the longest day I live.'

The words were choking me but I got them out somehow.
I turned to go but Andy's voice halted me.

'Jim,' he said. 'Would you have it in you to forgive the
presumption of a lonely foolish old man?'

I stayed silent.

He went on:

'Will you listen before you go to one last passage from the

Book? I promise you it's the last one I'll ever trouble you with.'

I refused to answer, fearing the treachery of speech.

He closed the Bible slowly, with a gesture of finality.

'*He that despiseth his friend is mean of heart*,' he said, speaking the words very slowly and without trace of emotion. 'It was Solomon said that, Jim. And he was the wisest man in all Israel.'

As I made off with the tears spurting from my eyes, I heard him call after me:

'You'll be in the morrow on your way past.'

But I did not call in the next day. Nor the day after. Nor ever again. Coming back from school I kept to the far side of the street with my face averted. Before very long I had joined a group of boys, more daring than the rest, and was shouting 'Scar-face, Heel-ball, Poxy-puss' with the best of them. I was mean of heart, as Andy had foreseen. Mean and cowardly and bitter. But how else could I exorcise the limping miserable ghosts that haunted my memory—the sound of Andy, snuffling and whining like a terrier bitch that my mother, for some reason or other, locked into an outhouse and the stealthy conniving note in his voice when he whispered: 'Hush, Jim.'?

The Metal Man

A FUNERAL thirst is a poor thing to have when you're carrying light. And when it's five pubs from the graveyard before you strike oil, it needs to be a proper gusher. But so it was, though you'd never have guessed it when you saw the two clients sitting up at the far end of Jonty's poky little bar—Scroggy Johnson with his long neck arched over a pint and the little Tailor, grinning like a hungry wolf into his empty glass. A nice pair of cronies. A hedgehog wouldn't be safe with Tailor around and there's bloody few quills on Scroggy's young cuddy of a wife. The cutting-out table could tell a few tales if it had a tongue. They even say she gives Scroggy a share of the take.

Anyway you could hardly describe either of them as a fogey, fully fledged and ready for plucking, so there seemed to be nothing for it but to sneak off quietly, leaving the pair of vultures to devour each other. But Tailor happens to turn round. He lets a gulder out of him:

'Hey there, Iscariot! Draw up your stool to the board. We can start the Last Supper now.'

'What are you taking?' he says.

He's an insulting bloody man when he's half-jarred, but there was no getting away from the little weasel. It was a case of join up and hope for the best.

'Not to be too sore on you, Tailor, a modest pint.'

'Give him a pint and a glass of whiskey. A glass of whiskey for myself. And for Scroggy here, I think another basin of stirabout would be in order.'

Now when Tailor is carrying he will buy with the best of them. And sure enough he produced a sheaf of crinklers— enough to set your two hips solidly on the bar stool till closing time. The bloody idiot starts waving the notes and making a bloody sermon.

'You are quite wrong, my friends. I came by this sudden windfall in the lawful pursuit of my ancient craft. The worthy proprietor of this establishment, Mr. Jonty Donoghue—ale, wine and spirit dealer, whom God preserve from the onslaughts of tinkers, policemen and tick-merchants—'

'Amen to that,' says Scroggy into his glass, as if every man-jack in the company didn't know bloody well that he had tapped to drying-up point all the publicans of the village. He's a polished hypocrite, that one.

'This gentleman,' says Tailor, bowing to Jonty who was filling up the glasses with flat porter from a dirty old enamelled jug, a stalactite worthy of the caves of Templemore dangling from one nostril—sweetener for some poor bugger's pint, 'has very wisely decided to entrust me with his personal adornment, for which purpose I have taken his measurements for a single-breasted, three-button suit of the best navy-blue serge—allowance being made in the pants for a fly swung to the left, a very rare tailoring job in a country where the starboard testicle is generally the lower slung—the whole to be fitted and supplied in time for first Mass on Sunday week. As a token of his trust and esteem. Mr. Donoghue has very fairly made a little down payment.' He peels off a note and slaps it on the counter. 'Take the drinks out of that, Boss. And may you wear the suit to the altar if ever you see fit to enter the holy state of matrimony.'

To listen to the flowery talk of him you'd have thought it was the Fifty Shilling Tailor was buying the drink instead of a little drunken scut of a country fit-me-tight.

Scroggy lifts his muzzle out of the pint.

'You'll mebbe have my own suit finished before that day dawns,' he says. 'It's paid for this six months now.'

Trust Scroggy to discharge a rasper. He'd skin you with

one lick of his tongue. But it didn't take a shake out of the Tailor. He turns to Johnson and says, sweet as pie:

'You'll not fatten up much, biting the hand that feeds you.'

We all sat watching Jonty put the Roman collars on the pints with a few skites of fresh porter from the barrel. No one spoke till the drinks were well-lowered. Then Jonty says, addressing Tailor:

'It's a wonder you weren't at the Doctor's funeral. The pair of you were great butties.'

They were the scandal of the parish, if the truth were told. Drinking and carousing at all hours of the day and night. You could call them a right pair of blackguards.

Tailor threw back his whiskey and ordered another round —a large whiskey for the celebrant and a couple of pints for the mass-clerks. Hadn't even the decency to ask the company what they were having. He says:

'I'm full sure if the Doctor—wish him rest—had any say in the matter, he would as soon have me drinking in here as listening to the clods hopping off his coffin.'

'Aye,' says Scroggy, between mouthfuls of porter. 'He was a powerful drouth. He would drink the cross off an ass.'

'What harm was there in that? Didn't he pay for every sup he got? And as much again to fill the guts of ungrateful gougers like yourself,' says Tailor.

Anyone else would have been daunted by a remark like that but if Mr. Long Neck gets anchored to a fogey, nothing short of the death-rattle of the victim's last shilling on the counter will release him. Oh, a deadly man! He could squeeze drink out of a fogey just by aggravating him. As he was doing now.

'He was free with his chippens all right, but he was a proper nuisance with a few jars in him. No need to tell *you* that—you had a bellyful of him in your time,' says Scroggy.

'People were always rubbing him the wrong way,' says Tailor.

'D'ye mind the time he had the row in Downey's pub with the wee jewman from up the country somewhere,' says Scroggy. 'He was rubbed the wrong way that night for sure. It took us the most of an hour pulling and hauling at his lower jaw to free his false teeth after your-man had finished with him.'

'He was a bit sharp with the tongue, all right,' says Tailor.

'He was sharp with his charges too,' says Scroggy. 'It was always cash before delivery on a maternity case. No fee, no foal, that was his motto.'

The two of them got stuck into each other over the merits of the dear departed. The best doctor in the country: couldn't cure you of the itch; lashing his money round on a crowd of gabshites: a cute hawk if ever there was one; the greatest joker of all time: a walking menace to the community; Tailor praising him to the skies, Scroggy running him down and drinks coming up for further orders. It took you sinking your pint middling rapid to keep pace with them.

Scroggy was dredging his memory for more stories about the Doctor so that the porter would keep flowing.

'D'ye mind yon night in Cleary's of the Gap?' he says. 'Yourself and myself and the Doctor. And that glubbadhaun, Kreuger Doyle. He wasn't long home out of the British Army at the time. Every bit as mad as he is now. The Doctor was throwing whiskey into him and getting him to demonstrate rifle drill. With a broomstick.'

'What put that into your head, Johnson? Sure that must be in old God's time,' says Tailor, real sharp.

You could see him taking a hold of himself, screwing up his face in a frown of suspicion, his wee buttony eyes blinking away in an effort to sober up. Scroggy had him taped right away.

'I suppose it was seeing Kreuger roving around after the funeral today that put me in mind of it,' says Scroggy. 'It was a funny night, that one. I can still see the big slob staggering around the bar shouting out all manner of commands at himself and falling over the broomstick, trying to obey them. I think it was some kind of bayonet drill he was tricking at.'

It was Scroggy was doing the drilling. And he'd keep drilling away at the Tailor till he had the whole story out of him.

He goes on:

'At the rear the Doctor gets tired of this caper and lugs old Kreuger over to the bar counter. Starts stuffing large brandies into him. All the time jagging at him about women—the women he must have met in foreign parts—Frenchies, darkies, Chinks. You know the class of chat he was always at. And poor old Kreuger, that didn't know what he had it for, lapping up the brandy and letting on to be an arch-hoormaster. You surely can't have forgotten, Tailor?'

'I'm hazy enough about that night. I was paralytic drunk the most of the time,' Tailor says.

Well, the bloody humbug! Pleading drunk and incapable with extenuating circumstances. That hare won't sit for long once Master Scroggy starts delving in the undergrowth.

'Indeed I wasn't too sober myself,' says Scroggy. 'About the last thing I can remember is Cleary oxtering Kreuger out the bar door. He couldn't have travelled far the state he was in. He was pure footless.'

'He slept the night in the byre,' says Tailor.

'Did he now!' says Scroggy. 'And how are you so sure of that?'

'We came across him and we leaving,' says Tailor.

Tailor bought a round of whiskies, probably hoping it might change the conversation. It was no use. Scroggy got stuck in him again.

'It's running through my head,' he says, 'that Doyle took

to the bed after that episode. Of course the Doctor must have told you what was the matter with him. When he was all the time broadcasting everyone else's ailments, he was hardly likely to keep his trap shut about Kreuger's.'

He takes a long look at the Tailor and picks up his glass.

'Unless,' says Scroggy, talking very civil and nice into his half-one of whiskey. 'Unless for one reason or another he wanted it kept quiet. Knowing he was in some way to blame.'

He throws back the whiskey and puts down the glass carefully. 'I'd be thinking, Tailor, that would leave you an accessory before or after the fact. Maybe both.' He sounded like a hanging judge rolling the death sentence round his mouth.

You could have found it in your heart to be sorry for the Tailor standing there with a haunted look on his face and his mouth gaping as if he had lock-jaw.

Suddenly Scroggy lets a roar out of him:

'Would you look at who's here? The wanted man himself. How are you, Kreuger, me old segotia?'

With that Doyle comes tramping in, about three quarters bluthered, his bloody great flat feet rising the dust off the floor, muttering to himself: 'Left! Right! Left! Right!' Looking at him you could well believe he was drawing a disability pension, for the bloody Germans must have wore themselves out belting hell out of his big baldy head with rifle butts to drive it down to the ears between his shoulder-blades. When he gets to the top end of the bar, he stops and shouts:

'Halt! Who goes there?'

Scroggy says out of the side of his mouth:

'Are you going to give him the countersign, Tailor?'

Tailor turns round and as sure as God is my judge says:

'Would you face a pint, Kreuger?'

Would a duck swim?

'Yes, sir. I would indeed, sir. I would surely. God bless you, sir.'

65

He kept up this toucher's litany in his hoarse growling voice till he got the pint in his fist. After that all you could hear was the sound of him wolfing it down. He's the dirtiest drinker in the parish. The porter was splashing over his face and hands and running down his neck. The greedy gulpin always tore his way through a drink for fear he'd miss the chance of another one going buckshee.

When he had sunk the pint what did the bowsie do but raise the empty tumbler to the Tailor.

'Good luck sir. Good luck to the donor,' says he.

For a notorious madman he makes bloody few mistakes as far as needling for drink is concerned, even the Scroggyman would be put to the pin of his collar to best him.

'Three buckets of porter,' says Tailor. 'And a ball of malt for myself.'

So we were relegated to the pints again. You could see Scroggy was annoyed. If he's in tow with a legitimate fogey he can't stand sharing the loot. And here was Tailor putting Kreuger on the round every time he bought. It was barbarous. It's a shame to see good drink going to waste, and there was more good-looking porter on the bar floor than in Kreuger's swollen gut.

By this time Tailor was well lit. The whiskey was beginning to put him into talking form—confidential talking form. Scroggy had gammed on to this also, for he suddenly says:

'Why the hell are you forever buying drinks for yon halfwitted savage? Sure you'd as lief be carrying guts to a bear as pouring drinks into that porter-shark.'

Jonty must have heard him for he pipes up:

'Get along to the other end of the bar, Doyle, and stop bothering these gentlemen.'

What's seldom is wonderful. *Gentlemen,* no less. It takes the folding dough to put manners on a publican.

'That poor angashore is on my conscience,' says Tailor.

66

You could see Scroggy stiffening like a pointer dog. He had nosed out the bird and it was only a matter of moving in to flush it up.

'Where did you meet up again with Kreuger after you left Cleary's thon night?' says Scroggy, just as if he knew the story, entire and complete, and only wanted to fill in a few minor details.

Tailor swallowed it—cheese, mouse-trap and book of instructions. Out he comes with the whole bloody history as if he had been waiting for the chance to get it off his chest.

It seems the Doctor was cranking up the car when they heard the snoring coming from the byre. The two of them went over to see who was in it, and when the Doctor flashed on his torch there was the Kreuger-man stretched out in a drunken stupor on the cow-house floor, his fly wide open and his credentials exhibited for all the world to see. The silly bugger must have folded up after having a pumpship.

The Doctor lets a whistle out of him.

'Did you ever in your natural life meet up with the like of that?' he says.

'A clear case of indecent exposure,' says he. 'One of the sins that cry to heaven for vengeance.'

Says he:

'Stay here a minute. We'll have to do something to remedy this situation.'

Off he goes to the car and when he comes back he has the black bag with him.

'Tailor,' says he, 'Scripture lays it down that if thy right hand scandalise thee, cut it off and cast it from thee. If thy right eye, pluck it out and do likewise. And what have we here? A more flagrant case of scandalisation would be hard to find. We must prune, my dear fellow. Prune ruthessly. The bill-hook is the only solution.'

He keeps ranting away like a madman, and as he's talking,

peels off his jacket, spreads it out on the straw and starts laying out the tools of his trade in an orderly fashion.

'Now, Tailor,' says he, handing him the torch, 'keep that
light steady or I'll hammer a job on you instead.'

Scroggy chipped in:

'Are you trying to tell me that you helped to dismember
a fellow-Christian?'

'I saw nothing of what happened,' says Tailor. 'I kept my
eyes tight shut all the time, even when the Doctor roared at
me to steady up the light.'

Tailor was out to make a general confession and nothing
was going to stop him. He described Kreuger snoring away all
the time, except for an odd grunt out of him as if someone
was stirring him with the toe of a boot.

At length the Doctor says:

'You can open your cowardly optics now, Tailor. The job's
done.'

He had his jacket on, the black bag was shut and, decently
enough, he had heaped straw over Doyle to keep him warm.

'Do you know what it is,' he says. 'If the entire College of
Surgeons were turned loose on your-man here, I defy them to
do a neater job.'

'He'll never have a day's trouble after this,' he says.

'Come on away,' says he. 'We'll be off home.'

And away with with the pair of butchers in the car. Oh, a
nice edifying story. No wonder the Tailor was never done
buying drinks for Kreuger. A poor enough penance for a
bloody deed the like of that.

Scroggy was still trying to ferret out the rest of the story.

'Why the hell did Kreuger keep his trap shut all these
years?' he asks.

'The Doctor saw to that,' says Tailor.

Apparently the bloody cut-throat had the brass neck to
call to see Kreuger next day. Spun him some cock-and-bull

story that he heard he was laid up with a sick stomach.

'I'll have a look at you,' he says. 'There's a bad class of a flu going the rounds.'

Kreuger strips off and the Doctor starts to examine him. 'Hullo!' says he. 'What's this? You're minus your rattley box, my good man. Where did you sleep last night?'

'I woke up in Cleary's byre,' says Kreuger. 'I had this terrible pain in my fork. I just managed to cripple home a few hours back and throw myself on the bed. Is it anything serious, Doctor?'

'A byre?' says the Doctor. 'That might account for it. Cattle are queer creatures. They have been known to crop the ears off a drunk man sleeping in a cowshed.'

'But it is more likely,' says he, 'that you contracted some filthy disorder from that French girl you were telling us about last night. Advanced gangrene must have set in and eaten the whole apparatus away.

'I'll put a dressing on anyway,' he says. 'But it's too late to save them.'

'What will I do at all?' says Kreuger.

'If you take my advice,' says the Doctor, 'you'll breathe a word of this to no one. If it gets out, you would have to go to the Bishop for absolution. Or maybe even to Rome itself.'

And he charged him five shillings for medical attendance.

'After all,' he told Tailor, 'the vet would have charged him a half-note for the same job and used the crusher on him.'

To think of that barbarous bloody quack, fit only for stirring ointment or mixing black-jack, chancing his arm at a minute job like removing a body's testaments and then charging the wretched victim a fee for making a bullock of him. It's tramped in a bog-hole he should have been instead of getting Christian burial. And that henchman of his, the bloody little measuring man, that's codding half the country with his tape and chalk and his ready-by-Sunday chat—there he is sitting up on the tall stool like a penitent waiting for absolution.

Scroggy was eyeing him with a cagey look.

'D'ye tell me, Tailor,' he says, 'you never riz an eyelid during the whole operation?'

'That's right,' says Tailor.

'Well how are you so full sure that the Doctor ever docked him at all?' says Scroggy.

'Hey, Kreuger! he shouts down the bar. 'D'ye mind thon night in Cleary's of the Gap? The night the Doctor—God be good to his soul—did the wee job on you?'

'I mind it well, sir. A powerful night, sir. A wonderful decent man, the Doctor.'

Kreuger kept babbling on, lifting his empty glass in salutation. 'Good luck, sir. Your health, Mr. Johnson.'

Much chance he had of getting a drink out of Scroggy, that registered blood-sucker.

'D'ye hear that voice?' says Scroggy. 'A gravelly rasp the like of yon never came from a gelding.'

'You've been codded, Tailor,' he says. 'That spoiled surgeon was making a right fool of you. To think of you pouring porter into that sluice-box for half a lifetime. To ease your conscience, no less.'

Scroggy into the laughing, squeezing out the words between outbursts of screeching:

'The poor wee Tailor . . . cute as a pet hawk . . . swallowing that joker's lies . . . Behold Kreuger! The stoneless wonder!'

'I declare to me God I'll die with the laughter,' he says.

He starts coughing and rakes up a ball of phlegm that must have been inside him these many months.

'That playboy in the graveyard must be splitting his sides this minute,' he says.

It would have done your heart good to see the Tailor. He

was fit to be tied. His face was screwed up into a knot with rage.

Scroggy kept after him.

'Give the poor old bags another pint, Tailor. He's been nursing the empty tumbler this hour past.'

The Tailor got his voice back at last. You'd have thought he was spitting out a razor blade with every word.

'I'll give that bocketty hoor a drink he'll not forget in a hurry,' he says.

'Come with me out the back, Scroggy,' he says. 'And take your tumbler with you.'

When the pair came back. Scroggy asks as casual as if he'd been calling every round:

'Will you take a black and tan this time, Kreuger?'

'God bless you, Mr. Johnson. I will indeed, sir.'

'A black and tan for my old friend, Kreuger,' Scroggy says, reaching out his tumbler. 'You can top it up with porter, Mr. Donoghue, the beer's in it already.'

Jonty nearly foaled a fiddler when he saw the steam rising off the glass. It was easy telling what the two bucks were doing out the back.

'What kind of a caper is this?' says Jonty. 'Do you want to poison the poor man.'

'God send him better,' says Tailor. 'If he lives to be a hundred he'll never sup a stronger pint. Sure the most of it is pure whiskey, double distilled. Damn the bit harm it'll do him.'

Jonty gave the glass a couple of skites of the porter jug and left it up on the counter to cool off. But before you could bat an eyelid the Kreuger-man had grabbed the tumbler—he maybe thought Scroggy might change his mind—and wolfed down a wheen of mouthfuls of the foulest and flattest porter known to man.

There wasn't a mute out of the company till Kreuger bangs

down the glass on the counter, fetched up a class of a moaning sigh that could easily have come from his croup and then starts puffing and blowing as if the bloody pint was laced with thunder and lightning.

'That'll soften his cough, the scrounging get,' says Tailor. 'It's time someone halted his gallop.' Scroggy into the laughing again. Wheezing as if he had the asthma. Says he:

'The miraculous draft of piss and porter . . . guaranteed to remove paint off a door . . . or the balls off a canon.'

'Do you think will he be all right, lads?' says Jonty.

He needn't have been wasting his sympathy, for when the bloody bashi-bazouk gets his breath back he reaches for the pint again and proceeds to baptise himself once more with fortified porter. It was a horrid sight to see him lapping up a pagan mixture the like of that, smacking his lips as if he enjoyed it. When he had sucked the last drop out of the tumbler, as sure as Jaysus didn't he raise the empty glass and start up his bloody old war cry again:

'Your health, Mr Johnson. Good luck to you, sir.'

No one paid a bit heed to him, and in the latter end he dried up. For a while it looked as if the porter seam had dried up too, for there was nothing but empty glasses decorating the counter. Scroggy must have thought the same, for he fixes his eye on a bloody old prop-up on the top shelf, advertising a whiskey that's defunct since the year duck and starts talking to himself.

'It's a poor bucking country this too. No wonder they're swarming out of it in their millions. Damn the bit thanks you get for staying. A land of ungrateful bastards. Lighten the load on their backs and they wouldn't so much as ask you had you a mouth on you.'

Believe it or not, he drew the badger. A fine plump brock it was too—balls of malt and pint chasers. You have to hand it to Scroggy, he's a proper artist with the needle.

The whiskey was sunk and all hands busy negotiating the pints when this bloody clocking hen starts giving out the pay at the other end of the bar.

Chook! Chook! Chook! You'd think you were in a bloody fowl-house. It was your-man, of course. Sitting on the bench, with his hands on his knees and his eyes tight shut, hiccuping away to beat the band. The cold sweat was starting to come out and every so often he would draw the back of his hand across his forehead to clean off the pickles of dew but mostly he just chooked. That is until he started to rift.

Chook! Chook! Rift! As God is my judge, it was the kind of sound you'd hear coming from a wild animal's cage. A class of a watery growl, finishing with a cough, like the poor brute was not entirely mad with rage but just in a sour kind of mood, lashing its tail and baring its gums. But it was when his guts started glugging and rattling that the music really started.

Chook! Chook! Rattle! Rift! It would put you in mind of a fidgety old farmer huddled over the fire, impatiently rattling the bars of the grate with the kitchen tongs, while he waited for a big pot of thick, bubbling, spitting stirabout to come properly to the boil, his ears deafened with the screeches of fox-ridden poultry and the hungry roaring of a sow that was after devouring its last bonham.

Scroggy was the first to pass judgment. He says:

'It's borne in on me that the contents of Strongbow's stomach will shortly see the light of day.'

Sure enough, Doyle has got to the swallowing stage. Mouth tight shut, cheeks blown out with puke, thrapple jigging like a step-dancer's diddies, he somehow managed to swallow every gulch—never let as much as a dribble past his lips. Oh, the real regimental porter-shark—too mean to clear his belly of a load of drink by letting it fly on the bar-room floor.

'That he may puke till his ass-hole chokes him,' says Tailor.

'Amen!' says Scroggy.

'Get him out of here before he destroys the place,' says Jonty.

Scroggy leans over and hisses: 'Would you for Jaysus sake lamp the antics of the inn-keeper!'

Jonty was gaping at Doyle with his mouth ajar. Every time the patient's guts gave a heave, Jonty's face would twist in agony and he would clap an anguished hand over his quaking lips.

Suddenly Doyle hoists himself to his feet like a dromedary.

'Atten . . . shun!' he bawls.

'Mother of God,' says Scroggy. 'Is that guzzling cossack going to start up his capers again?'

'Corplar Doyle's pleasure for a song,' says Kreuger, banging one foot down in front of him as if he was lunging with a bayonet.

'Since when did they start dishing out stripes for peeling spuds and scrubbing shit-houses?' says Tailor.

The little weasel was raging because it began to look as if Kreuger was going to go home with a gutful of free porter after all.

Kreuger into the singing, if you can call it that. A plain chant, if ever there was one, with only the one note to it—like a bagpipe drone.

> '*Floating about on the briny*
> *About on the briny waves*
> *Out on the briny ocean*
> *Out in the deep blue sea . . .*'

He was pulled up short by a woeful bloody belch that went all the way from bassoon to piccolo before it stopped. It took him a full minute, swallowing mad, with the bubbles coming to his mouth and nose and eyes before he could quell the mutiny.

'That was a near one,' says Scroggy, out of the side of his mouth. 'I'll lay six to four he dirties his bib before he quits the gowling.'

'Rise her, Kreuger. Rise her,' says he. 'Give her the loud pedal!'

'Good, you boy you!' says he.

Tailor says:

'Don't encourage the old cod. Let him get to hell out of here and stop pestering us.'

Kreuger starts off again but there was a hole in the ballad somewhere for the words of the bloody song were gone all baw-ways.

> '*Up in a lonely attic*
> *Far from the head of the stair*
> *There's many a man*
> *With another man's wife*
> *Floating about on the briny—*'

He broke off and fell to plucking his lower lip, making out he had forgotten the rest of the words, though God knows he couldn't have made his meaning clearer if he had put it on vellum and had it sworn by a notary.

It was a shrewd well-aimed shaft coming from a half-wit. It not only took a belt at Mr Long Neck for peddling his wife's person for gain and at the Tailor for taking advantage of, and having illicit traffic with same: but it also took a powerful side-swipe at *Mine Host,* the Jonty-fellow, who you can be sure thought his own dealings with Mrs. Scroggy had gone on unbeknownst, whereas any wean in the village could have told you that it wasn't only for the wee drop of extra milk that she came carrying her can to the side-door after hours, allowing, of course, that the craw-thumping hypocrite could take time off from smelling after that old crone that does the housekeeping.

Kreuger had surely put the ball in the back of the net in Army v. The Rest. You could safely say that Mr. Bloody Doyle is a solid cast-iron hundred-per-cent Metal Man—what's known in other parts of the country as an ' iron fool '—and if you're still in invincible ignorance, it's the title given to a wolf that has no need to wear sheep's clothing because it happens to have been born complete with fleece and double stomach.

You should have seen the dials of the three jokers. Mr. Whey-Face behind the bar, with his eyebrows up into his hair, the Tailor, busy seeing spooks and Scroggy—if a vulture could lick its chops at the sight of a nice steaming mess of human tripes, that was what the bold Scrog was doing. You could hear the free ones clicking up on that cash register he has behind his forehead.

Kreuger lifts the empty glass. Says he:

' Good health to the company. And to the poor gentleman beyond in the graveyard. If fair was fair and all paid up, he'd have the queer headstone over him.'

His guts were glugging away as bad as ever but he was holding down the porter like a true militiaman.

Tailor turns on him girning with rage.

' Would you clear to hell out of here, you double-faced scrounger,' he says. ' Damn the drink more you'll ever get from me the longest day you live. Not if your tongue was hanging down to your navel.'

What else could the Tailor say? Though he might have put it a wee-shade milder. Iron fools are not popular around these parts, for who's going to lash porter into a Metal Man who'll turn and reef you at the finish.

Kreuger puts down the glass on the counter.

' Good-bye, Mr Donoghue,' he says, shrugging his shoulders

till you'd think his head would be jammed between them.

Back from nightmare-land comes John Terence Donoghue, member of the Sodality of the Sacred Heart, St. Conail's section, local secretary of the Saint Vincent de Paul Society, generous subscriber to parochial charities and one-time—it is to be hoped—forgatherer with hoors of the wedded class.

'Come here, Doyle,' he says, 'I want you a minute.'

Kreuger shambled back to the counter and, as true as a gun's iron, didn't Jonty slip him half-a-bloody-dollar.

'Good-bye now, Corporal,' he says.

Could you beat it. There goes Kreuger with a never-ending seam of porter drying up on him through his own impudence and before he has gone three paces, lo and behold, the skies open and half-dollars rain down on him. Truly when God closes one door, he opens another. Though in Scroggy's case you could say two doors were on the latch—Tailor's and Jonty's.

Off again goes Kreuger, but he wheels round at the door.

'Corplar Doyle's no pickpocket,' he says real cheeky. 'He knows his place as well as any man.'

Suffering duck, to listen to that bloody gallow-glass striking his breast like a tom-tom, you'd never guess that the gable-ends of half the houses in the village are ready to fall with ground damp from the weight of buckshee liquor he has pissed against them.

He gives one more porter rift and makes across the street to the barracks where he squats down, as always, on the sill of the day-room window.

Good riddance, you might say, to his glugging guts and his porter splashing and his mean, lousy, hyena habits. You get well browned off with a mouse-about like him skulking around, mopping up free ones.

He put paid to the evening's entertainment for when Tailor ordered again, Jonty says:

At Night All Cats Are Grey

'Go home now, men, I think you've all had enough.'

The commotion started then. The two greedy gluttons, still hungering for more drink, insisted on service, but Jonty every bit as thick as themselves, refused to relent. They were so busy cribbing and chawing the fat that they paid no more attention to Legionnaire Doyle sweating it out across the street than they would to an ass rolling in the dust. None of them saw him pull out of his trouser pocket a bloody great workhouse handkerchief and start mopping his forehead. They didn't pass the least bit remark when he dropped down on his two knees, scrabbling about on the pavement. They seemed to think it the most natural thing in the world for a body to say and him leaving the bar: 'It's mebbe as well for someone to see old Kreuger home—the state he's in.'

It's likely they were gassing away when Doyle had been helped to his feet, the last half-note gathered up from the gutter and stuffed into his grateful fist. They were maybe still hard at it when Kreuger stood up like a man in the hotel bar and ordered: 'Two glasses of your best whiskey for this decent man and meself.'

He was still buying drink at closing time. You could hardly blame him. After all even a Metal Man can have a proper sense of his obligations. Especially when it is the day he draws his disability pension and he's carrying heavy.

You'd think a miserly cleg the like of Doyle would be more careful with his money. But then with all the trucking and huckstering that went on that day he was what you would describe as miraculous drunk, staggering about, falling over barrels, spilling drinks and generally making a proper fluke of himself.

It's a God's charity that someone with a bit of foresight was on the salvage job outside the barracks or the last pound of the poor bugger's pension would have found its way into the Hotel-man's till.

The Window

I MUST have sat through a brave few wasted Masses in the
parish church of our little fishing village before I took proper
stock of the stained-glass window over the high altar. And
small wonder. I was too taken up with the whole parapher-
nalia of worship—the barbaric ritual and regalia, the curious
statues, the Stations of the Cross with their absorbing scenes
of cruelty and terror, but above all the worshippers themselves, so startling in the variety of their devotions—old
women kneeling erect, their jaws champing as they launched
their incessant appeals to the closed door of the tabernacle;
big lazy lumps of young fellows hunkering back against the
seats as if they were hip-shot cripples; girls ploughing their
way through prayer-books stuffed with pictures and memorial
cards; cute hawks twiddling a single bead of a motionless
rosary to give the impression of religious fervour.

From hip to hip I would swivel around in my seat, gawk-
ing about me in every direction, until my mother would pluck
my sleeve and whisper:

' Stop fidgeting, Mick, and say your prayers.'

At which I would fall to muttering childish incantations and
disjointed prayers whilst I swung my rosary beads viciously
backwards and forwards between my bare knees till I would
put them cracking off the seat beneath me. But soon I would
tire of this and, after making sure that mother was once more
intent on her missal, would again commence staring around
me.

It was the summer sun pouring through the stained-glass
window that first tethered my restless gaze. It turned the
window into a seething cauldron of colour—a glorious jumble
of scarlet and purple and spun gold and blue—too dazzling

to fit its jigsaw hues into any significant design. Only later, the sun gone, did I notice the strangely clad figures, foreign-faced and haloed, that filled the window from top to bottom. When I asked my father who they were he looked startled, cleared his throat, but before he could reply mother cut in sharply:

'The Twelve Apostles, of course.'

I knew better than to argue with mother, but she was wrong—there were really only eleven. Grim and purposeful, they were marshalled in columns of four as though they were the last files of a regiment of marching Apostles who had come tramping down the glass and out into the church—a rear-guard cut off from freedom and imprisoned for ever and ever Amen by the fall of a leaden-barred portcullis.

The four in the front rank were tall splendid fellows tower-ing half-way up the window, above them four more carved off at the·waist, then three heads and finally, between two third row heads, a little faceless half-halo, covering, I felt sure, a poor undersized Judas standing up on tip toe in an attempt to get into the picture. All except one of them were grey-bearded and he had long, brown, silky hair and a woman's face. Two were baldy, one skelly-eyed and one had six distinct and separate fingers on his left hand, three of them being nailless. A commanding figure in the front rank with two enormous keys, one of silver and one of gold, strung from his waist, pointed upwards at something outside the frame of the window. Trying to guess what all the upturned haloed heads were looking at became my favourite Mass-time game.

Still I suppose I would have soon tired of these bearded foreigners had not Jimmy the Master told us all one day about the miraculous draught of fishes caught with a single shot of the net by the Apostles.

From that moment these grave-faced men came to life before my eyes. I knew each one of them like the palm of my hand.

I could have described the cottage in which he lived; the food he ate; his slow quiet-spoken way of talking; what he did from the time he got up in the morning till he went to bed dog-tired at night. I could even have told you how he acted with a drop of drink in him.

And what is there queer about that? Were not these old men plain, decent, fisher-folk like every man-jack in the village? Hadn't I often seen my father and my Uncle Ned jump up in the boat and point excitedly at the sight of a snowstorm of plunging gannets or the twinkling silver of mackerel breaking on the water just as these stained-glass figures stared and pointed at the beamed roof of the chapel? And wasn't the old rusted key of the rocket house hanging on our dresser at home every bit as big and important looking as the keys dangling from Saint Peter's girdle?

No wonder I sat Sunday after Sunday with never a stir out of me till Mass was over, gazing up at the gleaming window with all sorts of daft notions chasing each other like eels through my head. Mother began to think there was the makings of a priest in me and indeed it seemed the only way I could become as good a fisherman as my father or Uncle Ned.

A year after my First Communion I lost all interest in the window, went back to my fidgeting and decided to become a trawlerman. This is how it came about.

A mission was held in the parish and on the opening Sunday the chapel was so packed we were forced to march the whole way up the aisle and into the very front seat.

Now in our village the front row of seats was, by a sort of unwritten law, reserved for religious cranks and half-wits. Oddities like Ellen Tierney—the May Queen we used to call her—whose custom it was to genuflect first to the high altar, then to either side and lastly to the congregation after which with a gracious inclination of her head, as though acknowledging our silent applause, she would take her seat. Or Musky Burke—a harmless poor gawm, the recognised pet of the village—who every evening made the round of the Stations on his bare benders, muttering and whispering away to himself all the time, his rolled-up trousers flapping and rustling on the stone flags. Many a devout old woman had had the living daylights scared out of her, for Musky, in the gathering darkness of a winter evening, must have seemed like a great, black, wounded bird, hissing and spitting as it dragged itself painfully along, broken wings trailing the ground.

It was Musky's seat that mother pushed me into ahead of herself, so that I was right beside him under the pulpit. Her reason for this unusual manoeuvre was obvious—she wished to be one person away from the notorious reek that had given Musky his nickname. But for my part I was too interested in Musky's antics to pay much heed to such a small matter as a bad smell.

He had at least a dozen rosaries draped along the ledge in front of him and every so often he would pick up a different one and commence running the beads through his fingers at the rate of no man's business, muttering at each jerk of his scampering fingers: 'Go ye by! Go ye by!' and at the large Our-Father bead: 'Go ye big un by!' Between whiles he would stand up and kneel down and stand up again and thump his breast and bless himself till it would make you dizzy looking at him. All the time keeping up the eternal litany of belches and tail-skutters that helped to make people keep their distance.

So engrossed was I in Musky's queer behaviour that I failed to notice the missioner open the sacristy door. One moment Father Brady was leaving the altar. The next, this tall, bearded figure, gowned and girdled and tonsured, was striding across to the pulpit. I tell you the heart near leapt out of my mouth at the sight of him, for here was the living comrade of the painted Galilean fishermen and could have stepped down that very instant from the sun-drenched window.

Now, I said to myself, this is what you will look like when you grow up. And stuffed with pride, I watched as he leaned out over the pulpit, hushing without effort every sound and movement in the church.

At last he commenced to speak.

My father used to say that a man's voice should be like the sea—soft and calm and slow-spoken but lifted to a bellow when he stormed with rage.

This voice was neither. It rose and fell in rounded measured cadences that put me in mind of the high-stepping trot of the kind of pony you would be apt to see at a show. It rolled over our heads and back from the roof and walls till we sat dazed under a whirling stupefying cloud of word and echo. Whilst he spoke, his hands moved in graceful eloquent gestures like the slow sweep of seaweed fronds in the swell of the tide.

For a while I tried hard to understand what he was saying but his city accent and the way he mouthed and hissed completely defeated me.

Musky was in the same fix. At the start of the sermon he sat, frowning with concentration, one hand to his ear, the other dangling a rosary halted about the third decade. There was not a mute out of him and even his agitated guts seemed to be under control. But soon, like myself, he gave up and I saw him begin to move an Our-Father bead, very gently, very gingerly, back towards the heart of his fist. Before very long a Hail-Mary bead was on its way. And then, like an overloaded goods train, the beads began to creak and clank with ever gathering speed as his avid twitching fingers sent them whirling against the timbered pew.

By the time he started on a fresh rosary, Musky was going full blast, belting his breast madly with his free hand, crossing

himself at the close of every decade with such furious abandon
that his right arm whirled like a windmill, whilst he urged
himself to even greater speed by his whispered exhortations.
The grumbling of his stomach recommenced though he
seemed to be trying successfully to keep it down to a reasonable pitch.

I saw the missioner shake his head a couple of times as if
tormented by flies but not until he leant out over the pulpit
to emphasise the gravity of his words, was the full enormity
of Musky's unorthodox devotion revealed to him. His head
jerked up like a startled horse and he broke off in mid-sentence
with a gasp. It must have taken him three deep breaths before
he was able to resume his sermon. But the damage was done.
More and more frequently, under the remorseless pressure of
Musky's rattling beads and gabbled ' Go-ye-by ' litany, was
the even flow of his discourse broken. He began to stumble, to
hesitate, to repeat himself : as if the hackneyed phrases rolling
from his lips had suddenly become unfamiliar and dangerous.

The heat of the church seemed to be affecting him too, for
repeatedly he pulled out a large, white handkerchief and
mopped his brow, though he always finished by patting his
mouth with finicky precision to let us all know that he was
really only drying his lips.

The war of attrition might have gone on long enough if
Musky, by this time completely isolated in his cosy world of
ritual, had not been suddenly overwhelmed by a violent
high-pitched hiccup, which attacked him as he was dealing
with an Our-Father bead.

If you can imagine a guinea-hen with the power of speech
you will have some conception of the dramatic effect of
Musky's sucked-in screech: ' Gooooohhhhh!' followed by the
rest of the pious ejaculation in a loud relieved voice: ' Ye big
un by!' It reined the missioner back on his haunches and so
shocked the congregation that no one even thought to laugh.

The tense silence that followed put an end to Musky's gallop. He huddled in a frozen terrified stupor, hugging his stomach with his clasped hands, the rosary beads that had been his undoing, wrapped around his knuckles. You could see him waiting for the hand of God to strike him down.

And indeed no wonder, for above him the missioner, his head held high, his stern gaze doggedly fixed on the rose window of the gallery, could well have been standing on Sinai, his eyes averted, in angry and offended majesty, from the calf-worshippers below. The only evidence of his mounting wrath was the slight movement of his jaws as he silently ground his teeth.

At last, after clearing his throat in a manner deliberate and menacing, he recommenced speaking but Musky, too terrified to relax, sat on in stricken immobility. I could see his lips pressed tight and his knuckles white from tugging at his craw and it came to me that he was holding his breath for fear of a worse calamity.

His eyes commenced to bulge, his cheeks to redden. The tightly-pressed lips, clamped ever more tightly shut, gave the lower part of his face a foolish grinning appearance utterly belied by the sick despairing eyes.

I prayed as I had never prayed before—not to God or His holy Mother, nor to Saint Anthony, uncomplaining holder of so many of my unredeemed pledges, but to the haloed fisher-men of the painted window, surely the trusty patrons of those in dire and instant peril.

Please, I begged, transport this angry monk to the altar steps where he will be able, like the sensible priests of the parish, to preach in peace with the bulk of the pulpit between himself and the antics of a poor foolish ghomey. Or else, I prayed, grant to your servant, Musky, the grace that he may hold out in silence until the sermon is over.

But when I felt the bench beneath me vibrate with the

violence of Musky's convulsive trembling, I guessed he was at the end of his tether.

And so he was. His mouth shot open and his tortured lungs and puddings had leave at last to bellow their furious protest.

Since then I have heard men of many nations, often full to the gills with porter or maybe gorged with bacon and cabbage, voiding the wind from their churning stomachs, but never a voidance so loud and prolonged as the one that filled the chapel that morning. When the last grumble had died away, a person would have been hard put to it to say which end of Musky was the real culprit.

The missioner's reaction was immediate. Leaning right out over the pulpit he addressed himself to Musky's bent shame-stricken head. He spoke in a low clear voice, meant, I am sure, to carry no further than the front seat but yet reaching, in the startled silence of the church, the straining lugs of every scandal-monger in the congregation. So perfect was his self-control that not the least trace of his pent-up fury was allowed to ruffle the smooth flow of his words.

' My good man,' he said. ' Your conduct is vulgar, scandalous and intolerable. If you cannot comport yourself any better than the beasts of the field, you should at least have the manners to sit at the back of the church where your behaviour will not be the cause of distraction to myself and the good people of the parish.'

Musky cowered down, head in hands, shamed and outraged by the awesome corrective of being read from the pulpit. His shoulders jerked spasmodically in the manner of someone trying to strangle a fit of sobbing and I edged along the bench towards him, snuggling against his dirty smelly body in an instinctive gesture of solidarity.

It was a queer feeling came over me then as I sat glaring up at the clever bearded hateful face that I had so wished

might one day look back at me from the mirror. Inside me
was a cold aching emptiness. I felt that I had been robbed of
something—something that lurked deep down in the pit of my
stomach. I had often thought of it as a small furry wild
creature, that spent most of its time tucked up in a corner of
my insides sleeping peacefully until suddenly a quite ordinary
familiar thing—the silver phosphorescence dripping from an
oar blade or the gleam of the monstrance swung slowly in
benediction: rain hissing on the sea or drumming on the roof
of an empty church: the tang of tarred rope or the heady perfume of incense—would send it scampering around madly
inside my tummy, tearing and scratching in a frantic effort to
get out. I had always taken it for the mysterious inner tumult
you had to have before you could become a priest.

With scalding eyes I blinked up at the stained glass window
but there was no comfort to be found there. The company of
brave, bearded giants had dwindled to a group of dispirited
old men, lost and frightened and leaderless, huddled together
against the onset of loneliness and despair. Their robes that
I had once thought so rich with colour now seemed tawdry
and outlandish. Their faces were wan and sickly and their
hands a scholarly white—like the missioner's.

I looked up at the hands resting on the pulpit-top—hands
smooth, well-cared, white, the fingers long and tapering;
hands that surely smelt of soap and sanctity. I looked down
at my own grubby hands with their black-ringed finger-nails
and at my mother's, dark and coarse and ugly, knuckled with
rheumatism and roughened with work. I looked at the brown
gnarled stubby-fingered hands of my father. I looked down
along the seat at the line of swarthy weather-beaten hands
and black-avised faces and it came to me that I had been
fooled and cheated.

These whey-faced men had been house-bound all their
lives, perhaps chained to book-littered desks or to counters

clotted with silks or furs or great bars of yellow gold. They had never seen a tall mast reel across the sky or heard the creak of straining timber or felt the pulse-beat of a tiller. They had never learned the kindly tolerance of those indentured to the sea.

No, I decided with a scornful sniff, these painted figures were not fishermen at all. It takes sun and wind and the salt spray to stretch hide on a man's skull instead of skin. And a lifetime's wringing a living from the sea to give him the neck and shoulders and powerful crab-claws of a man the like of my father.

Great men they might have been—great and holy and learned beyond measure—but they were strangers to the sea. Oh, indeed it was far from the sea they were reared!

I sniffed again with lordly condescension and huddled into the comforting warmth of Musky's rancid jacket.

My mother's angry whisper brought me back to earth.

'Wipe your nose, boy,' she hissed. 'And pay attention to the holy Father.'

Myko

You'd GET people to say that a barman couldn't put a foot wrong. That all he has to do is stick to the old reliable two-for-myself-and-one-for-the-boss system and he'll have a business of his own in no time. Well, God grant them better sense. It's well seen they don't know the Boss. If ever there was a skinflint born, bred and come to maturity—it's Myko Connors. You'd have a poor chance of ringing up a double on the cash register with him prowling around, breathing down the back of your neck like a jealous husband.

He runs a funeral undertaking business as a side line but believe you me, he has as little regard for a coffined Christian as he has for the relatives walking overground. And of all mankind, alive or dead, the class he has least time for are travelling gentry. He wouldn't serve a drink to a tinker, not if the seat of his trousers was patched with ten pound notes.

So you can imagine my feelings when the first person to darken the door on a Monday morning turns out to be the Cracker, son of old Maggot Feeney, the head bombardier of a notorious band of tinkers who camp out every winter a couple of miles outside the village.

'You'll get no drink here,' says I, giving him no time to open his mouth. 'So about turn and on your way.'

'I want to see the Boss,' says he, as cheeky as you like.

'It's a matter of business,' he says.

'Is it the measures you want to check? Or are you collecting for the Foreign Missions?' says I.

'It's a coffin I want,' he says. 'Me ould fellah's after dying.'

'Why the hell didn't you say that when you came in?' I says, when I got my second wind. 'I'll get the Boss for you now.'

'I'm sorry for your trouble,' I says, making for the door.

You should have seen Myko's face when I told him that the Maggot Feeney was dead and looking burial.

'Is it that bloody little ruffian?' he says. 'Why didn't he die at the Galway races? Or in his ancestral home in Granard where every tinker from hell to Bedlam was spawned? It'll give that Feeney menagerie a foot in the door if he's buried beyond in the graveyard.'

'Did you leave that young marauder on his tod in the bar?' he says. 'Get down to hell at once or he'll have the shelves stripped.'

When I got down to the bar I slipped young Cracker a right dart of whiskey for decency's sake.

'Drink it up before the Boss comes down,' I says. 'Poor ould Maggot wasn't the worst of them.'

The young buck was still licking his chops when Myko comes into the bar and tears into him.

'What's this I hear about you wanting a coffin?' he says, as if it was a criminal offence to die.

'Much use a coffin would be when you've no place to bury it. Are you going to put it standing in a corner of the caravan like a grandfather clock?'

'Or maybe,' he says, and you could nearly taste the vinegar on his tongue, 'Maybe you've a plot taken, beyond in the cemetery?'

'Me brother's away up to the Parochial House to fix up that end of it,' says Cracker, without turning a hair.

'What's that?' says Myko and you could have snared his two eyes with a hay rope. 'A plot in the graveyard. It's late in the day for your father to be thinking of settling down.'

'It was me ould fellah's last wish. He picked the spot himself a while back. And put aside enough to pay for it.'

Myko changed his tack.

'Funerals are an expensive item these days,' he says. 'D'you know you couldn't put a man under the clay for less than twenty pounds. And that would be little better than a pauper's funeral. Coffin, hearse and a single mourning car.'

'You'd be better,' says he, ' to phone your uncle in Galway. He was very devoted to your poor father, they tell me. I'm certain sure he'd rather the body was brought to Galway. From what they say, he can well afford the funeral expenses.'

'It's the coffin I want,' says Cracker. 'No hearse. No car.'

'And how d'you propose transporting the remains to the church? Are you going to hoist the coffin on your back like a creel of turf?'

'We can take him in the spring-cart. The coffin's all we want.'

'Aren't you the callous young brute! You'd expose your poor dead father to the wind and the weather and the jeers of the populace.'

'Never mind that. How much for the coffin? The cheapest you've got?'

'Ten pounds for a job in spruce. Including breast-plate, handles and the rest of the gear. To be padded, trimmed and caulked before delivery—'

Myko was going into his sales talk when Feeney pulled him to a halt.

'How much for the bare boards, put together and varnished?' says he.

'Cash down,' he added.

Myko's frown came apart at the seams and he started rubbing his hands together like a courting cricket.

'Eight pounds,' says he. 'That's the best I can do. And I'd be losing money at that figure.'

The Cracker bid him four and they chewed the fat till the differ was split at five pounds ten.

The young fellow paid up like a man. Myko told me to go

out to the store and help get the coffin on to the spring-cart.
Only when we pulled the coffin out from under the heap of
lumber where it had lain since Adam was a pup, could you
see the full extent of the robbery the Boss was after committing. You wouldn't put a brute beast in it let alone a Christian.
It was warped and twisted and knotted and there were cracks
gaping open that did away with the privacy a person's entitled
to—dead or alive. If there came rain the deceased would be
afloat before he reached the graveyard.

'There's nothing here that a lick of a paint-brush won't
cure,' says I, to cheer up the bereaved.

'Of course,' I says, 'it's maybe a bit on the large size,' (It
could have housed Finn McCool let alone a wee runt like
Maggot Feeney) 'but some padding here and there'll do the
job for you. You can't have him rattling about like a pea in a
whistle.'

As we were hoisting the wooden monster on to the cart
Feeney says:

'I'm not holding this against you, chum. I know you're
only the ha'penny boy around here.'

'So's your sister,' was all the answer I could rake up.

I went back to the Monday morning work, but all the time
I was dusting shelves and replacing bottles, polishing the bar
mirrors, serving the odd drink, with my ears deeved by the
bloody drivel that the first pint of the day provokes in a craw-
sick customer, I was debating in my own mind the case of
Feeney v Connors and I felt sure there would be an appeal
lodged.

I was right. Around five o'clock, with the bar packed and
the Boss and myself going like a pair of red-shanks who
should come sloping in but the Cracker and slinking in after
him his young brother Merley—a shifty-eyed jackal, if ever
there was one. They pushed their way up the crowded bar to
where Myko was serving. Cracker leans over and says:

'Are ye busy, Mr Connors? Could I speak to ye a minute?'

Myko looked up from filling a pint. When he saw who was in it he ducked under the counter again.

'I did what you told me, Boss,' says Cracker. 'I phoned the Uncle and they're sending down a coffin and hearse. We're taking the remains to Galway the night.'

Myko pushed the pint over to the waiting customer, got him his change and turned to Cracker.

'What's that to do with me?' he says, acting it out real cagey.

'We'll not be wanting the coffin now,' says Cracker. 'It's outside on the spring-cart. Will we leave it in the shed?'

By this time all hands were earwigging. Drinks were sitting untouched on the counter: conversation had dried up.

Myko took the ball on the hop. He says:

'It's all one to me what you do.'

'You'll refund the money, of course,' says Cracker.

Myko ignored him. He turns to me.

'Go out to the shed,' he says, 'and see what damage the coffin has suffered since it left the premises.'

I finished serving a round of drinks and when I got out to the shed the Feeneys had brought in the coffin. I got them to help me throw the lumber back on it, till it was decently hidden.

'To tell you nothing but the truth, men,' says I, when we had the wretched thing shrouded with broken boards, crushed cardboard boxes and empty ten-glass bottles 'I'm just as glad you returned this bloody horse-box. No one but a hungry cleg would have let it out of here in the first place.'

'Amen,' says Merley, the impudent whelp.

'Will that ould miser cough up the dough?' says Cracker. 'He's liable to get a belt of a porter bottle if he tries to renegue.'

'Don't be getting your dander up over nothing,' I says.

'The Boss may be a hard man but he's always straight in his dealings.'

'He'd better be,' says Cracker.

When the two Feeney boys came in by the street door, the crowd at Myko's end of the bar pushed back to let them in to the counter. Leaving them room to swing a bottle, I figured.

It was the Boss who went into the attack first.

'What's it like?' he calls down to me. 'Is it badly scratched? How many dents in the timber?'

It would make you doubt the existence of God when a man can come out with the like of that without being struck dead.

'Nothing that I could see,' I says, and I couldn't resist adding, 'it's in no worse shape than it was leaving the storehouse.'

Myko never let on to feel that kick in the fork. He goes to the till and takes out a sheaf of notes.

'Well,' says he, for the benefit of the congregation. 'In that case I must fulfil my obligations.'

He starts slapping the notes down on the counter under Cracker's nose.

'One . . . two . . . three . . . four . . . five . . .' he counts. 'Now the ship's on an even keel again.'

So help me loving Jasus, I nearly foaled a fiddler.

Cracker made no move to lift the notes. He eyed Myko thoughtfully, as if trying to decide what part of the bald skull he'd split open with the first crack of the bottle.

'There's another ten bob,' he says. 'You were paid five, ten.'

'I'm well aware of that,' Myko says, taking it nice and cool.

'You can divvy up so,' says Cracker.

Myko puts his thumbs into the arm-holes of his waistcoat and starts playing four finger exercises on his chest.

'Listen here, young Feeney,' he says. 'We'd better get this matter straightened out. You didn't get that coffin out on appro. You bought it from me for five pounds, ten. Right? Then I buy a coffin from you for five pounds. Right? If you don't like the price you can take it home to the caravan and use it for a settle-bed.'

I won't deny I was proud of Myko at that moment. With a wig and gown he'd have passed for the attorney general himself.

Cracker was shaken, but there was fight left in him still.

'The bloody coffin was bought and brought back the same day. How hell d'you make that out two separate deals?' he says.

Myko blew out his chest and addressed the bar customers as though they were a bench of jurymen.

'D'you mind the Harvest Fair a year back? D'you mind a jack donkey changing hands that day? The Feeneys sold it to Charlie Ruadh from the back of the mountain. And him too drunk to know whether he was buying an ass or an African elephant. Sure everyone at the Fair thought it was only a bit of a joke. But when Charlie sobered up and searched out the Feeneys at the tail-end of the Fair, how did they treat the poor old fellow? Did they refund him his money? They did in my arse. He bloody near had to go on his benders to get them to take it back for three pounds less than he paid for it. No use in Charlie saying he was only returning something he had bought that day but didn't want. He'd never have showed up at a Fair again if he had renegued on a deal like that.'

It was a masterly performance. Daniel O'Connell himself couldn't have bettered it. It was more like that cold lantern-jawed Northerner, Carson, larding into some poor quaking sinner for breaking laws that he himself meant to break before nightfall.

The steam was taken out of young Cracker. He hadn't a word to say. It was Merley came to the rescue.

'That was different, Mr Connors,' he says. He had the real tinker's voice, half-whine, half-bluster. 'That was different. It was the ould fellah sold the donk. This deal's between yourself and himself here. And leave the ould fellah out of it. If he was here to speak up for himself, there'd be no chawing the fat about the price of coffins.' He finishes up with a sneering kind of a laugh.

Cracker gives a gulp, as if he'd been kicked in the stomach. 'Who the hell asked you to butt in?' he says. I could see him getting set to play welt at Merley. 'You keep out of this or I'll plaster you to the wall.'

Myko chipped in at once.

'Now, now, boys!' he says. 'No fighting in the bar.

'Here you,' he calls down to me. 'Draw a couple of pints for the two lads.'

When the tumblers were in front of them he says:

'Drink up now, lads, and no hard feelings. You've the sympathy of all here in your sad bereavement.'

'And don't be leaving the money lying on the counter,' he says.

Could you beat it? The soft word and the kindly advice. Like a ministering angel. It wouldn't have surprised me if he had poked his head under one wing and started picking out fluff.

Cracker takes up the notes and the two play-boys start negotiating their pints.

I have always held that you could tell the form a man is in by the way he deals with his drink. Well, if you'd heard the clatter of the two Adam's apples glugging up and down as the Feeneys laid into the porter, gulching it back as if they couldn't get finished and away quick enough, you'd have known they were a beaten and a sorry pair.

When they put down their empty glasses, Myko says:

'Let you be on your way now. It's a long distance to Galway and you wouldn't know how the weather would turn.'

It wasn't the bum's rush, I'll grant you, but if he'd kicked them out with his stocking feet, it would have been much the same thing.

It was just a week afterwards to the day, that the smell started. The kind of smell that would put you wrinkling your nose wondering should you change your socks. The Boss was snoking around the yard all morning trying to trace the broken sewer-pipe. There was a shelf of stout to be labelled. I was taking it easy, with a bottle in one hand and the racing page of the *Press* in the other trying to pick out a likely double for Hurst Park when Myko burst in from the yard with a face the colour of putty. I was so startled I put the bottle under the counter instead of the paper.

'What's wrong, Boss?' I says.

'I'm ruined,' he says. 'I'm destroyed completely.'

'I'll never live this down till the day I die,' he says.

'What's eating you?' I says.

'Come out to the shed,' he says, 'and you'll soon see what's eating me.'

'And stir your stumps,' he shouts back at me from the yard.

When I got out to the shed, it was to find the five-ten job in spruce cleared of litter and the Boss standing over it horror-stricken. And no wonder. There was a cuckoo in the nest. A bloody coffin-dweller, no less. Not the usual one—to be coffined, conveyed, and dumped underground before there was time, so to speak, for your-man to warm the timbers. Oh, no! This was a real old residenter, long enough on the premises to claim squatter's rights. There was no need to unscrew the coffin-lid to put a name on the tenant. Myko might as well slap a breast-plate worded: *James (Maggot) Feeney* on the lid and be done with it.

It dawned on me that Myko's obligations wouldn't end there.

'Boss,' says I. 'You'll have to bury the little weasel. The Health Inspector'll be around if he stays here much longer.'

Myko was muttering away to himself. It sounded like:

'Oh, the dirty tinkerous tribesman and his treacherous gets!'

'Hadn't he a grave-plot bespoke?'

At the thought of that disreputable tomtit—never a creature of fixed abode—coiled up, in an odour of respectability, in a corner of the graveyard, with maybe a granite headstone over him erected by his sorrowing relatives, I could do nothing else, God forgive me, but laugh, I tried to gasp out an explanation:

'The Feeney clan'll be doing a pilgrimage . . . to ould Maggot's grave every year . . . and tinkers from every art and part . . . will be lined along the bar counter . . . drinking and fighting and smashing bottles and glasses . . . to do honour to the decent man that buried the Maggot Feeney.'

Odorous Perfume Her Harbinger

THE ACRID tang of freshly-spilled ink: the mingled odours of food, flowers and unwashed dishes: the musty reek of overcoats huddled together on a hall-stand: above all, the dry scourging scent of eau-de-Cologne evoke for me the leering ribald features of my dead grandfather, the deplorable behaviour of my always so correct aunts and—with blinding shocking clarity—the sight of my adored and lovely Granny, her bereavement forgotten, rocking back and forth in helpless mocking laughter whilst she thumped her perfume flask gleefully on her knee.

A few months before Granpa's death, the oddness that had been budding in Granny came to full flower. Maybe it was more apparent to me than to the others. I had been orphaned in a car crash and had lived with my grandparents since infancy, accepting them without question as my real parents.

Certainly Aunt Ellen, a kind homely wee body, noticed nothing wrong for she was all the time, even when tending bar, poring over silly old love stories.

And Aunt Sarah—a simple, poor creature, stone deaf and so short-sighted that her eyes nuzzled at the thick steel-rimmed glasses like hungry pike—Armageddon itself could be raging without an echo reaching the attic bedroom where she sat, winter and summer, dumpy legs swinging as she riffled through an old magazine or gazed stolidly into space or answered your unheard question with vehemently nodding head and a smile of singular sweetness.

As for Granpa, he must have wondered when Granny stopped coming to the bottling-store to help out with the bottling. They had always worked together from the time that he—land steward to her impoverished and prolific father—had made off with his employer's daughter, perhaps in full settlement of arrears of salary. He swept her from an easy-going pleasure-loving South to the dour flinty North, where he bought a licensed premises and installed his beautiful, exotic, giddy, not-yet-seventeen-year-old bride as a village publican's wife. She tended bar, helped at the bottling and the bookkeeping, cooked, kept house and, like her mother before her, reared a squad of youngsters of whom Aunt Ellen and Aunt Sarah were the only ones left husbandless and at home.

Granny never mentioned her girlhood in the big old country house pictured in the framed photograph above the drawing-room mantelpiece and few relics of this ancient splendour remained. A fox's mask, the silver-mounted hoof of a pony, a riding crop and, strangest of all, a pile of dog-eared ballad music, the front sheets of which portrayed, in stilted posture, ladies and gentlemen of a world far removed from my own.

One piece of sheet music—'Love's Secret'—showed a tall elegant officer leaning over the shoulder of a ringletted girl seated at a magnificent concert grand, who, to judge by her drooping wrists, was languidly, swooningly accompanying the rich thrilling voice of her soldier lover. Written on the top left-hand corner—beside the title—was the message: 'This for you.' It was signed 'John.'

Though Granpa's name was John and the copperplate writing was undoubtedly his, I found it impossible to imagine him turning the pages of a sheet of music, let alone singing a romantic ballad.

He was a small man. Small, bearded, sallow-faced. He walked flat-footed, without dignity and was continually puffing out the white whiskers ringing his mouth, like a bird ruffling its feathers. Indeed with his bright, glittering swift-blinking eyes gazing at you from side-cocked head, he was not unlike an aged but sprightly eagle.

He spoke gravely, deliberately, chewing over the facts first with munching gums (he seldom wore his teeth) before delivering judgment.

Before Granny began to go queer in the head, the routine for bottling stout had settled into a traditional pattern.

Granpa sits with his back to us, cases of empty bottles stacked within easy reach. Granny sits, stirring in a zinc bath a porridgey mess of steaming corks. I stand between the pair of them. Waiting.

Granpa picks up a bottle, rams its neck up the long narrow-stemmed tap, glances over his shoulder and says:

'All ship-shape and battened down?'

'Aye aye, sir!' we say.

'Full speed ahead then.'

He turns on the tap and with the same movement swings his hand over to the case for another bottle. The production line has been set in motion.

In a cracked voice he chants an accompaniment to the milking movements of his hands:

> *'What will we do with the drunken sailor?*
> *'What will we do with the drunken sailor? . . .'*

As each bottle is filled he drops it into an empty case beside him. The last bottle in place, I lug the case over to the zinc bath where Granny is waiting to insert the softened cork.

I give her a start of six corks before I start malleting. No word is spoken. Thudding mallet, jingling bottles, clattering of cases being shifted around. The air thick with the acrid tang of fresh porter.

When the three-dozen case has been corked, I shift it and pull into place another case that Granpa is after bottling. Always he keeps ahead of us, necking each bottle to the gushing tap so swiftly and smoothly that there is scarcely a drop of overspill.

Three cases corked, he turns off the tap and wheels around.

'Well, young fellow,' he says. 'What did the Master hammer into your thick skull today?'

'The metric system. He says if it hadn't been for one man there'd be no metric system in the world at all.'

'Small loss that would be. With their milli and kilo and whack-fol-de-diddle-dido.'

Granny asks: 'Who was it, Jim?'

'The Master says it was the French emperor. Napoleon.'

Granpa puffs out his cheeks, blowing loudly through his whiskers.

'Napoleon, is it?' he says. 'Now let me tell you something. If that quarrelsome little French ferret had gone oftener to the stool, the world would be a happier place today.'

'And where did you learn that piece of gossip, John?' says Granny.

'Sure the whole world knows that when he was opened up they found his guts were blocked solid with . . .'

'John!' Granny says sharply, nodding a warning in my direction.

'I know. I know,' he says impatiently.

Granny lifts a steaming cork and rolls it round with her fingers. She says:

'I can't see why there was any need to open the body. After all, he didn't die a violent death.'

Her lips move silently as though conning her multiplication tables.

'Un-less . . .' She drops the cork back into the bath.

'Surely they weren't looking for traces of poison?'

Granpa reaches behind him and grasps a bottle.

'How else would they stuff him if they didn't open the carcase?' he says, swinging round on his stool.

'Bear a hand, mates!' he says, necking the bottle and turning on the tap.

'Embalm!' Granny shouts, trying to make herself heard above the jingle of the bottles. 'Embalm! Not stuff!'

But Granpa is singing away to himself in time with the bottling:

> '*Oh, the French are on the sea, says the shan-van-vocht.*
> *Oh, the French are on the sea, says the shan-van-vocht...*'

Another three cases and he stops work again.

'Does he teach you nothing but French history, Jim?'

'Oh, no. We're doing Daniel O'Connell these days.'

'The Liberator, is it? And what has he to say about *him*?'

'He says his name should be taken out of the history books.'

'For why now, would there be any harm in asking?'

'He says he never drew sober breath from the time he broke his confirmation pledge till they pulled the britches off him for the last time in Derrynane. And between whiles he ran up a mountain of debt from card-playing, horses and fancy women.'

'So that's all he has to say about poor O'Connell.'

He turns to Granny.

'Did you hear that? Yon lemonade-drinking string of misery would condemn a man because he was fond of a jar and a bit of skirt. Well, listen to me ...'

'Hush, John! You'll only ...'

'I'll not hush. Drink and women were never the downfall of the Liberator.'

'John dear, you're surely not suggesting that Daniel O'Connell failed to achieve Catholic Emancipation.'

Granpa scratches his head frantically.

'I'm only trying to explain that he could have been a true Liberator ...'

'But sure he must have been or they wouldn't call him one?'

'I mean he could have liberated his country instead of his church.'

'There you go again. Off on your old hobby-horse. The Church.'

It is painful to watch the look of frustration on Granpa's face. His Adam's apple bobbles as he swallows his impatience. At length he says, very slowly:

'I'm not talking of the Church. Just the bishops.'

'I know, dear. The bishops.'

'By the time those playboys had finished with him, poor Dan was sapped of courage and manhood. Squeezed dry by a clerical octopus.'

'Is it not a grizzly you mean, John? Or one of those snakes that hang from trees? The big ones.'

'The snakes, of course. Not the trees,' she adds.

'They're in the Zoo. You know the ones I mean,' she elaborates.

Granpa's lips move. If I could lip-read, they would say:

'Snakes? Trees? Zoo?'

He looks at Granny. At me.

'Where was I?' he asks.

'I'm not at all sure. Somebody was being squeezed dry. A bishop, could it be?' she says, gazing at him gravely, her eyebrows raised in polite enquiry.

'A bishop?' Desperately he rasps his lips with a finger-tip.

'That's what I gathered,' she says. 'Could it be that this was preparatory to opening the carcase and stuffing it?

'Or if you prefer to put it that way embalming it?' she says.

You could count ten before his astonished face breaks into a grin. A grin of reluctant admiration.

'It beats out,' he says, shaking his head slowly. 'You'd make a penny-boy out of Solomon himself.'

He wheels round again to the porter tap. Over his shoulder he says:

'I'll bet when they opened him up there wasn't a straight bone in his archiepiscopal body.'

'And I don't mean Solomon,' he says.

Granny bursts out laughing. He joins in. And there they are, the pair of them, like a couple of school kids, skitting and laughing and making proper jackasses of themselves. When they begin to quiet down, something happens to start them off again. Maybe Granny will point a shaking finger at me and say:

'Look at old Sobersides. Sitting there in judgment like a stuffed Solomon. He thinks we're mad.'

Off they go again, as bad as ever.

This was all before the slow change came over her, transforming her from someone content to pass her days in quiet routine into the uneasy spirit that prowled the house from top to bottom in search of God knows what.

The first recognisable oddity in her behaviour was the way she would switch from daft gaiety to sudden frowning gloom. Her conversation would dribble to a halt and she would look at you silently with bemused, unseeing eyes. They were the eyes of a caged animal opaquely staring through you and the wall behind you at the barely remembered vision of freedom.

This trance was easily dispelled.

'What did you say, Granny?' in a loud voice would bring her back to reality.

Not so the next stage in her drift away from us. For now you could never meet her eyes. Her glance slid away from you like quicksilver and you found yourself staring instead at a handsome beaked nose and an ivory-smooth cheek without ever seeing her turn away her head.

Nevertheless the sensation of being constantly watched was always there. It was as if the awful Eye of God—confined so far to the coloured plates of prayer books from which it glared insanely down from the domed roof of a church at the unfortunate mass-servers beneath—had now become flesh and dwelt amongst us.

Let you sit down to eat with unwashed hands and an itch like the sting of a carefully-trained burning-glass attacks them curbing their flight from plate to mouth. Look up and her gaze is elsewhere, studying Granpa's movements as with finicky precision he cuts and jumbles, jumbles and cuts, churning up the diced meat, the bruised potatoes, the vegetables reduced to pulp by his busy fork, until all is in fit state for transfer to his toothless gums.

Try reading the folded pages of a comic whilst you hunker down over the seat of an armchair, droning out the responses to the rosary, and at once the burning-glass is steadied on the back of your neck. Glance round and she is stooped in concentration over the rosary beads sliding through her lean elegant fingers.

The final symptom of what I now decided was dotage was this constant prowling from room to room of the house. Every time I heard, in the prayers at the end of Mass, the priest's invocation to Michael the Archangel to ' thrust Satan down to hell and with him the other wicked spirits, who wander through the world for the rui. of souls,' I used to shiver. Not that my adored Granny coula ver be wicked. Much less be a party to the ruination of anyone. It was just that she was too much like a wandering spirit for my peace of mind.

Rarely would you actually meet up with her in her wanderings, though the whisper of her skirts was forever ahead of you.

She was climbing the flight of stairs you had not yet reached: the landing boards above you were creaking softly from her tread. She rounded the corridor just ahead of you: was behind the door you were always too late to see closing so stealthily. As you passed it you could sense her standing tensed, be-ringed fingers gripping the door-knob, grey eyes narrowed in an expression of distaste rather than alarm.

When you did chance to meet her on the stairs and squeezed against the banister to let her pass, you could see the puzzled questing look on her face, as though she were trying to remember what she was searching for, before she passed you with a wary glance, a brief smile and a murmured: 'That's a good boy!' Behind her trailed the antiseptic smell of the perfume she was continually dabbing on her temples, lips and hands from the flask in her handbag.

When I questioned Granpa he said:

'Eau-de-Cologne. Your poor Granny thinks it's a protection against everything—headaches, chapped hands, blistered lips, roughened skin.'

These moods of Granny's were not constant but were punctuated by intervals of normality, during which she fussed over us all with extravagant affection as though she hoped by this means to shed the burden of guilt and remorse mirrored in her anxious gaze.

But soon she was caught up once more in wild senseless gaiety and the wretched cycle would begin again. I came to dread the sound of her laughter and to pray, God forgive me, for some miracle that would silence it altogether.

In her absence Granpa and I continued bottling porter but now I must cork and mallet. We work quicker. There is little talk between us.

I have worked out a system of my own. A handful of corks I insert in succession before driving them home with the mallet. My fingers become deft. Often I pull ahead of Granpa and am forced to wait till he catches up. On these occasions I feel I am entitled to jack-act.

Once, with only half a dozen uncorked bottles left in the case, I fumble slyly in the basin for the smallest, spongiest cork, inserting it carefully so that it will not concertina. Then:

'Hey, Granpa!' I call.

When he looks, I drive home the cork with the heel of my fist.

'Now!' I crow. 'Match that!'

He turns off the tap and gets up. At random he lifts four corks from the cooling water, necks them and . . . Thud! Thud! Thud! Thud! They are fisted home.

'It's only money wasted, buying mallets for the likes of us,' he says.

He sits down on the stool. Facing me. I ready my mind for his questions, wondering what shape William Ewart Gladstone will be in when Granpa has finished with him.

'Look, son,' he says, leaning towards me. 'Your Granny's not herself these days. Pay no heed to her.'

He starts to wheel round to the bottling tap but changes his mind.

'You've seen the antics of a broody hen, Jim?' he says, picking his words very carefully. 'Nothing satisfies her. Mooching around from Billy to Jack with a neb on her like a wet week.' He clears his throat. 'Well, women are the same. They get moody. Nothing you say or do will make a bit of differ. You can only wait till the craving leaves them and they're themselves again.'

I pick my words every bit as carefully as him. I say:

'Are you trying to tell me that Granny is craving to clock?'

He bursts out laughing.

'Be Janey, son,' he splutters, 'you're as quick on the uptake as herself.'

Into the bottling again and him coughing and wheezing with laughter. Over his shoulder he shouts, above the jingle of the bottles:

'No need to worry, Jim. Her nesting days are over.'

That was the first laugh out of him in three months.

Come to think of it, it was the last. In two days time he was dead. Of a heart attack.

It was on the Harvest Fair day, a dragging old fair with the cattle still bawling on the streets at teatime. As Granpa had not come down from the study—a room part-office, part-library, where he attended to his ledgers and his correspondence—I was sent upstairs to fetch him.

When I opened the door I knew immediately that something awful had happened. He was still perched on the high stool pulled into the desk, but his head had fallen on the sloping lid. His cheek rested on the unfinished letter, over which the ink from the overturned inkwell had flowed. Ink had stained his sideburns, the top of his nose and the greater part of his beard and collected, like sour unshed tears, in the lower corner of one eye. The other watched me with cold indifference.

Even as I stood horror-stricken at the door, a drop of ink splashed to the carpet and, almost simultaneously, a sustained hysterical squealing broke out from the cartload of young pigs parked at the pavement edge outside. I had time before I too screamed, to think that this dreadful menacing clamour could well have been the last sound allotted to Granpa by a cruel and contemptuous Deity.

Granny—suddenly brisk, alert, composed—took charge of everything. Aunt Ellen was sent running for the priest, Aunt Sarah for the doctor. I was dispatched to bed, after swallowing back an enormous whiskey toddy, the glass clinking against my chattering teeth.

Then Granny was tucking the cool sheet around my glowing, weightless body, kissing me with paper-dry lips and murmuring:

'Try to sleep, darling.'

My last recollection was of the bedroom door closing softly on the clean comforting fragrance of cologne.

The next two days were crowded and eventful. From morning to night the stairs creaked with visitors. Strange faces—

grave, indifferent, nervously smiling—stooped, spoke and were gone. All day long meals were cooked, tables laid, dishes washed. Cars kept drawing to the kerb, shedding relatives.

Aunt Fanny—small, dainty, vivacious, elegantly dressed in dark well-cut city clothes. Aunt Bridget, my country aunt— fat and weather-beaten, with bulging spaniel eyes and with hands rough and broken-nailed. Aunt Rose from England, tall, as handsome as Granny but with a prim buttoned-up mouth. Her mourning clothes, like Aunt Bridget's, sat uneasily as though newly bought.

All brought husbands with them who spent most of their time in the bar or the drinking room, only appearing at meal-time.

Cables had been sent to the aunts and uncles in America, Australia and New Zealand and the door-bell was nearly pulled out of its socket by the Post-Office messengers with telegrams of sympathy.

For these two days the four aunts were rushed off their feet so that even Aunt Sarah was called on to bring in fuel or dry dishes. I ran messages—to the Post-Office, the grocer, the butcher. Only Granny remained tranquil and unruffled.

She sat in the drawing-room on a high-winged chair beneath her wedding photograph, little older, you would think than the precocious schoolgirl linked so determinedly to the jaunty bewhiskered bridegroom.

Gravely and lucidly she talked to the visitors, so different from the poor sick ghost of a few days back. Her only wanderings were to the corpse-room, where she shuttled back and forth with those who wished to kneel at the bedside in prayer.

My turn came before the coffin-lid was screwed down. I was below in the kitchen, daunted by the sudden hush that had come over a house crammed full with people. Granny came rustling in from upstairs. She said:

'Look, pet, would it upset you terribly to say goodbye to Granpa? You were his favourite, you know.'

Her voice was low, composed, but you could have squeezed, like a sponge, her glittering eyes. I followed her though the press of mourners on stairs and landings till we stood at the bedside.

When I was younger I had once buried a dead canary. In a shoe-box. As I looked at the tall sides of the coffin, walling in the tiny brown-clad figure, I thought wildly of the cotton wool I had stuffed round the dead bird till it was wedged— warm, secure, imperishable.

This thought came between me and my prayers as I knelt, with face buried in hands, at the foot of the bed.

The airless oppressive room would have been unbearable but for the fresh tang of Granny's perfume.

I was glad when she signalled me to get up and I followed her from the room without a backward glance.

In our part of the world, public displays of grief are frowned on. Funerals are dour, dry-eyed affairs, attended only by the men-folk: the women stay behind to cry their eyes out at will in the darkened memory-haunted house.

So I took my place in the top-hatted frock-coated assembly that followed the coffin to the church. For the whole journey —a solid mile—the coffin was shouldered by relays of bearers, tramping behind the empty hearse. I knew this to be a signal honour and, fattened with importance, I revelled in my role of sorrowing next-of-kin. Even the hollow thud of clay on coffin-lid was made bearable by my position among the front row of mourners, at the very lip of the grave.

When we returned the house was back to normal—blinds up, smell of cooking, the turmoil of the wake already swept and dusted away.

After dinner the men retired, with a bottle of whiskey, to the bar parlour. Aunt Sarah disappeared to her eyrie in the attic. Aunt Ellen and the other three aunts sat around the kitchen exchanging family news that soon trickled to exhaustion. Granny sat listening.

At last Aunt Rose got to her feet.

' I'd like a little souvenir of Father,' she said in her odd clipped English accent, ' before I go back tomorrow. I'll just take a look around upstairs.'

Aunt Bridget suggested:

' Perhaps, Rose. I could give you a hand,' and in the end they all went upstairs, leaving Granny and me below in the kitchen.

She sat at the kitchen table staring down at her moving fingers as they pulled and twisted one ring after another over the knuckles of each finger. The house was quiet except for the sound of the women's steps as they moved from room to room upstairs.

The footsteps changed from the continuous creak of a group of people moving around leisurely, to the purposeful tread of a single person. There was a hint of tension in the sound. I decided to investigate.

Through the banisters of the landing I witnessed the strange conduct of the four sisters. Like bees outside a hive, three of them hovered around the study door. As I watched, Aunt Rose came out, carrying a large gilt-framed painting. She stalked past her sisters without a word or glance, nodding her head continually as though applauding her own curious behaviour. She marched into the drawing-room where she placed the picture under a little heap of souvenirs, returning at once to the study. Soon she re-appeared with a pair of bronze lion-headed book-ends which joined the mounting pile on the window-sill. As she returned to the study, I heard Aunt Bridget say:

' This is going too far!'

She followed Aunt Rose into the room. They re-appeared

together, Aunt Rose with Granpa's marble inkstand: Aunt Bridget with a photograph, which she left on the piano top.

Now Aunt Ellen joined in. Her first foray produced two books and a silver paper-knife. These were deposited on a chair in the drawing-room. She nearly bumped into Aunt Rose on the return journey.

Soon the three aunts were scurrying back and forth, dodging each other as they passed, adding paintings, photographs, statuettes, but mainly books, to the growing heaps of souvenirs on sill, chair and piano top. And all the time in grim, sulky silence.

Only once did Aunt Fanny take part in this wild scramble. Caught up by the other three as they converged on the study door, she was whirled in with them, to re-appear in a few minutes clutching Granpa's battered old prayer-book. Hugging the book to her breast, she stood back squeezed against the wall, watching first in nervous frozen-smiled bewilderment and then in wide-eyed alarm the increasing agitation of the others. It was evident that the situation was out of control. An explosion was surely imminent.

I beat a cautious retreat back to the kitchen, where Granny, just after freshening up, was replacing the perfume flask in her handbag. The room, purged of the last trace of death by the wry pervasive smell of cologne, was quiet and restful as she leafed through the pages of an illustrated magazine.

It wasn't long before the hubbub began. Faint at first, and then louder as the aunts came streaming down the stairs.

Headed by Aunt Rose, they burst into the kitchen and fanned out around Granny. It was Aunt Bridget who went into the attack.

'Rose is behaving abominably,' she said. 'She'll have all away to England with her if you don't stop her.'

Aunt Rose's thin lips curled up in a sour smile.

'You're hardly the one to complain,' she said. 'Your feet

113

must be sore running around like a squirrel hiding things away.'

I thought Aunt Bridget would burst.

'Do you hear her?' she appealed. 'The drawing-room window-sill is piled high with loot and she accuses me . . .'

'That's right,' Aunt Ellen interrupted. 'She's got all of any value stacked away.'

Aunt Rose turned on her like an angry swan.

'Listen to Civil Ellen' she hissed. 'You haven't changed much over the years, have you? The little mouse with the sharp teeth.' She gave a contemptuous sniff. 'There was no need for *you* to hunt for keepsakes when you had all these years at home to skim the cream.'

Aunt Fanny gasped.

'And don't you try to sound so shocked, Fanny. If your home wasn't bursting with vulgar extravagance, you wouldn't be satisfied with a humble prayerbook as a keepsake.'

Blushing with shame, Aunt Fanny slid the prayer-book to the kitchen table.

Aunt Bridget, making a great effort to keep her composure, said:

'You know perfectly well, Rose, that this row is all your fault. You said you only wanted a little keepsake of Pappa, God be good to him.'

'And you all followed me upstairs to make sure that was all I would take. I know you did. If I hadn't come home for the funeral, I would have got nothing more than a memorial card as a souvenir.'

'We only wanted to help you' someone said.

'You were spying on me. As you always did. The three of you were continually taking sides against me when we were young. Apparently it's still the same.'

A babble of voices.

'Oh no, Rose!'

'You shouldn't say that.'

'We never took sides against you.'

Aunt Rose surveyed them scornfully.

'Jealous creatures. That's all you ever were.'

Through the indignant clamour a sharp voice cut in:

'Stop this vulgar brawling at once!'

We had all forgotten Granny.

'It seems I have had the misfortune to rear a family of tinkers. Quarrelsome, abusive tinkers.'

I had never heard the steel in Granny's voice before. This voice, I felt, had the authentic ring of riding-crop and jodhpurs.

'Rose,' she said, 'you seem the most glib-tongued. Perhaps you would explain what this unseemly squabble is about?'

Aunt Rose was unabashed.

'Oh, it's all a storm in a teacup, Mamma,' she said airily. 'Just a silly fuss over a little relic to remind me of Pappa, God rest him.'

She stared at Aunt Bridget daring her to speak.

'Can I see it, Rose?' said Granny, holding out her hand.

There was no need for me to wait for Granny to open the small purple box. I knew what it contained. The crystal and gold crucifix, with the glass panel at the back, through which you could glimpse a minute sliver of wood—a tiny splinter from the centuries-old timber gallows of Golgotha. A relic of the True Cross. This was the gift of the Mother Superior of a convent in Rome, in acknowledgement of some extraordinary but undisclosed kindness of my grandparents, when on pilgrimage in that city. It was kept in a drawer of Granpa's desk along with a parchment certificate, signed by the Mother Provincial, guaranteeing in sonorous Latin phrases, the authenticity of the relic.

No one spoke whilst Granny turned the crucifix over and

over in the palm of her hand. At length she turned to me.

'Run upstairs to your grandfather's room and bring down the Latin certificate in the top drawer of his desk. The Mother Superior warned us that if we ever parted with the relic, the documentary proof must go with it.'

Aunt Rose's face was wreathed in a smile of pure benevolence.

As I reached the door, Granny called after me:

'When you're up that far, tell your Aunt Sarah I want her.'

Granpa's room looked like a mouthful of teeth after a visit to the dentist. There were empty sockets everywhere. No photographs or paintings remained on the walls. The desk was stripped bare. The jade and ivory figures were gone from the mantelpiece. The bookshelves were grinning with gaps.

Before I left with the certificate, I pocketed a small leather-bound seventeenth-century treatise on 'The Perception, Treatment and Cure of the Melancholie Madness and like Ailments.'

In the attic bedroom I was forced to place my lips to Aunt Sarah's ear and shout my message. At last the puzzled expression left her face. She nodded her head triumphantly.

'Mamma want me? Is that it, Jim?'

I nodded agreement. And kept ahead of her, nodding encouragement, as she waddled out of the room and down the stairs.

The four aunts were standing as I had left them. Granny was still fiddling with the relic. She did not look up as I placed the certificate on the table.

Aunt Sarah took up her position at Granny's shoulder. With her piously-clasped hands and downcast gaze she could have been an altar-boy, patiently awaiting the signal to shift the Mass-book.

'Aunt Sarah's here,' I said at length.

Granny looked up.

'What is it, Sarah?' she asked.

Aunt Sarah smiled. She nodded her head vigorously.

'Yes, mam,' she said. 'Yes, mam.'

Granny's gaze travelled back to the tiny crystal and gold crucifix.

'Oh, yes,' she said. 'I had almost forgotten.'

She beckoned to Aunt Sarah.

'I suppose no one thought to give you a memento of poor Pappa?'

She spoke in a low clear voice, her lips carefully moulding each word.

Nodding and beaming with delight, Aunt Sarah said:

'No, mam. No, mam.'

Granny held out the crucifix.

'Here, child,' she said.

She picked up the parchment certificate.

'You'd better have this too.'

She flapped her hands like you'd shoo hens away from the half-door.

'And now, run along with you.'

Aunt Sarah must have reached the first landing before the clamour broke out.

'You can't do it, Mamma! You simply can't!'

'It's blasphemous. A holy relic like that.'

'God knows what Sarah will do with it.'

'She'll lose it.'

'Or throw it away.'

One voice dominated the others. Aunt Rose's.

'I knew it! I knew it! I knew it!' she said. 'You are jealous things. Low mean begrudging cheats. And now you have poor silly Mamma roped into your schemes.'

Granny said mildly:

'Poor silly Mamma. Is that what you think of me, Rose?'

Aunt Rose was unabashed. She stared back at Granny,

surely seeing, as in a mirror, the same haughty upthrust chin and stubborn grey eyes.

'You may be fooling the others,' she said, 'but you aren't fooling me. You know that, Mamma, don't you?'

She held Granny's gaze.

'You've started again, haven't you?' she said.

She leaned forward.

'Was it worry that brought on Pappa's heart attack?' She spoke in a calm reasonable voice.

The shocked silence lasted a bare second.

'How dare you, Rose?' Granny burst out. 'How dare you speak that way to your own mother!' Her anger was as spurious as Aunt Rose's equanimity. 'Now listen, all of you. If you must squabble like corbies over your father's few treasures on the very day of his burial, it will not be in my kitchen. At least I am mistress here.' She picked up the magazine again.

Aunt Rose smiled—a thin-lipped humourless smile.

'Oh, if that's how you feel . . .' she said. She stalked off, her straight back and shrugging shoulders expressing her own feelings.

The others drifted after her, Aunt Fanny last of all.

When they had gone, Granny laid down the magazine.

'Pay no heed to Aunt Rose or the others, Jim,' she said. 'Death seems to set folk quarrelling, instead of drawing them together.'

'It's not that' I said. 'It's just . . . Aunt Sarah . . . she's not fit . . . she's not . . . the right person . . .'

Granny interrupted.

'If it's the relic that's on your mind, you can stop worrying. It's a fraud.'

'Don't look so horrified, child,' she said. 'Relics can be faked as easily as antiques.'

'But how about Granpa—surely he wasn't fooled?'

'Your grandfather was an extraordinary man, Jim. He had a soft spot in his heart for swindlers and sharks. Any type of a crook was always sure of a welcome. Why, there are letters in his desk . . .' she coughed, 'from tricksters . . .' she coughed again, sharp and gritty, 'all over the world.'

'Slip into the pantry, honey, and get me a glass of milk. I've a frog in my throat' she wheezed.

'And don't fill the glass too full,' she called after me.

Her voice came to me as I lifted off the glass-beaded muslin cover from the milk-jug and commenced to pour.

'I think it became a hobby. Like his book-collecting. Not that they ever managed to swindle him out of anything. No. He just kept them on the hook, asking for more information, promising a substantial investment until . . . Thanks, dear. Just put it down there.' She was rooting around in her handbag.

'Where did I leave my glasses? They should be here. I distinctly remember . . . Oh, yes! I know where they are. On the dressing-table in my bedroom. Would you ever . . .?'

From upstairs came the low steady drone of voices.

'Wait a moment, Jim. Try the hall-stand. I could have left them there.'

As I left she called after me:

'If they're not in the hall-stand, look in the pockets of my waterproof.'

The hall-stand, a few steps away from the kitchen door, was swamped with strange coats. I burrowed into them.

'I can still hear John chuckling as we left the convent,' I heard her say.

The unfamiliar use of Granpa's given name brought my head up with a jerk. And there she was, in the tiny mirror of the hall-stand—the ricochetted reflection from a mirror someone had left on the kitchen dresser. She was easing out the cork from a half-pint bottle of whiskey (I'd have recognised the Jameson label at twice the distance).

'He said he had met crooks in every walk of life. In business, in politics, in the professions. But never before in a nunnery.'

The cork was out. Very carefully she was lowering the neck of the bottle into the tilted glass.

'He went straight to the Irish College in the Via . . . I forget the name of the street. He knew a Father Dempsey there. See would they maybe be in my grey tweed coat, Jim? He was from the West somewhere.'

The glass of milk was now topped up: the corked bottle back in her handbag. She lifted the glass to her lips.

'You should have heard the priest giving out. (sip) "A relic of the first class in the hands of a lay person. (sip). The very idea of it is beyond belief. (sip). It would be a sacrilege, John!"'

Still sipping, she took out the spectacle-case from her handbag with her free hand.

'And when John produced the certificate and said: "How about this, Father?" he nearly went through the roof. Oh, Jim! I've a head like a pin. The glasses were in my handbag all the time.'

Back in the kitchen, I found her, glass in hand, the open spectacle-case at her elbow.

'He told your grandfather that the Italians had turned the faking of relics into a national industry. "They have managed to convince themselves," he said, "that fraud for pious purposes has moral sanctions." He was from Galway I think . . . or was it Westport . . . tall . . . delicate . . . handsome . . .'

She put down the almost empty glass. Her caged eyes, scorning the years, squinted at the blinding Roman sunlight.

'You were saying, Granny?' I raised my voice.

'What's that, Jim?' she asked.

'What happened about the relic?' I asked.

'Oh, the relic!' she said.

She finished the last of the milk in two slow mouthfuls.

'Father Dempsey said that exposure of the fraud would cause too great a scandal.'

From her handbag she took the perfume flask. She unscrewed the metal top.

'But the nuns,' I persisted. 'Were they punished?'

She sprinkled her balled-up handkerchief. She said:

'God send you better wit, child. You'd have an easier job punishing the elements.'

With the scent-soaked handkerchief she patted her temples, her cheeks, her lips, her neck.

'I never had much time for nuns after that. Deep, deceitful creatures.'

Tipping up the flask, she shook it cautiously. One . . . two . . . three large drops of cologne were distilled on the back of her left hand. Stooping she lapped with rapid flicking tongue.

'How would it be if the priest was wrong and the nuns were right?' I asked.

She stared at me, slack-jawed, wide-eyed.

'That'd be the queer sacrilege!' I said.

Slowly her face creased into a grin. She rocked forward in helpless laughter.

I watched the small silver-casqued head bobbing and swaying, and the perfume flask, clutched by long, slender fingers, thumping against her knee in wild merriment. My throat went dry and my hands damp and the spurting tears scalded my eyes.

She looked up, gasping with laughter.

'You're as sharp . . . as a needle, Jim . . . When your Granpa hears this . . . he'll be tickled to . . .'

The flask slipped from her fingers, shattering to pieces on the tile floor, filling the kitchen with the clean astringent fragrance of cologne.

Meles Vulgaris

'WHAT ARE you reading, darling?'

Her voice was muffled by the turtle-necked sweater out of which she was struggling.

He pulled the bedclothes further up his chest, adjusted the pillow and turned a page.

'Come again?'

'There wasn't a cheep—' her chin emerged—'out of you—' the sweater was peeled from her rolled back ears— 'all evening. It must be—' a last effort and she was free— 'a powerful book.'

'Uh-huh.'

She pitched the sweater on to a chair seat shook out her wiry black hair and examined herself critically in the mirror.

'Sitting hunched up over an old book since tea-time,' she told the frowning sun-tanned reflection, 'without a word to say for yourself.' Eyes—sloe-black, deep set, heavy lidded—gazed back at her appraisingly. 'You know, darling, it's lonely all day in the house by yourself.' With tentative fingertips, she smoothed out the crow's feet. 'No one to talk to till you're home for the weekends.' Her gaze slid over the tiny frightening folds and wrinkles of the neck and sought comfort in the firm brown flesh of arms and shoulders. The mirrored face smiled ruefully. 'It's a wonder I don't start talking to myself.'

'Uh-huh.' With finger and thumb, he rasped gently the lifted ready-to-be-turned leaf.

She swung round.

'I belive you weren't listening to a word I said.'

'Sorry, honey. I wasn't paying attention.'

She reached out a hand. Curious.

'What's it about, anyway?'

He handed her the book.

' *The Badger.*' She leafed the pages rapidly. 'It looks like some sort of a text book.'

' So it is.'

Frowning, she studied the stylised animal on the jacket.

' Why the sudden interest in badgers?' she asked.

' I saw it—' he nodded towards the book 'displayed in a book shop window.'

' But what on earth induced you to buy it?'

' A sudden impulse. It reminded me of that holiday we had in the Blue Stack mountains. When we saw the badger fight.'

Her face lit up.

' But that was years ago.'

He rolled over on his side, tucked the bedclothes in round his shoulders and burrowed into the pillow.

' Oh,' he mumbled, ' I remember it—remember it right well.'

He yawned.

' The book tells you how the little fellows tick.'

The common badger—meles vulgaris—a genus of burrow-ing carnivores, is found in hilly or wooded districts in almost every part of the country. More common in the West than in the East.

Sunday morning after Mass. Around the church gate the usual crowd of men standing about in groups, talking football, greyhounds, hangovers, weather. From the outskirts Micky Hogan beckoning. Moving away from the crowd before he spoke.

' Are you for the match the day?'

' I don't know. Why?'

' They're drawing a badger up at Johnny John's.'

' D'you tell me! What dogs have they got? Mind you, it's not everyone will chance getting his dog mauled or maybe killed by a brock.'

' Hawker Downey is bringing along that treacherous whelp of a Kerry Blue of his. A right mauling might put manners on it.'

' Any others?'

' They have another Kerry Blue lined up. A good one.'

' Whose?'

' The curate's. The boys are going to whip it when he's gone to the match.'

' Och, go to God. There'll be the queer rumpus when he finds out.'

' The dog'll be at the gate to meet him when he gets back from the game. It might be a wee scratch or two the worse for the trip but sure the silly brute is always in trouble. You should take the car and we'll head into the Blue Stacks. It'll be right gas.'

' How did they catch the badger?'

' D'you mind the Johnny Johns complaining about the fox slaughtering their fowl?'

' Aye.'

' Well, they found pad marks yesterday morning outside the hen house. The tracks led to a badger's earth not a stone's throw from the house. The nest was dug up, the sow and the three cubs killed and Mister Brock himself is for the high jump this afternoon.'

The badger is a member of the order Carnivora and has large canine teeth but, contrary to popular belief, it does not prey on poultry or young lambs. It feeds on insects, small mammals, molluscs and earthworms, supplemented by veget-able material such as fruit, nuts and grass.

Still riffling the pages of the book, she stared blindly at the unfamiliar photographs. Tenderness welled up inside her, tearing at throat and eyes. Perhaps he too was thinking of their first holiday together after they were married. When he had taken the firm's car and they had driven into the foothills of Croaghgorm to his Aunt Ellen's tiny farm-house. There was no money to go any place else. But who cared? They had spent three weeks there, coddled and fussed over by Aunt Ellen.

They had moved round together in a daze. Drunk with love. Shouting their crazy enchantment at the echoing hills. Bound together with such hunger for each other that the warmth left the blazing summer sun if they moved apart.

For those three weeks they had only one body between them—a parched thirsty body that soaked up happiness like a sponge. It was on the last day of that unforgettable holiday that they brought Micky with them to the badger fight in the Blue Stacks.

The baiting had already started when the car bumped and slithered up the last stretch of track and into Johnny John's yard. A crowd of mountainy men stood around watching Hawker Downey—a fussy, wee, know-all—trying to coax, drag, push his stupid gulpin of a dog into an overturned barrel. Each time he got the Kerry Blue's forequarters inside the barrel, the dog would wriggle free dashing around among the onlookers, wagging its stumpy tail.

The crowd hooted and jeered.

'Put your shoulder to him, Downey.'

'Take away the cowardly cur.'

'Give the curate's dog a trial.'

'Crawl into the barrel yourself, Hawker.'

Downey was nettled. He got the dog by the scruff of the neck and the skin of the rump and fairly hurled it into the barrel.

'Sic him, Garry!' he urged. 'Sic the brock!'

Never did dog react quicker. It bounced back out of the barrel, shot between Downey's splayed legs and never cried halt till it reached the safety of the dunghill, where it ploutered about in the soggy muck, wagging a doubtful,

125

disillusioned tail. Whistles, threats, curses, wouldn't shift it.

There was nothing for it but to try out the curate's dog. Much against his will Micky Hogan, who sometimes exercised the dog for Father Bradley, was prevailed on to handle it.

'I'll gamble the curate will blame me for this day's work, if he gets to hear of it. So keep your traps shut. All of you,' he said.

The Kerry Blue trotted at his heels to the barrel mouth. He patted its flank.

'In you go, champ,' he said.

The dog moved in willingly enough. For as long as it took Micky to straighten up, take a cigarette butt from behind his ear and light it, the dog stayed stiff-legged, tail quivering, before it backed out slowly. Once clear of the barrel it stopped, shaking its head violently.

Micky grabbed it. Examined the muzzle.

'Not a scratch,' he announced. 'There's only one remedy for this disease. The toe of me boot.'

'You may give over, Hogan,' a querulous voice called. It was the old fellow himself. Johnny John. He was standing at the kitchen door, watching the proceedings with a sardonic smile. 'I told the young fellows to get fox-terriers. But of course they knew better. Those dogs you've got aren't worth a curse. They'll never face the barrel.'

'For why?'

'The smell of the brock has them stomached.'

One of the characteristics of the badger is the possession of musk- or stink-glands. These anal glands are used as a result of fear or excitement. The recognition of danger will stimulate secretion and trigger off the defence mechanism.

A hand ruffled his hair.

'Unhook me, will you, honey.'

Reaching up a hand towards the voice, he pawed the air blindly.

' Come on, lazy-bones,' she urged. ' I can't get this wretched thing off.'

His eyes opened to black bra straps biting into sun-browned skin. As he fumbled with the hooks, buried deep in flesh, she chattered on:

' How's that for a tan? I was the whole week stretched out on the lawn. Sun-bathing. We get so little sun it would be a shame not to make the most of this hot spell. God knows, it's hard enough to get a decent tan up. Olive oil helps, of course. But then you must be careful not to fall asleep or you'll get fried. Properly fried.'

The loosened bra fell away. With outstretched arms she spun around.

' Becoming, isn't it?'

The brown body appeared to be encompassed by a monstrous pair of white plastic goggles out of which glared two angry bulging bloodshot eyes.

His flesh crept with embarrassment.

' Most exotic,' he said.

She flushed with pleasure.

' You really think so?'

He yawned wide and loud.

' Sure.'

His head dropped back on the pillow.

It was decided to let the dogs attack in the open where the rank smell would be dispersed. The crowd scattered back from the barrel. The two dogs were leashed.

One of the young Johnny Johns gripped the bottom of the barrel. Tilted it. Slowly. To knee level. Scrabbling noises. Higher still. More scrabbling noises. Up to hip level. Silence.

' He's lodged, boy,' called Johnny John. ' You may shake him out of it.'

The young fellow shook the barrel. Cautiously. Nothing happened. Harder this time. Still no result.

' You'll get no windfalls that way,' someone shouted.

' Slew the barrel round, Peter,' the old man ordered.

A murmur of appreciation went round.

' Sound man.'

' The old dog for the hard road.'

' It takes yourself Johnny.'

Slowly Peter swung the barrel on its base. The crowd began to close in. The old man moved out from the porch. One of the dogs whimpered.

At the quarter turn the badger came slithering out, still clawing wildly for purchase.

It crouched, facing its tormentors, the grey-black hair on its body bristling like a hedgehog, its black and white head flat to the ground. Although it remained motionless, its whole body, from snout to stumpy tail seethed with controlled energy.

This fierce smothered tension dominated the crowd with a threatening fist. No one moved. Peter still held up the tilted barrel. Hogan's smoked down butt scorched the palm of his hand unheeded. Halted in mid-stride Johnny John waited, ash-plant poised.

Again a dog whimpered.

The crouching badger leaped forward. It picked no gap in the ranks of its enemies. It hurled itself at them and they broke before it. Shouting and cursing: shouldering, elbowing, pushing each other, in their anxiety to get out of the path of this savage creature running amuck; they backed away.

Through this opening dashed the badger. Ahead lay freedom. A length of laneway a thick hedge, a familiar track reeking with the smell of its kind, the safety—somewhere— of an unravaged set.

There was one enemy left. Johnny John.

Wily and tough as the brock itself, he had moved out towards the yard gate and now, with stamping feet and flailing ash-plant, he headed the badger back towards the closed and bolted outhouses.

Baffled, uncertain, the badger slowed down, scuttling along with a lurching, waddling gait. The length of the outhouses it ran, seeking shelter—scurrying, hesitating, scurrying again —like a business man hunting for a seat in a crowded train.

The feet of the badger are plantigrade: the animal walks on the flat of its feet, including the heel, in contrast to the Ungulates, which walk on their toes.

He clung doggedly to his share of the bedclothes as she plunged into bed, wriggling and threshing around, till she was coiled up under the glow of the bed light, an open magazine held between pillow and bedclothes.

The glossy leaves crackled imposingly as she flicked them over, seeing not mink-coated figures, luscious dishes of food, enormous luxury automobiles, but grim, hungry, plush-covered hills.

' Why don't we go back there again?' she said. ' Sometime.'

' Where?' His voice was muffled by the pillow.

' Croaghgorm.'

The bed springs creaked as he shifted peevishly.

' What would we be going there for? Aunt Ellen's dead.'

' We could stay some place else. A farm-house in the hills.'

Again he shifted. Rolling over on his back. To the ceiling he spoke—patiently, reasonably, wearily.

'Look, Sheila. In a cottage in Croaghgorm you would last exactly one night. No hot water. No foam rubber mattress. No thick pile carpets. No radiogram. Above all nothing to do. Except you tramp the mountains, helping them to herd sheep.'

Her heart contracted as she felt the spring of the moss under her bare feet, the cool squelch of mud oozing between her toes.

' Or sit in the house all day blinded by a smoking turf fire.'

She drew in her breath, sniffing the acrid, heady, wholly delicious, fragrance of burning turf: watched with sleepy eyes the flames die down as the brown ash formed: heard the tired sigh as the burnt out sods collapsed.

' Not forgetting the peaceful night's rest you'll have with sheep dogs barking, cattle bawling and roosters crowing their heads off at day-break.'

She rolled over facing him.

' We must go, dear. Sometime. If it's only for the day.'

' All right. All right.'

He pulled the bedclothes over his head.

The badger disappeared into the opening between two outhouses.

' He's got away.'

' Why didn't you mill him, Johnny?'

' Loose the dogs.'

The old man pranced about in the gap, waving the stick.

' He picked the baiting-pitch himself,' he said, as the crowd gathered in the opening. ' And a better choice he couldn't have made if he'd searched all Ireland.'

It was a cul-de-sac. The gable ends of two outhouses—one of concrete, the other galvanised iron—a few yards apart, linked by a man-high stone wall.

Around these confines the badger sniffed, scratching the ground here and there with a tentative forepaw. Where the zinc shed met the wall, it started digging.

By the time the decision had been reached to send in Hawker's dog first, the badger had rooted out a hole large enough to warrant the use of its hind paws. With these it scattered back the uprooted clay into an ever-rising parapet.

When the Kerry Blue came charging in, the badger wheeled around, keeping to the shelter of its burrow, to face its assailant, teeth bared in a silent snarl.

It crouched motionless but for the grinning muzzle that swung from side to side parrying the probing onslaughts of the dog. This swaying exotically-striped head, slender, graceful, compact with fierce vigilance seemed to repudiate the huddled body, craven, lumpish, dingy, belonging surely to a different and inferior species.

The dog pounced. It grabbed the badger at the back of the head where the long grey body-hairs begin. Secure from the snapping jaws by this shrewd grip, it whipped up the striped head, shook it violently and slammed it back to the ground. It pinned down the badger's head, pressing it into the loose clay whilst it gnawed and grunted, grunted and gnawed, shifting its grip deeper and deeper through the thick hair, as if it sought to sink its teeth into solid flesh.

Always it was thwarted. Choked by the mass of coarse wiry hair, it was forced to loosen its hold, gulping in a quick mouthful of air before it pounced again.

The badger crouched supine, muzzle buried in the clay. Waiting.

At last the gasping dog released its hold. For one vulnerable second it loomed over its enemy, its slavering jaws content to threaten. In that second the badger struck.

The striped head reared up. Snapping jaws closed on a dangling ear. A yelp. Frenzied scuffling as the growling dog sought to free itself. A wild howl. The badger, still gripping the torn ear, had lashed out with one of its fore-feet, raking the dog's muzzle—once, twice—with its long gouging claws before the poor brute broke free. Bleeding from lacerated ear and jowl, it backed away yapping.

Johnny John struck the ground with his stick.

'You may take the cowardly brute to hell out of that,' he

said. 'A Kerry Blue's no use to fight once it starts giving tongue.'

Downey grabbed his dog and lugged it away. The badger went back to its burrowing. Micky Hogan started to unleash the second dog, now trembling and straining at the lead.

'You mightn't bother your barney, Hogan,' said Johnny John. 'That dog'll never best a brock. Didn't I tell you it was a soople, snapping animal you wanted. Not a big lazy get the like of thon, that'll fall asleep on the grip.'

Micky looked up.

'I'm surprised at you, Johnny,' he said. 'Have you no respect for the cloth?' He stooped over the dog. 'Go in there, Father Fergus, and show this anti-clerical gentleman how you handle a heretic.' He released the dog. 'Off you go, chum.'

The dog advanced cautiously. Every few paces it paused, straddle-legged, watchful, snarling muzzle out-thrust, its gaze fastened on the badger, now faced round awaiting its attacker. It advanced to within arm's length of the striped muzzle before it came to a halt, crouched on stiffened forefeet. It growled softly, continuously—a growl so far back in its throat that it sounded like a harmless gentle purr.

The badger held its ground, beady eyes bright, alert, muzzle cocked, lips drawn back in its soundless snarl.

The two animals crouched, locked into stasis by the hate and fear that glared back at them from alien eyes. So long did they remain poised that a shout went up when the tension was broken at last by the pouncing dog.

'He's nailed him!'

'Good on you, Fergus!'

'Hold tight to him!'

Johnny John said quietly:

'There'll be trouble when he loosens yon grip.'

The dog had gripped the badger by the snout and was

tugging it from its burrow into open ground. The badger with splayed feet, resisted. It was of no avail. Heaving and jerking, the Kerry Blue drew the badger inch by struggling inch over the clay parapet until it had the thirty pound carcase out on level ground. At this moment the dog's hindfeet lost their purchase on the moiled ground.

The sudden skid loosened the hold of the dog's jaws. It was the badger's chance. Teeth crunched. A yelp of pain from the dog. The badger's clumsy body came to life—squirming, wriggling, jerking. At last it was free. Snout torn and bleeding. One eye damaged. Dragged from its sheltering burrow. But free.

It began to sidle towards the uprooted trench. The dog blocked its path, menacing the badger with bared and bloody teeth.

' The brock has relieved the poor bugger of half his bucking tongue,' someone said in an awe-stricken voice.

' What did I tell you?' said Johnny John.

This time there was no preliminary sparring. The dog closed in at once, only manoeuvring so that his attack came from the badger's rear, safe from the deadly teeth and claws. Like a boxer using his reach, the dog took advantage of longer legs and greater agility. It leapt around the badger, darting out and in, feinting to charge until it lured its enemy into position. Then it pounced.

Sometimes it succeeded in straddling the badger, flattening it on the ground, where it could tear and maul the defenceless animal's head. But not for long. The badger would break free, roll over on its back and rip with lethal claws the dog's unprotected belly.

Slow, ungainly, its heavy stumpy-legged body unsuited to swift exchanges, the badger was content to remain on the defensive. But always it was dangerous. Let the Kerry Blue fail to duck away quick enough after releasing its grip and another gash was added to its scored and bleeding body.

Except for the scuffle of paws on the trampled clay, the panting of the dog as it sparred for an opening, an occasional grunt from either animal, the struggle was fought out with quiet decorum. Indeed for long stretches there was complete silence as the two animals lay locked together, jerking spasmodically as the dog strove to deepen its grip or the badger to free itself.

If both had not been so mired and bloodied—the badger's slender elegant head being so plastered with blood and clay that the parti-coloured striping could no longer be discerned —they could have been tricking together harmlessly. Or dozing in the sun. Or even coupling.

It was evident that the strain of continual attack was wearying the dog. Its movements were now clumsy, sluggish: its lithe evasions slowing down. At last the inevitable happened.

The Kerry Blue came charging in obliquely. Swerved to escape the grinning expectant muzzle. Halted. A moment of teetering indecision. A shout from the crowd.

'The brock has got him!'

'It'll tear the throat out of him!'

'Maybe we should separate them, lads?'

'Throw Downey's craven cur in on top of them.'

Hawker called:

'Will I let Garry have another go at him, Johnny?'

The old man squirted a jet of tobacco-juice towards the straining dog. Said he:

'Damn the differ it'll make. The brock is the boss. He'll beat the two of them.'

Hawker loosed the dog.

'Sic him!' he said. 'Sic the bastard!'

The dog went in, running low to the ground, watching its comrade back away, dragging after it the badger, in a frantic effort to break the throttling hold. Ignoring threats, jeers and pleadings, it waited its opportunity. An unexpected jerk put the badger's legs sprawling. The wary dog pounced, grabbing the badger by a hind leg. Tugging at its hold, it swung the badger off the ground till it dangled belly up, its teeth still sunk in its enemy's throat.

Before the badger could right itself, the dog slammed the helpless body down on its back and, shifting its hold, bit deep into the tender flesh of the groin.

So swiftly did the badger release its grip and lash out with scourging claws at the already lacerated muzzle of its new assailant that the agonised yapping of both dogs—the throttled and the mauled—broke out simultaneously. Still yapping, they fled to either side of the enclosure where they wheeled round, barking and growling. They were in poor shape. Bloody. Mangled. Shivering with fright.

'That burrowing bastard has made a slaughter-house job of them,' said Micky Hogan.

Johnny John spat, a quick explosive spurt. He said:

'Didn't I warn you the brock would master the pair of them? Better if you call in your wretched curs before he drives them ahead of him into the village.'

The badger had limped back into the scooped out trench. It commenced digging again. With its forepaws only. Soon its claws could be heard rasping on the cement foundation of the shed. It stopped. Changed position and burrowed again till once more stopped by the cement. Twice more it tried, before it started on the galvanised iron. Inserting a paw under the bottom of the sheeting it commenced to tear at it, tearing and tugging until at last it managed to secure a purchase for its jaws.

'In the name of God,' someone said, with a nervous laugh, 'does it mean to pull down the building over its head like Samson?'

The badger was worrying at the metal sheeting—tugging,

snapping, gnawing—its body coiling and uncoiling, as it strove to chew or tear its way to freedom.

'You'd think it was crunching biscuits,' one of the young Johnny Johns said. 'With jaws the like of yon, it'd chaw itself out of Sing Sing.'

The badger has extremely powerful jaws. A peculiar feature of the lower jaw is that it locks in a transverse elongated socket in such a complete manner that it will not dislocate: if it comes away at all the skull will be fractured.

An elbow jogged him.

'Are you asleep?'

'Eugh! . . . Eh? . . . Aye!' A long sighing breath. Part moan, part fretful wail.

'Come off it, Brer Fox. You're codding nobody. Lying awake there brooding on the silly old badgers you were reading about all evening.'

She ran a teasing finger down the bones of his spine.

'Wha's-a-matter? Wha-dja-want?'

'Oh, nothing. I thought you were asleep.'

'Darling. I've had a long, hard day. I'm jaded out. Beat to the ropes. Let's go to sleep, what d'you say?'

He clutched the bedclothes. Huddled down lower in the bed. Breathed loudly, steadily, through his nose.

The men were debating the fate of the badger.

'Destroy the brute. That's the only thing to be done.'

'Look at the shape it's left the dogs.'

'What'll the curate say when he sees the cut of Fergus?'

'Small odds about those whining hoors,' said Johnny John. 'Didn't the brock lather the daylights out of the pair of them? We'd be poor sports to slaughter it after that.'

'Let it go,' he urged.

'So that it can raid more hen-houses?'

'Or spread ruin round the district with its burrowing?'

'Aye! Or maybe start attacking the young lambs?'

Johnny John was overborne.

'All right' he said. 'Fetch out a mattock.'

It was decided that Clarke, the village butcher, would dispatch the badger. Mattock at the ready, he moved in towards the gnawing animal. A few paces from the burrow he halted as the badger swung round to face him. Three cautious steps brought him within striking distance of the snarling muzzle. He hefted the mattock. Balanced it carefully, judging his target. Brought the blade smashing down square on the badger's poll, driving its head deep into the clay. A neat professional stroke.

The butcher stood over the motionless body, leaning on the shaft of the mattock. He was about to turn away, satisfied with a job well done, when the badger stirred. Raised its bloodied muzzle from the clay. Struggled erect.

Again Clarke chopped the heavy-bladed weapon down on the badger's skull, crushing the mangled head to the ground. Slowly, painfully, the snarling muzzle was raised in defiance.

Twice more the butcher swung down the mattock before Johnny John's shouts penetrated his shocked bewilderment.

'In God's name, give over, Butcher. You'll never do away with the brute that way.'

The old man rushed into the enclosure.

'Gimme that tool, man,' he said, grabbing the mattock. 'You'll take the edge off the blade. D'you not know that a brock's skull will stand up to a charge of buckshot?'

A feature of the badger is the extraordinary growth of the interparietal ridge of bone on the dorsal surface of the skull in the mid line. This ridge is half an inch deep in places and serves to protect the main surface of the skull from blows delivered directly from above, though its prime purpose is for the attachment of the powerful jaw muscles.

'Tell me,' she murmured, her breath fanning his ear, 'what attraction a badger has got that the rest of us lack?'

She had rolled over, cuddling herself against his back.

'Can't you let a fellow sleep?' He edged away unobtrusively.

'What has it got?' she insisted, snuggling closer.

'It's got courage. Courage. Tenacity. Fortitude.'

'Where do the rest of us come in?' Her hand burrowed into the jacket of his pyjamas. 'Wouldn't we all act the same way with our back to the wall? Courage and ferocity!' She sniffed. 'There's more to it than that. Surely?' Her fingers drummed an urgent message on his chest. 'You'd never ask someone to take second place to a stupid old badger.' A warm leg slid over his own. 'Would you, darling?'

'Sheila . . . please!'

He shook himself free. Reached up and switched off the light. Fists clenched, eyes squeezed shut—he lay, trying to ignore the reproach in her rigid outstretched body. When at last her breathing had steadied to the rhythm of sleep, he tugged the bedclothes back over himself, relaxed and opened his eyes to the dark.

Queer, he thought, how she had got to the core of things. Unwittingly. For surely, without tenacity, courage and ferocity were futile.

The courage of the badger is legendary. A shy, inoffensive animal, with no natural enemies, it will yet, if cornered, exhibit a ferocity noteworthy in a creature of such small dimensions. It is utterly fearless. Whether bird, beast or reptile: the forces of nature or the savagery of man—nothing can daunt it.

Johnny John was standing an arm's length from the badger.

'There's only one way to kill a brock,' he said, over his shoulder.

He raised the mattock. 'A clout on the muzzle.'

He swung down the blade.

At the same instant the badger charged. The squelch of the blade on the animal's back and the cry of dismay from the old man came together.

'So help me God,' he wailed, 'I didn't mean to do it.'

He dropped the mattock. With horror-stricken gaze he watched the badger. Hindquarters flattened to the ground, girning muzzle still lifted in challenge, it continued towards him, dragging its helpless body forward on stubborn forepaws.

'A wee tap on the nose. As God is my judge, that's what I tried to do,' Johnny John pleaded.

'Come away out of that, Da, or it'll maybe maul you,' one of the boys called out.

The mattock lay across the badger's path. An insurmountable barrier to the crippled beast. Feebly it pawed at the heavy implement striving to push or pull it aside. Without success. At last, the infuriated animal sank its teeth in the wooden shaft, lifting the handle clear of the ground. Unable to drag itself further forward, it lay stretched out, eyes glaring madly ahead, clenched jaws holding aloft the murderous weapon. The matted, filthy, blood-stained animal had already the ugly anonymous appearance of death.

The old man was near to tears. In his distress he shuffled a few steps to either side, beating the fist of one hand into the palm of the other.

'Where's my stick?' he muttered. 'Where hell's my stick?'

He shook his fist at the watching crowd.

'It's all your fault, you ignorant pack of hallions. Didn't I pray and plead with you to let the brock go? Now look what you've done.'

He moved back towards them, changing direction aimlessly, his gaze scanning the ground.

'Where did I drop my stick? It must be someplace hereabouts.'

He looked up.

' Let none of you ever boast of this day's work. It was pure butchery, that's what it was. A cowardly bit of blackguardism. There's more spunk in the brock than in the whole bloody issue of you.'

He halted.

' Will some of you find me stick . . . or some other implement . . . He looked back over his shoulder, as though fearful of being overhead. ' Till I put an end to its . . . Oh, Mother of God!'

The badger had released its grip on the mattock. It rolled over on its back. Screaming.

It kept screaming—a loud sustained yell of defiance that not even the onslaught of death could subdue to a whimper: that ceased abruptly only with the slack-jaw and the glazing eye.

There are many conflicting theories regarding the signifi-cance of the badger's peculiar yell. Some naturalists believe it to have sexual origins: others that it has some connection with the death or funeral rites of this strange animal. All are agreed on the blood-curdling quality of the cry.

Lying wide-eyed and sleepless, he tried to close his ears to the appalling sound. It was no use. The voice of the dying badger refused to be silenced.

For all these years it had resounded in his memory with the urgency of a trumpet call—the wild defiant shout of an animal ringed about with enemies. He had thought to cast himself in this heroic mould. To be a maverick. Forever in the ranks of the embattled minority. Instead there had been a slow erosion of ideals, a cowardly retreat from one decent belief after another until at last he found himself in the ranks of the majority. The ring of craven curs that hemmed in and crushed the unruly, those few who dared cry: ' *Non serviam!*'

The badger cry was now a pitiful sound. A shrill squeal of protest. The rage tinged with terror: the defiance with despair. The cry of something crushed, defeated, abandoned.

Desolation—a grey waste of futility and failure—engulfed him. His skin crawled. His limbs cringed in revulsion at the extent of his betrayal. Shivering, he eased over towards the warmth beside him. At once the rhythm of her breathing changed. She was awake. Had been all along. Lying there. Listening. Waiting to smother him with forgiveness. To hell with that for a caper. There was no absolution needed in this case.

The springs creaked as he shifted back, dragging the bed-clothes with him. It would be the price of her if she got her death of cold. The answer to her prayer. He coiled himself up, tucking in round his neck the bedclothes stretched between them.

Hardly was he settled down for sleep than the tranquil breathing became intolerable. He could envisage the patient, anguished, uncomplaining eyes of a holy picture staring into the darkness. Nursing its bitter wounds. God knows, you'd find it hard not to pity her.

He turned towards her.

' Sheila,' he whispered.

Once more the tiny catch in her breathing.

Gently he stroked the tense stubborn body, feeling it yield to his touch. She rolled over. Facing him.

' What's wrong?' she murmured.

Disconcerted, he stammered:

' Are . . . are . . . are you awake?'

She snuggled closer.

Feebly he grappled with her questing hand, warm and sticky with sweat. Lips fastened on his. Murmured:

' You *do* . . . want me . . . don't you?'

She buried her face in his neck.

'Grrrr!' she growled happily. 'It's good to know I'm still on the wanted list.'

Acting out the familiar prologue, he held her in his arms, seeing only a mangled body mired and misshapen, bloodied muzzle grinning senselessly at a senseless sky: hearing only the scream of agony that death alone could arrest.

A feeling of loneliness swept over him. A bitter hopeless loneliness that he knew to be surrender. The sin of Judas. The ultimate and unforgivable catastrophe.

He shivered.

'Darling!' Hoarse, breathless, she clutched at him with avid, furious hands. 'Oh, darling! Darling!'

The Pishogue

WITHOUT warning it tore in from the south-east—a mean, black, murderous storm that pounced on our fishing fleet, driving the boats before it, sails reefed down to the merest rags as they scuttled for the shelter of Sheephaven dock. For a day and a night the wind did its worst to us, resentful that anything could escape its fury. It seemed to me—a youngster just starting school—that all the waves of the world, a mad tormented host were being rounded up and driven down on us in a terrified stampede—huge bull-like waves that charged bellowing with lowered crests; monsters that reared their green bulk high over the sea wall to stamp their foaming hoofs on the boats not yet hauled up to safety; as far out as the eye could see an ocean of plunging waves with overhead a whirling curtain of mist—the sweat from their steaming flanks.

* * *

That night I woke with a queer sensation of just-having-missed-hearing-something. Not the storm which still howled round the house, but something unfamiliar and much more important. Tense and expectant I waited for the sound to be repeated. At last it came—from far out to sea—a high, wailing, human scream muted by the storm but still clear and distinct. It could have been the cry of a curlew or a solitary homing sea-gull, there was in it such an awful desolation of loneliness and futility. For what seemed ages there was nothing to be heard but the wind and the sea and the clawing gusts of rain on the window. Then it came again, urgent and shrill with terror, voicing its bitter protest—a poor lost thing, naked and shivering and doomed, that yet dared to bare its teeth at eternity. The next I knew was a gasping shout that must have been my own, candle-light dazzling my eyes and my mother sitting on the bed telling me it was all only a nightmare.

* * *

WHEN I heard that the *Bessie Morgan* had been driven on the rocks during the night, I bolted my breakfast and raced down to the quay. I knew the *Bessie Morgan* well. A two-masted schooner of around one hundred tons, she was in the coal-carrying trade between Swansea and the south coast of Ireland. She had a crew of three—the skipper and owner, a grim taciturn man, seldom seen and always avoided; the mate, whom I can only remember as a burly figure forever pacing the deck, and Ginger, the deck-hand. Ginger was a friendly soul, cheerful as a cricket. Never have I known anyone so blatantly alive. He shouted and cursed and worked like a demon all day and at night swaggered off up the village to Jonty Gallagher's where he would drink pints of draught till it almost ran out of his eyes. Everybody liked him, even the old people. To me he was an immortal—a roystering, guzzling, benevolent demi-god.

Four or five times a year the *Bessie Morgan* put in to Sheep-haven, spent about four days unloading and waddled off again in ballast like an enormous black duck. Though clumsy, she was stoutly built—squat and beamy, capable of weather-ing the worst that sea and wind could do to her.

Yet there she was, a couple of cable-lengths out to sea, crushed and broken on the rocks guarding the bay. She leaned over drunkenly on her port beam exposing a mangled deck from which everything had been swept away—ship's dinghy, ventilators, donkey-engine, hatches. Even the wheel-house was gone. Of her after-mast there was only a jagged stump; her foremast, snapped off at man's height, trailed dejectedly in the sea, an unholy tangle of gear and tattered canvas preventing it from being washed away; her hold gaped open and from it a trickling saliva of coal and sea-water streaked the deck at every lurch she gave. Her figure-head—a sooty full-breasted female—had been carried away along with the bowsprit, so I started off at once up the beach to look for it. For all I knew or cared the *Bessie Morgan's* crew might still have been sleeping safe and sound in their bunks.

* * *

They found two bodies that day. The mate's washed up on Ballyvawn beach, Ginger's in a deep pool among the rocks farther up the coast. I was at the dock when they brought Ginger's body in—a sodden, swollen, inert heap stretched face downwards across the thwarts. Death, I had always thought, was something cold and impersonal and not at all frightening; it stretched out decently in bed, brown-shrouded and unfamiliar, on its features the smug waxen serenity of a holy picture; not a poor sea-ravaged thing, without manhood or dignity, its head lolling on the floor-boards, the sea-water drooling from the gaping mouth.

One of the fishermen told me they found him kneeling down with his face buried in the sand—' like he was praying.' For nights afterwards I used to dream of cool, green depths and a dark figure outlined against white sand, a figure that crouched on its hams, head bent and arms outflung, in an attitude of grotesque adoration.

* * *

A Sunday afternoon three weeks after the wreck. The sea nearly dead calm drowsing under a mild September sun. The beach dotted with knots of excited men and women, gabbling away sixteen to the dozen. A constant shifting and changing as people moved round from group to group gleaning information.

Scanty enough it was. Listening to Mick Donnelly holding forth to a few cronies, I had learnt all there was to know—an old priest living in retirement in the village had been persuaded to attempt the recovery of the skipper's body.

Mick, of course, poured scorn on the whole project, but then with Mick, disbelief was a matter of principle. A life-time of argument and contrariness had turned him into a fanatical sceptic. He sat now, a sour-faced, thin-lipped little runt of a man, hunched up on a rock moodily eyeing the crowd.

'Pishogues!' he snorted contemptuously. 'Them and their bloody pishogues! It's bad enough for crazy ould faggots of women to be mixin' muggard and slaughterin' cocks on Martin's night and buryin' hoofs and hen eggs in their neighbours' fields, but to be draggin' poor Father Brady down here on an errand of the sort '—he paused and shook his head sorrowfully—' it's not Christian.'

A shocked chorus of protest broke out. 'Go aisy now, Mick.' 'Sure Father Brady wouldn't have dealings with the like.' 'Take care how ye insult the cloth.'

'What's pishogues?' I inquired timidly.

Mick ignored me. 'I'm not sayin' one word against Father Brady,' he resumed. 'No more he's off the mission these ten years and must be goin' on ninety now. No! I'll tell ye who's at the back of all this. It's the same ignorant gulpins who've been goin' round preachin' that as long as a drowned man stops in the water there'll be no luck in the fishin'. Better for us if the whole bloody coast were alive with corpses—there'd be a run of mackerel to beat the band. And now these prime boys think they've got some pishogue that'll bring the body leppin' up out of the water like a trout. Mark my words . . .' He broke off suddenly and pointed up the beach.

'Here he comes now, lads,' he exclaimed. 'And would ye

for pity's sake take a look at what's along with him. That ould cod Clancy. And him preenin' himself like a newly-trod laverock. Oh, I knew well he'd be stuck in this business somewhere.'

Clancy, tall, straight-backed, thin as a lath, looked youthful beside the stooped figure of the priest. Never before had I seen anyone so old, so incredibly old and shrunken and withered up.

He must have been a big man in his day, but the years had done their work and all that was now left was the massive head sunk, as if by its own weight, into the tired drooping shoulders. You got the impression that this huge incumbrance of a head might at any moment plunge down through the crumbling framework of bone and sagging flesh that had once been a plump clerical body on to the tottering legs beneath. The flesh on the face sagged too and formed a vast dewlap that made the head seem even bigger than it was. Leaning heavily on Clancy's arm, he shuffled along with quick dragging steps the while he champed and mumbled continuously at his toothless gums. Older than time itself he looked. Even his clothes, wrinkled and faded and hanging around him in slack listless folds, seemed like himself to have long since given up the struggle against the intolerable burden of the years.

All the more startling it was when you noticed his eyes—bright and unblinking and ageless as a bird's. They were utterly incongruous—like an owl with the eyes of a canary—but in some queer way they made your heart grow big in your body. I often try to recapture the expression in them. Candour there certainly was. And a childish trust. And tolerance. But there was something else—something fierce and unbeatable and strangely heroic that I'd be the better for remembering.

The two men halted at high-water mark. Around them in

a half-circle the crowd ranged itself, silent, watchful, curious.

Clancy faced about. ' Get down on yer knees, all of ye,' he commanded in a loud domineering voice. Everyone obeyed.

He now produced from under his coat a beautifully-fashioned laurel wreath and from an inside pocket, a candle. Fixing the candle upright in the close-plaited stems he handed the wreath to the priest, his manner a mixture of acolyte and ring-master. With a final flourish he struck a match and, shielding the flame in his cupped hands, lit the candle.

In the bright sunlight the flame was invisible and Father Brady remained for a long time gazing in bewilderment at the candle as if wondering if it were really lit. At last he roused himself. Carrying the laurel wreath stiffly at arm's length he shuffled down the shelving beach into the fringe of the receding tide. Tiny wavelets lapped and hissed over the shingle and over his old worn boots but he paid no heed. Carefully, almost tenderly, he placed the wreath on the surface of the water. Then he stepped back and waited.

Almost at once the wreath commenced to drift out on the ebb-tide. It skipped and curtseyed and bobbed up and down on the water, twirling round and round in either direction, stopping and starting in convulsive jerks as though it were dancing a highly-indecorous Roger de Coverley. The glossy leaves shone with a wicked sleekness. The little candle flaunted its slim satin-white nakedness before the sun and sea. Gay, impudent, very lovely it was, but without motive or meaning—a bunch of twigs at the mercy of wind and tide; a wretched little pishogue; a tired old man's dream.

As it drifted on and on out to sea I could sense this feeling in the restless crowd. I could see it in Mick Donnelly's sardonic grin. But Father Brady, still standing motionless at the water's edge, had about him an air of certainty, of dogged unswerving certainty.

A sudden stir of excitement drew my attention back to

the wreath. It had stopped about twenty fathoms from the shore and was bobbing up and down excitedly, struggling frantically, I thought, to free itself from some obstruction—seaweed or the like. Eventually it seemed to get clear for it drifted off again.

But now its behaviour became entirely abnormal. It commenced to range around in every direction, methodically quartering the surface of the sea, backwards and forwards, this way and that like a hound casting about in a covert. It seemed to quiver with excitement.

Behind me I heard Mick mutter something about whirlpools, but whirlpools or freakish eddys would hardly account for what happened next. As though it had at last picked up the scent the wreath started off across the bay heading for Seal Island, a tall gaunt rock only a stone's throw from the cliffs. This meant that not only was it holding its own against the pull of the swiftly-running ebb-tide but, crazier still, it was sailing right into the eye of a breeze that had just now blown up from the west. Slowly, doggedly, it pushed its way through the water, never once deviating from its self-chosen course. It seemed to have acquired a will and purpose of its own that drove it forward against wind and tide. The more you looked at it the more you became certain that it was a live thing, a thing relentless, single-minded, terrifyingly unselfish like an ant or bee or mayfly—the incarnation of a single overwhelming desire that could only end in fulfilment.

The wreath continued on across the bay into the shadow of Seal Island. There it appeared to hesitate. For perhaps a minute it circled round uncertainly. Then it stopped, lying inertly on the water as though resting on solid ground. Freed from the blurring dazzle of the sun it stood out clear and distinct against the dark background of the rock glowing with a rich warm secret glow—a milk-white opal set in a cameo of jade.

At Night All Cats Are Grey

You could not imagine the queer hush that came over all of us. At dusk, when the gulls are straggling home, grey-dim and quiet and ghostly, gliding out and in along the curves of the cliffs, you get the same kind of hush. It is universal. Every sound is muffled and apologetic, an instinctive cringing away from the onslaught of darkness. This was different. Around us the ordinary everyday noises went on as usual— the waves fussing over the shingle, the rumble of a cart on the road above us, a dog barking monotonously, distant voices—but we were cut off in a small world of silence, a world narrowed down to a motionless green and white speck, a strip of glittering wind-wrinkled sea and the sombre druid-like figure of the old priest.

Clancy's arrogant voice broke the spell. He had got to his feet and was shouting orders, instructions, warnings. No one paid the slightest attention to him. The kneeling crowd broke up, scattering in all directions, some towards Seal Island for a better view of the wreath, others making for the quay where already the first boat was nosing out of the harbour entrance. Only Father Brady remained, lonely and unheeded, waiting patiently at the foot of the beach.

* * *

It is turning dusk. The lamps in the harbour have just been lit. Inside the boat-house all that the hungry sea has left of the skipper's body is laid out on planks stretched across a couple of trestles, where it will stay till after tomorrow's inquest. Up on the cliff a group of fishermen loll on the grass, their backs against a ditch, listening tolerantly to Mick Donnelly laying down the law.

'I don't know what kind of men ye are at all,' he was saying. 'Ye'd swallow back, so ye would, any kind of an ould fairy-tale that would come yer way. Sure ye know fine well the whole business was a bit of play-actin'. Mebbe ye'll tell me I'm a liar when I remind ye that there's always a sweep of water running across the bay to Seal Island on an ebb-tide. Wasn't that how the Doctor's son was drowned a few years back?'

Someone interrupted: 'Aye, Mick, but it's only after a storm ye'll get the run.'

He is crushed at once. 'Why don't ye go down to the dock and try for yourself? Throw in a bit of a cork and see where it'll land.'

There is an uneasy silence.

Another voice asks: 'What about the wind? Wasn't it blowin' dead against it? And wasn't the candle lightnin' when they picked it up?'

'Wind!' There is a world of scorn in Mick's voice. 'Wind be damned. There wasn't what wind would shift the smell of a fart. Sure the sea was as smooth as a baby's bottom.'

He squirts out a jet of tobacco juice with an air of finality, leans his head back on the ditch and pretends to doze off.

No one speaks for a long time. The only sound is the contented gurgling of spittle-choked pipes.

At last Corney Gallagher speaks up: 'Ye're disrememberin' one thing Mick,' he says in a dreamy offhand kind of way as though talking to himself. Mick just gives a grunt. Corney rambles on as cool as you like: 'Ye know we found the poor ould captain, God rest him, wedged tight under a rock. And I'm thinkin' only for the priest and his bit of greenery he'd be lyin' there still. Aye, and would be till the Day of Judgment.'

Mick sits up furious, nearly choking with rage. 'Ach!' he splutters. 'I don't give a button or a hen's tongue, and that's a damned small piece of meat, whether or which. It was all a pishogue. And a bloody poor one at that.'

151

The Betrayers

'She's lying down.'

I never grasped the true significance of this statement until the summer I was packed off to spend the entire school holidays with my Aunt Mary at Benowen Strand, near the narrows of Lough Foyle, where you could stand on the shore and see, due North, the coastline of Southern Ireland. You got the impression that a good spit with the wind behind it, would carry across the narrow neck of sea and river to that poor priest-ridden country.

Aunt Mary's big old stone-built house and Willie Nesbitt's thatched cottage were the only dwellings in this tiny settlement, perched in the middle of a bleak stretch of wind-swept dunes. It was here I first learned that 'lying down' did not mean merely the assumption of a prone or horizontal position. It meant also a closed door past which one must always tiptoe. It meant drawn blinds at mid-day in an airless bedroom. It meant my aunt's voice resolutely uncomplaining:

'Leave the tray down beside the bed, Jim. And darling, *do* try to close the door quietly behind you.'

She suffered from attacks of migraine, especially during hot weather and the continuous spell of sweltering sunshine that characterised that summer, kept her confined to her room most days with splitting headaches. 'She's lying down' had become part of the normal routine of the house. I had long since ceased to question her prolonged absences. One of the by-products of her ill-health was that I was forced, through sheer boredom, to spend most of my evenings in the kitchen, with the only other occupant of the house—the maid.

This was all very well when Jane, Willie Nesbitt's sister,

was the maid. But then she was a long string of pump-water, with clinker-built teeth, sallow skin and an ironed out chest. When she went to work in England and the new girl from the County Donegal came, it was a different kettle of fish. Her name was Cassie, Cassie Moran. She arrived the same day as the piebald mare, a drunken purchase of Willie Nesbitt's.

Cassie seemed to materialise in the kitchen, without ever having gone through the process of arrival. I came on her sitting straddle-legged before the kitchen range, reading a woman's magazine. She looked up, said: 'Hi!' and went back to her reading.

As for the piebald, I saw her first by torchlight as Willie, blethering away like a ha'penny book and near smothering me with the smell of porter, opened the half-door of the stable.

'I hear tell your new girl arrived the day,' he said, flashing his torch on the mare.

'What d'you think of her?' he asked.

I looked at the sleek exotic creature, sidling away from the beam of light, ears flattened, nostrils flared, her whole body shivering with nervous tension.

'She's a proper beaut!' I said, not rightly knowing if I meant Cassie or the mare.

Next morning, in the broad light of day you could have faulted neither of them.

The mare was a lovely creature, a skewbald actually, patched brown and white with a narrow strip of black separating the two colours. With her air of dainty elegance she had the appearance of a circus pony—a beast that no farmer in his right senses and with a proper regard for the dignity of his craft, would allow into his yard.

Cassie too looked a thoroughbred. Small, dainty, raven-haired, she had the kind of complexion seen only on the covers of the glossier women's magazines. Willie Nesbitt gave his verdict as we watched her carrying water back from the well:

'She's a well set up wee cuddy, all right. As neat a pair of hocks as you'd wish to see. They're two of a kind, herself and the pony!'

And indeed it was true. Cassie never moved from place to place like an orthodox biped. She plunged. With the frisky abandon of a colt she would dart across a room or fly up the stairs, taking them two at a time. Prowling among the sand-hills, she progressed in little scuttling rushes, as though chasing a barking terrier. She had an animal wariness that showed in the sudden tilt of the head as she listened to some sound that only the cocked ear of a horse could discern.

For the first couple of weeks I was too busy to investigate Cassie. Every spare minute was devoted to watching Willie working on the pony. Up till now she had been treated as a pet, never broken to saddle or harness. But Willie was confident he could master her.

'I'll have her drawing gravel and sea-weed before the summer's out,' he said.

There was every chance of it. Willie—a squat, baldy, chin-less forty—who lived with his widowed mother, ran a few score of sheep and three scrawney bullocks on the surrounding warren of sand-dunes. He milked one cow and each spring he went to the moss to cut and rear his turf. He laboured a rood or so of garden which he set in main-crop potatoes, savoy cabbage and swedes. That was the extent of his farming. But he had other gifts. He could set snares, lobster pots or a long line better than anyone in the locality. He could lift a salmon out of the river under the nose of the water-bailiff. He had an old-fashioned single-barrelled shotgun that, in his hands, was every bit as accurate as the most expensive Purdey. Above all he had an understanding of animals, especially horses, that was uncanny.

Willie felt there was one thing needed altering before he

started in to break the pony to harness. To keep calling her Sally, a name that called up her pampered past would only be a handicap. A new name was required. As usual, Willie consulted the Bible.

'Sheba!' he announced at last. 'That's what we'll call her. After Solomon's woman that brought him the apes and the peacocks and the Arabian horses. Yon wee pony has Arab blood in her, I'd stake my solemn oath.'

So Sheba she became. But if Willie thought a change of name would effect a change of nature, he was soon proved wrong. For once the pony got used to her new owner and surroundings, she became temperamental and capricious. If thwarted she would paw the ground, shaking her head violently till her mane rose in a crest of foam. It was the behaviour of a spoiled brat and, as an only child, I could not but admire her performance.

Each morning she was released into the wire-fenced paddock beside the cottage where, after kicking up her heels and whinnying with delight, she would settle down contentedly enough to graze.

She took to the bridle with the minimum of trouble, allowing the bit to be forced between her jaws with little more than token resistance. Willie led her round and round the paddock at walking pace the mare occasionally breaking into little jigging sidesteps, through sheer high spirits. Once when he stooped to tie up a trailing bootlace, she butted him playfully on the rump. Moving a pace or two away he tried once more to knot the lace. Again Sheba butted the tempting target. He flung the reins over her head and moved away. The pony kept at his heels, her mincing gait a contrast to Willie's flat-footed slouch. When he stopped, Sheba sidled up to him, craving attention with sniffing muzzle. He started off round the paddock, Sheba still at his heels. Each time he halted, the pony went through the same nuzzling act.

At Night All Cats Are Grey

Willie made a great pretence of repelling these attentions but it was easy to see that he was delighted by the pony's show of affection. When we were stabling Sheba, he said to me:

'The wee mare's bulging with brains. You can see that, Jim? There'll be no trouble in the world breaking her to harness. It's just a matter of going easy and not rushing her.'

So for a week Willie and the pony performed their circus act each afternoon in the paddock, with Mrs. Nesbitt, Cassie and myself for audience. Mrs Nesbitt, a bitter-tongued old wasp gave out the pay as we stood at the gate watching.

'Boys-a-boys, thon's a queer looking yoke,' she said, out of the side of her uptwisted toothless mouth. 'I'll hould ye yon lady never cut a furrow or drew a load of dung. A plaything of the gentry, that's what she was.'

'Willie says he'll have her hauling before the end of the summer,' I said.

'I'm telling him to bring her back and take what he can get for her. He could plead he had a sup of drink taken when he made the bargain. I don't doubt he could even law them for fraud forby.'

'Maybe he's going to enter her for some of the Shows. There's big prizes to be won, they say.'

'Would you hould your tongue about Shows. He's wasted time enough on that daft creature without you putting ideas intil his head.'

Cassie never spoke. She stayed watching till Willie took the bridle off the mare, then ran back to the house.

Willie tackled me about her.

'You should give me a knock-down to her,' he said. 'When the old one's not around.'

He scratched his head thoughtfully.

'I'll tell you what we'll do, Jim. I'll try out the mare with the long reins in the morning. I've a notion she'll take to them. If she does I'll bring her down to the strand the morrow night. Let you pass the word on to the wee cuddy.'

I gave her the message that night. She was sitting, as always hunched over the dying fire, stuck into a paper-backed romance. Mooching around the kitchen I had rooted out a package of cream crackers and was buttering a rising column. I spoke over my shoulder:

'Willie's trying Sheba out on the long reins tomorrow night. Down on the strand. He thought you might like to come.'

I slapped the last of the butter on the one remaining biscuit.

'D'you think would there be a hunk of cheese in the joint, Cassie?' I said.

'He wants a knock-down to you,' I said.

There was no answer. Flinging down the knife, I turned round. The book lay open on her lap. As I watched, a leaf swung slowly back from left to right. She made no move to turn it back.

'Is there wax in your ears?' I said. 'Or are you struck dumb with longing for some silly old story-book hero?'

'There's cheese on the top shelf of the pantry, Master Jim,' she said, without budging.

I moved to the back of her chair.

'What's in these ruddy books anyway that keeps you re-reading every page as if you were revising your homework?'

I reached over her shoulder to flick back the vagrant page. Our heads were close together, her hair soft against my cheek. I froze into an attitude of attention, my outstretched fingers on the open page, repeating to myself the ridiculous words that caught my gaze:

'Love is the tenderness of the morning, not the madness of the night.'

I kept up the pretence of literary criticism even when she turned back to speak to me and I could no longer see the book.

'What sort of a chap is he, Jimmie?' she asked, her voice purring from deep in her throat.

My mouth was jammed against her cheek. I pulled back my head to reply.

'Who?' a high voice, surely not my own, squeaked.

She craned further back so that her cheek was once more pressed against my mouth.

'Don't be a silly goose. Willie Nesbitt, of course,' she said.

Her skin smelt of soap and rumpled pillows and the plunge-room after a match.

'Oh, he's all right.' My dry lips grazed her cheek as the shameful voice croaked out a reply.

I felt I was being swallowed by an exotic jungle flower from one of my science fiction stories.

'Has he a girl?' she persisted. 'Is he in love with anyone?'

Dazed and stupefied, I could only quote the words dancing across my closed eyelids.

'Love is the tenderness of the morning, not the madness of the night,' I said, hardly able to hear the silly words through the singing in my ears.

She swung round in her chair and faced me, her eyes all pupils, her lips puffed out like frost-stricken birds.

'You're a one,' she said, 'you sound like a story-book.'

Casually, as though I were a begging dog entitled to an encouraging pat for my cleverness, she leaned forward and kissed me full on the lips; calmly; expertly; leisurely. She got up, yawning and stretching. I stared hungrily at her tight-stretched nippled jumper. The blood hammered impatiently on my ear-drums: my insides weaved and lurched drunkenly. I felt shaky and weak. The cannibal flower had at last engulfed me, squeezing the very marrow from my bones.

'Ten o'clock,' she said, making for the scullery. 'The spuds still in their jackets and not a wean in the house washed.'

She moved with a slow voluptuous swagger, still twisting

and flexing her arms. Drugged with emotion, I slunk off. Before I closed the kitchen door she called out:

'Tell your pal I go for a walk along the beach every night.'

Willie was delighted when I gave him the message next day.

'We'll take the pony out this evening,' he said. 'I tried the gear on her this morning and she was as quiet as a lamb.'

Sure enough, when he took Sheba, already tackled with bridle and girth, down to the strand, she stood quietly while he tied on the rope reins and threaded them back through the metal eyes on the girth. Willie walked back the full length of the long reins, shook them gently and chirped:

'Get up, Sheba!' he said softly. 'Get up, honey!'

The pony's ears pricked up. Willie waited.

'Get up!' he coaxed and chirped again.

Still the pony refused to budge.

'Get up there, you silly girl! Stop acting the mohawk!' he pleaded, shaking the reins very gently in time with his words.

She started off at a brisk gait. We were forced to trot to keep up with her, until the soft sand forced her to a plodding walk. Out on the hard sand she still kept to walking pace.

Cassie was dawdling along at the edge of the tide. Long before we were near her, Willie commenced to rein Sheba in.

'Whoa there, Sheba!' he called easing back on the reins. 'Whoa, girl!'

The pony pulled up abruptly, nearly tripping Willie up.

'She has a good mouth,' he said. He was evidently disgusted at his failure to bring the mare to a halt at Cassie's side.

Cassie ignored him altogether when she reached us. She began patting Sheba's neck, rubbing her face against the pony's muzzle.

'Hullo, Pretty-puss!' she said. 'D'you think now would Willie let me handle you?'

She looked up.

'Your name's Willie, isn't it?' she said.

He reached out the reins to her.

'Here you are,' he said. There was a sappy grin on his face. 'You've had truck with horses before?'

'Wasn't I reared on a farm in Donegal!' she said.

He stayed close to her as furiously she shook and plucked at the reins, urging on the unheeding pony with clicking tongue and shouts of:

'Come on away! Come on away there!'

'Give over,' he said at last, taking the reins from her. 'You'll have her mouth torn to shreds if you keep on at that caper. You'd think you were bawling a drove of bullocks to the Fair.'

He turned to me.

'Will you chance your hand?' he said.

No matter how I tried—chirping, wheedling, twitching the reins—I could not stir the pony to more than a toss of the head.

Cassie was disgusted.

'What that Jezebel wants,' she said, 'is a lick of an ash-plant. That would put some of the notions out of her head.'

'You'd never train Sheba that way,' he said. 'She's been petted too much. One belt of a stick and she'd never work for you again.'

'You're too soft-hearted, Willie. My father used to say that no horse was ever rightly broken in till your name was inscribed with an ash-plant on its side.'

'I never whaled a horse yet. And I've put a brave few through my hands. It's wrong. Don't you know what the poet says?'

He cleared his throat and commenced to intone:

" If I had a donkey and it wouldn't go,
Would I belabour it? No! No! No!"

' You're as mad as a March hare, Willie Nesbitt. Coming out with that silly nursery rhyme. As if there was ever an ass foaled that didn't need a proper flaking before it would budge a foot!'

It was terrible to see the abject look on Willie's face. Like a cringing mongrel set on licking the boot that kicked it. Before he could disgrace himself further, I handed him back the reins.

' Take over yourself, Willie,' I said.

It was uncanny. One chirp and Sheba was off again. No coaxing, no fuss. And once more Wilie assumed dignity and authority.

For an hour he schooled the pony up and down the strand, concentrating solely on starting off and pulling up. As soon as she showed signs of ignoring his signals, he untied the reins.

' We'll knock off,' he said. ' No use working on her when she's getting browned off.'

' You have the patience of Job,' Cassie said. ' I don't know how you keep your temper with that saucy madam.'

With outstretched neck the pony sniffed and nuzzled at Cassie's face.

' Don't be trying to get round me, you old plaster,' she said, scratching Sheba's forehead. ' You'll not find me as soft as your boss.'

We started back up the strand with the mare pacing sedately behind, Willie holding forth non-stop.

' If you lift a hand in anger to a spoiled article the like of Sheba, you're goosed. You'd be well advised to sell her to the first man puts a price on her for she'll never do a day's work for you. No! This wee mare has got to be convinced that you're a class of a god—a decent kindly god that wouldn't rake her ribs with thunderbolts or start swearing at her out of the sky.'

By this time we were out on the metalled road.

' I'll leave yous and love yous!' said Cassie, branching off for the house.

Willie caught his breath.

' Eh?' he said.

' I'll maybe run into you the morrow night if you're below on the strand schooling the pony,' she called back.

While we were brushing down the mare Willie kept coming back to her last remarks.

' Did you hear what she said? She made a date for the morrow night. Isn't that what it amounts to, Jim? Eh? And what d'you think of her saying: " I'll love you and leave you ". That sounds good, doesn't it? We'll have to be out on the strand brave and early to not miss her.'

I never in my life heard such mushy talk. The silly smirk on his face sickened me about proper. On top of everything didn't he say to me as I left:

' Put in a good word for me will you, Jim? Like a decent man.'

When I got as far as the kitchen, Cassie was sitting, book on lap, as if she had never moved since the previous night.

' He's a gas man, the bould Willie,' she started off immediately. ' He thinks of nothing but his blooming old pony. I thought he would never stop talking about her.'

' Does he never go with girls, Jimmie?' she asked.

Hands gripping the back of her chair, I was leaning over her in what I hoped was the correct attitude of a practised libertine. I said:

' You've nice curly hair, Cassie. Is it all your own?' My voice sounded normal enough but I was breathing like a beaten runner.

'Find out for yourself, Mr Curious Cat. And don't forget what happened to *him* when he became inquisitive!'

With the outstretched fingers of one hand, I started combing through the curls on the back of her neck, watching them coil up again like the little furry caterpillars we call Hairy Mollies.

'Why are you always asking after Willie?' I said. 'Have you a notion of him?'

She shook her head free.

'It's queer notions I'd be having, falling for the likes of him!' she said. 'Sure I suppose his old mother wouldn't let him look at a girl?'

'If Willie brought a girl into her kitchen, Mrs Nesbitt would split her with the tongs,' I said.

I reached down and turned back the page of the book, as I had done the previous night.

'You're not making much headway with your home-work,' I said.

She twisted round, grinning.

'Maybe you should give me a hand with it,' she said.

This time I did not wait for her to take the initiative. Closing my eyes I made a grab. Cassie squealed and fended me off.

'Are you trying to pull the head off me?' she said, rubbing her neck. 'D'you think you're bottling a calf or what?'

'You'd be the better for a little practice,' she said.

I could feel my face burning.

'Put your hands behind your back!' she commanded.

I did so.

'Now!' she said, leaning back, eyes closed, mouth puckered.

There I stood, bolted to the ground with shame, until she opened her eyes. The mocking curl of her lips shrivelled up the remains of my self-respect. She jumped up from the chair.

'Nine o'clock. Better for me to ready the supper,' she said.

As she passed me on her way to the pantry, she suddenly flung her arms round my neck, kissed me and whispered in my ear:

'I must keep in with Jimmie, mustn't I? It's not fair to be teasing him.'

Before I had time to gather my wits, my aunt's voice called from the stairs:

'Jim! Where are you?'

'I'm here, Aunt Mary. In the kitchen.'

'Don't be staying up late now. You know your mother warned you not to!'

Cassie turned at the pantry door, pointed dramatically at the calling voice and whispered:

'He shouldn't be collogueing with the kitchen staff, should he, Ma'am?'

She stuck out her tongue derisively.

Aunt Mary's voice came again, further up the stairs.

'You could bring up the supper. It will save Cassie the trouble.'

There was the faint sound of a closing door. Cassie whistled—a long sibilant tribute.

'She's got you taped, Master Jimmie. I'll better give you the tray before she comes down and takes you up by the ear.'

As she opened the kitchen door for me she said:

'Tell Silly Billy I was asking for him,' and in a whispered rush of words: 'D'you think could he ever be prised loose from that old vampire of a mother of his?'

The next few weeks are blurred with a haze of happiness. All my time seems to have been divided between Sheba and Cassie, though I must have gulped down three meals a day and bathed, fished and explored much as usual. Willie, drawing turf from the moss with a borrowed horse was busy till tea-time so I had Sheba to myself all day. I spent hours in the paddock trying to coax the pony to do for me the things she would do so freely for Willie. I would give a finger-whistle every bit as shrill and curt as Willie's. The pony would merely lift her head, look at me with disinterest and go back to her grazing.

When, after lengthy stalking she allowed herself to be caught there was no doubt of her affectionate response to my petting. Yet halter her and she would neither lead nor drive. She would graze her way round the paddock attached to me by a dangling rope. At the slightest pull of the halter, up would go her head in the effort to tear the rope from my fist. Never was I permitted any control over her movements.

Cassie had no better luck. She would stand at the gate coaxing and cajoling. The pony only lifted her head when Cassie's voice rose to a shout.

It was different when Willie put in an appearance after ricking his last load of turf for the day. Before ever he reached the gate of the paddock, the mare's head was up and she was whinnying with excitement. Still she never stirred till Willie whistled her up. Sometimes he kept her waiting deliberately, perhaps lifting his fingers to his mouth to deceive her, until he had her pawing the ground with impatience. Then, at the sound of the liberating whistle, she would break into a gallop and finish up snorting into Willie's face.

She was becoming accustomed to the daily schooling on the strand. Already she had mastered the signals for starting and halting. She would stand motionless for minutes on end waiting for the chirp or the twitch of the reins that would start her off again along the strand. Willie was confident he would have her working in harness before the summer was up.

Cassie joined us every night she could get away. She always fell in on Willie's free side and always the conversation opened in the same stilted, ceremonious manner.

'Well! How are times, Cassie?'

'Not so bad. And how is it with yourself?'

'Can't complain. A body must take the rough with the smooth.'

'Aye! True for you, Willie. You might as well keep the good side turned out.'

You would think they had not seen each other in six months. We would tramp along in silence behind Sheba for a while but before long the harping would start.

'How's your mother, Willie?'

'Oh, as well as can be expected. She's a hardy old warrior, that one.'

'She's getting no younger, though. She should be taking it easy at her time of life. It's a mystery to me how she keeps going!'

'Och, she manages well enough. It would take a lot to put *her* on her back.'

'I don't know. An old woman is no manner of use round a farm-house. It takes a sturdy young country girl to get the work done.'

Cassie was always getting herself worked up about the hard lot of the old people.

'It's a crying shame, that's what it is. Old creatures the like of your mother, forced to slave on where even a working horse'd have been put out to pasture.'

At this stage Willie generally produced a bar of chocolate or a bag of sweets. While Cassie was munching he would explain:

'No use in wasting your sympathies on that old hairpin. Sure she might as well be out in pasture for all she's doing.'

Cassie was not going to be down-sayed by this class of talk. She harped on:

'Isn't that just what I'm trying to tell you. A man come to your time of life should have his family reared instead of being still tied to his mother's apron-strings. You should think shame of yourself, Willie Nesbitt!'

At this Willie would shake the reins.

'Get up there, Sheba! The women get the last word, don't they, girl?'

Stabling the mare he always quizzed me about Cassie:

'How old do you think is she?' 'Would she have a boy of her own back in County Donegal?' 'Do you think would she be a steady girl that would settle down on a farm?'

Silly questions like these get my goat. I told him he had a right to ask Cassie himself and not be trying to use me to ferret out information for him.

'I just thought you might know,' he said. 'You and she being so pack.'

I let that pass.

'Don't forget to keep her in mind of me, Jim. D'you hear now?'

'I'm never done talking to her about you,' I said.

'I know that. You're a good pal.'

Sure enough we talked about him, Cassie and I. And about Sheba and old Mrs Nesbitt. There was little else to talk about.

To be exact we did little talking. Most of our time was spent huddled over the kitchen range, acting out a charade that never got further than the first syllable. In bed each night, I planned its completion in a whirlwind seduction based on the scanty lore picked up at school from my fellow neophytes. Yet it only required a mild rebuke from Cassie: 'Where d'you think you're going with no bell on your bike?' to quell my cravings.

When my cowardly hands had surrendered their hard-won advantage and I had resumed my role as disinterested friend or bored voluptuary, she would close the book and say:

'I doubt they teach you more than your manners at school, Master Sly-boots, judging by your old-fashioned habits.'

The truth was, the stakes were too high. It meant risking my present small but certain happiness for the possibility of becoming a figure of distinction among the braggarts of the school jakes. And so, content enough with short rations, I made do with the small coinage of love—the strokings and nuzzlings and sudden casual pounces of affection that sent me reeling to bed when Aunt Mary called me.

Every night the call seemed to come earlier and from a lower step so that I kept my ears cocked for the creaking stair that would be the last warning of her approach.

Before I left for bed Cassie always said something like:

'Give the bronco-buster my love.'

Or:

'Tell Romeo that he has me put to loss with his attentions.'

Always I replied:

'Fat lot of use that would be! All Willie cares about is the pony. And his old mother, of course.'

* * *

The coming of the policeman with the census papers changed the routine of our ways. He stood for a solid hour talking to Cassie at the kitchen door—a tall young fellow, smiling and very sure of himself, hardly bothering to use the sheaf of census papers as an excuse.

That night, instead of giving me a message for Willie before I left the kitchen, Cassie said:

'What d'you think of Herbie?'

'Herbie who?' I said.

'Herbie Gibson, of course, the fellow doing the census.'

'Is it that peeler you were gassing to at the door? You weren't long worming the christian name out of him!'

'I could hardly call him " Constable Gibson " and him mad to square me for a date.'

'Do you mean to say he was trying to date you up and you only after meeting him?'

'He has me asked out for the morrow night. D'you think should I chance my arm and go out with him?'

'Well, if you are badly in need of exercise, a night on police patrol might limber you up.'

'Quit the codding Jimmie and pay attention!'

She was leaning towards me, scowling with the effort of concentration.

'Do you know what it is?' she said, speaking very fast. 'I'll go clean daft if I have to stay any longer cooped up in here every night. Sitting waiting for your friend, Willie, to pluck up the courage to ask me out. If I don't make a move very shortly I'll find myself sitting on the shelf.'

She paused for breath.

'If I went out with Herbie a couple of nights,' she went on, 'do you think would it put the skids under Willie? There must be some way to get him out of his pooshey habits.'

My mouth was so dry I could not answer at once. Eventually I managed to say in a breathless croak:

'Willie is so taken up . . . breaking in the pony . . . that he'll never notice . . . that you're gone. Or who you're gone with.'

'Oh, it will come to his notice all right. Trust that scheming old mother of his to nose it out and dish it up to him for breakfast, dinner and tea.'

'But isn't that what you want?'

'Och, you don't understand. What really matters is *who* he hears it from.'

She eyed me with the steady, tilted gaze of a bird.

'Now if *you* were to tell him it would be different,' she said. 'You could give it the right twist.'

'There would be no need of any of this hunker-sliding if you were to give that Herbie guy the brush-off.'

'But maybe I want to go out with him. After all he is a bit more exciting than cagey Willie. What do you think, Jimmie? Will I chance it?'

I tried to moisten my lips with the strip of linoleum that was once my tongue. When I spoke I found myself gobbling with rage.

'Little-heed-you'll-pay-to-any-advice-you-get.' I drew breath. 'You'll just do what suits your sweet self.' I managed to break off without adding: 'No matter who it hurts.'

Cassie flung her arms round me, murmuring:

'Is Mummy's darling feeling cranky? Perhaps sugar plum has wind in his poor wee tum-tum?'

She commenced to pat my back and make clucking noises. Aunt Mary's call saved me from further indignity. I broke free. As I started up the stairs, she put her head round the kitchen door.

'Psst!' she beckoned urgently. I leaned over the banisters. 'Don't forget to tell Willie my side of the story.'

For the next three days Willie had me deeved with enquiries about Cassie: 'What sudden notion has she taken to go walking into the village every night?' 'Could it be she's fashed about something?' 'Maybe it's because the pony won't take to her?' On the fourth day he heard the news.

I was helping Willie clean out the byre when Mrs Nesbitt came to the door. She stood watching us in silence, a humpy old witch, with crying red eyes and long grey hairs straggling over lips and chin, mumbling away at her toothless gums like a horse munching hay. At last she piped up:

'Postman's been!'

Willie ignored her and went on with the work.

'Letter from your sister. Four pages of excuses for not sending home any money. She was aye one for putting on the poor mouth.'

Willie grunted.

' Postman says he saw your friend Miss Fly-by-night walking the road with a polisman. I'll hould you it was the young blade was round with the tally sheets. He was chatting her for the best part of an hour the day he was here.'

Stupidly Willie stared at her, the dung-laden sprong, lifted to waist level, shedding its load unheeded.

Mrs Nesbitt went on:

' These mountainy young ones are woeful easy carried away. I dare swear nothing less than a uniform will do her now. She'll be too big in her boots for the like of a small farmer any more.'

She waited, munching furiously. Willie screwed up his eyes as if he had stared too long at the sun.

' They say in the village,' she continued ' that thon young polisman is the right blackguard. Does nothing from dawn to dusk but follow women. He's put down for poling Martha Fleming, yon sappy creature from the Crooked Bridge that finished up in the Mental Office. It's to be feared she's not the only silly young goose that'll be forced to hatch out that young fellow's goslings.'

She turned back to the house. Willie spat on his hands and commenced forking dung furiously.

' We'll start ringing Sheba this evening,' he said.

For the next fortnight he worked on the pony for a couple of hours every night. He would start Sheba up the strand. After a hundred yards or so he would put the pressure on one rein. Gently: steadily: he coaxed the pony until he had her wheeling around full circle, with himself as hub. Pivoting so that he always faced her, he signalled his instructions, calling or chirping, getting his results with an economy of effort that never failed to thrill me. A spell of walking, cantering, trotting, all in the same direction and he straightened out the mare once more. Again he gradually eased her round till he was ringing her in the opposite direction. Behind us we left a string of ploughed up circles for the incoming tide to wash away.

During all this time Cassie never appeared. Each evening after tea she would slip off up the road in the direction of the village. I have no idea what time she sneaked back. There was never anyone in the kitchen when I collected Aunt Mary's supper tray.

When I tried to speak to her between meals, she kept dashing about, plunging from kitchen to pantry, scullery to wash-house, banging saucepans, clattering delph, running taps—a picture of dedicated industry marred only by the all-too-frequent pause—standing perhaps over the scullery sink, plate in one hand, dripping cloth in the other, staring into the distance, the corners of her mouth quirked up in the beginnings of a smile, whether in recollection or anticipation I never waited to find out.

Meanwhile Willie, hurt at Cassie's continued absence, no longer ringed the pony within sight of the entrance to the strand as he had done the first days she stayed away. Instead he took Sheba to the Long Strand, a deserted beach a good mile round the Point.

Here, with no sound but the soft padding of hoofs, the occasional ring of metal as the pony shook the bridle, the gasping of wavelets as they collapsed in exhaustion on the sand, Sheba circled the pair of us.

Her madly heraldic appearance as she paced around with determined thrusting head and high-stepping hoofs, her cream and gold skin gleaming like porcelain, the furious sweep of her long tail lashing her fly-tormented flanks: all these things combined to lull me into a speechless stupor. Willie too must have been affected the same way, for only when he had Sheba straightened out between rings did he speak. Bitter complaining talk.

' She's a lazy lump, that one,' he would say of his mother.

" Scrooging over the fire all day, with her muzzle cocked into the heat like a crippled old hound. Wouldn't rise off her hip to get you a sup of tea. A man has a poor time in a house the like of that I can tell you. There's no fear of him bursting his breeches with the burden of food he'll have to contend with. And to crown and complete all, there she is the day long, sitting in the corner chawing and champing at her gums till it would put you mad with the hunger looking at her.'

Or he would start giving off about the police, never singling out any particular officer.

' They are a nosey lot of boys, those. Aye sniffing around after something. If it's not tail-lights on bicycles or the lack of a dog licence, it's the poaching. Plowtering along the brew of the river at all times of the day or night. You'd wonder what they expect to find when you would hear the clatter of them a mile away. Cute hawks, too. Catch one of them jokers marrying a girl in service. Not likely. It's a school-teacher or someone the like of that they want, with a job and a bit of money in the Bank. You'd wonder the young cuddies haven't them taped long since.'

Never once did he mention Cassie.

He did not take out his bitterness on the pony. In fact he was even more gentle and tolerant with her. It seemed to me he had come to rely on Sheba's affection as a prop for his tottering self-esteem. Each day at the paddock gate the pony's boisterous welcome, once a casually accepted tribute, became a more and more necessary demonstration of love and loyalty, and her ready obedience—a proof of devotion, not of intelligence. Perhaps that was how it was for though Sheba refused to work for me, in less than three weeks schooling Willie had her weaving from side to side at the slightest pressure of the reins and obeying his reiterated: ' Back up there, girl!' without ever squinting round in distrust.

At last a day came when Willie was able to announce:

'It's time the mare was put hauling. She is well enough mouthed by now. We'll try her out in the paddock this afternoon when I get back from stripping the snares I set last night up at the shooting lodge.'

'Why the paddock?' I asked.

'The strand is too heavy going. She might only lose heart,' he said.

I was so excited I rushed off at once to tell Cassie. She was in the kitchen making an apple pie for the dinner. I stood watching the deft hands knead and roll out the pastry on the bake-board. Her sleeves were pushed up, her bare arms dusted with flour so that the fine hair stood up in a white fuzz.

She looked round.

'Has the cat run away with your tongue?' she said. 'I thought by the way you rushed in here that you were bursting with news.'

Face flushed and beaded with perspiration from the heat of the kitchen, she stared at me. I could feel the blood swishing round my head, thudding in my ears like the plunger of a churn. I ran an arid tongue round my mouth.

'You should come to the paddock this afternoon,' I said. 'Willie is going to try the pony out hauling.'

She turned back to the bake-board, lifted the flattened pastry and draped it over the apple-filled dish like you'd spread out a wet bathing suit to dry on the rocks.

'What's wrong with Willie Nesbitt delivering his own invites?' she said. 'He has not spoken a civil word to me these two weeks.'

With a knife she trimmed the fringe of hanging pastry, shaped it into narrow strips, and set about decorating the pie-top.

'Willie did not send me,' I said. 'I just thought you would like to see Sheba working, now she is properly broken in. You used to like watching once . . . before you . . .'

Cassie lifted the pie-dish and brushed past me to the range.
I waited for the clang of the oven door shutting.

' Well,' I said. ' Seeing that you helped to train Sheba—'
Cassie laughed.

' Who do you think you're codding?' she said. ' Sure the
pony never paid a bit heed to me.'

' You will come anyway, won't you, Cassie?'

Behind me I heard her move. Her bare arms, warm and
sweet-smelling, were wound round my neck. She whispered,
her lips tickling my ear:

' I'm sorry, Jimmie. I won't be able. It's my afternoon off.
I have to go into the village to do a bit of shopping.'

' Honestly,' she added.

I broke free from the coaxing arms.

' I may get back in time,' she called after me.

' Back in time!' I shouted before I slammed the kitchen
door. ' That will be the day to go down in history.'

* * *

Dinner over, I went down to the beach. The tide was far out,
the sand mucked up with dead jellyfish. I gave up the idea of
bathing, climbed a dune overlooking the paddock and scraped
out a cool trough for myself in the roasting sand.

It was the hottest day of the summer. Oily whorls of heat,
swaying and twisting like tendrils of seaweed, reared up from
the baked ground. Everything you looked at shivered as if
reflected in rippling water.

Below in the paddock Sheba stood listlessly, head drooping,
tail swishing feebly. An old sheep-dog of Willie's cowered
under a farm cart, tail and lolling tongue flat to the ground.
Belly deep in the tide, a trio of wretched bullocks faced out to
sea, cudgelled to exhaustion by the drover-blows of the sun.
The sea, flat and milk-white tracked by a stretch of leaping

sparks as though swept by the flames of a welding lamp. A
world of torpor.

Yet I had but to close my eyes and all was seething, clam-
orous life. Overhead a plague of larks with their shrill, inter-
minable monologues. Sea birds screeching, wailing, moaning.
A solitary corn-crake clearing its throat monotonously. In the
background a throbbing drone of insects.

Sleepily I lay, chin knuckle-propped, soaking up the
warmth. I watched Cassie, fresh and cool in a lemon frock,
set off up the road to the village, breaking into little spurts of
running like a Wagtail and later I kept my blinking sun-
sodden eyes open long enough to see Willie start off
across the sand-hills, fresh snare wire coiled round his neck,
a bunch of rabbit traps slung from one shoulder.

I woke up dazed with the sun and made off for the shelter
of the house. From room to room I prowled opening doors
and cupboards, leafing through family photograph albums
of trapped and glaring relatives, reading old letters that told,
in the same scrupulous fashion, of weather or holidays: sickness or death. I read the titles of the sober leather-bound
volumes in the bookcase: shook, without much hope, the
locked drawer of my aunt's writing-desk: examined the hall-
marks on silver, the pottery marks on china. I took a swig
of sherry from the opened bottle in the liquor cabinet.

There remained one room I had never yet rummaged.
Taking off my sandals, I started up the stairs, taking them in
quick rushes of three or four steps at a time, being careful to
avoid treading on the creaking ones. Cassie's room was at the
end of the corridor, beyond the closed door of my aunt's room.
To reach it I had to negotiate a stretch of loose floor-boards,
one so noisy that the cat used to flinch when it padded over it.

I stuck close to the wall, balancing against it with my finger
tips, trying to creep along as close to the skirting-boards as
possible. I went flat-footed, placing the advancing foot down

gently, slowly easing the body weight onto it, ready to shift
back to the other foot at the slightest sound.

Teeth clenched, breath held in, I sidled past Aunt Mary's
room, taking advantage of every cough or rattling bedspring
that would cover the sound of my progress.

At Cassie's door, I gripped the handle with both hands and
turned it very, very gently till it would move no further, all
the time pulling the door towards me so that the latch could
move soundlessly.

At last I pushed inwards. The door gave. It was unlocked.

The curtains were drawn back from the open window: sunlight and the tang of seaweed filled the room. An iron bed, a
chair, a table with ewer and wash-basin, a curtained alcove:
that was the extent of the furnishings. Yet nothing was left
lying around. A line of shoes 'were arranged neatly under the
wash-stand, whose four corners held, like rooks on a chess-
board, a covered soap-dish, a glass containing tooth-paste and
brush, a plastic hair-brush and comb, both scrupulously
clean, a folded face-cloth with the nail-brush placed in the
exact centre. A suit-case was pushed under the bed.

Quietly I slid it out. It too was unlocked.

There was just time enough to note the neatly folded under-
clothes and the transparent plastic bag with its meagre reserve
of rolled-up nylon stockings before my aunt's voice put an end
to my ferret-work.

' Cassie!' she called. ' Is that you?'

Under cover of her repeated calls, I pushed back the suit-
case, scuttled out of the room leaving the door ajar and padded
to the head of the stairs, where I faced down and cried:

' Commmm-ing!'

I dragged the word up from the back of my throat and tried
to make it sound as if it was rising from the staircase well.

Waiting a few seconds, I marched up the corridor, burst
open my aunt's door and poked my head into the room.

'Were you calling?' I said.

The huge darkened room, with its high canopied bed and littered furnishings seemed close and oppressive after the bright austerity of Cassie's room.

'Oh, is that you, Jim!' she said. 'I thought Cassie was back. I could have sworn I heard her moving about in her room.'

She was sitting up in bed, pillow-propped, a green bed-jacket draped round her shoulders. Her hair, that I had discovered to be really bronze, was fluffed out madly over the pillows and she stared at me with such wide-eyed tragic intensity that I had to restrain an impulse to pull away the pillows and let her roll stiffly back with rattling eyeballs clicking shut and chest bleating: 'Maaa-maaa!'

'Darling,' she said. 'Would you mind terribly bringing me up a glass of milk? My throat is parched.'

I must have moved into the room slightly for she suddenly said:

'What is the idea of the bare feet? Were you snooping around again?'

'The sandals were hurting me,' I said, making off as quick as I could.

I was worried. Aunt Mary was as cute as a cut cat and I did not relish the way she said: 'Again.' Going downstairs I tried to figure out a way to distract the probing I was almost certain to get.

The inspiration came to me as I was buckling on my sandals in the hall. Aunt Mary was due the special treatment reserved for visitors. So when I returned to her room I carried a tray containing the sherry bottle, a wine-glass and a plate of digestive biscuits.

'They say a change is as good as a rest,' I said, edging out space for the tray amongst the jars and bottles on the bedside table.

' Our science master,' I said, ' is always preaching that nature intended cow's milk for calves.'

Aunt Mary was transformed. She was suddenly young and pretty, the lines of fret and worry swallowed up by a cheeky school-girl grin. She said:

' I am not a science teacher but I know it reflects on the quality of one's hospitality if a guest must sup alone. Run down, darling and bring up another glass.'

So I found myself sitting on the edge of the bed, sipping sherry and munching biscuits, whilst my aunt chattered on and on about her school-days, dreamily at first but soon with increasing bitterness and I watched her grow old again and the edge creep into her voice and I wondered could I get away before she started reefing me.

I was just getting to my feet when she said:

' How often must I tell you, Jim, that you should not sit on the edge of a bed.'

I eased myself up, trying to ignore the peevish protest of the mattress.

' You know perfectly well it is bad for the springs. You could even damage the base. I'm always warning Cassie about that.'

Here we go, I thought. Next stop—Paul Pryland.

' And when we are on that subject,' she continued, ' I would be thankful if you would spend less of your time in the kitchen. You have been haunting it ever since Cassie came.'

I smothered a sigh of relief. As Willie would put it— better bad than worse. Aunt Mary had spat up a bone that must have been stuck in her throat these many weeks past. I said:

' I don't know when I was talking to Cassie last. She has been out every night for the past three weeks. God knows where she goes to!'

What matter how many roosters I put crowing by my

denials. It was a case of: 'Man mind thyself, woman do thou likewise.' And Cassie was well able to do that.

Aunt Mary was off again:

'Too much familiarity—that is how the best of maids are spoiled. They must be taught to keep their distance. Be polite and considerate to them, of course, but beyond that—'

She eyed me significantly.

'Yes, Aunt Mary,' I said civilly, wondering to myself what hare she was trying to rise.

'It is a bad thing for two persons of very different states of life to become over-friendly. It leads inevitably to the moral corruption of one or the other.'

Well! Well! So I was caught out at last. Aunt Mary had unmasked the irresistible seducer who was preying on the kitchen staff. Corrupting an innocent country girl with hardly enough sense to come in out of the rain. What a pity it was not true! Still no one could accuse me of not trying. I shut my eyes tightly, not to avoid my aunt's accusing gaze but to close out the shameful picture of my defeat and disgrace.

My aunt's voice went on relentlessly:

'You know perfectly well that while you are in this house I am responsible to your mother for your moral welfare. What *are* you making silly monkey faces about?' She belched gently.

'Excuse me!' she said.

'It must be the sherry wine,' I said, opening my eyes. 'I feel dizzy.'

She was dabbing her mouth daintily with the edge of the sheet.

'I am not going to allow you—Oh, thank you!' she said, as I heeled up the bottle into her waiting glass. 'I cannot allow you to be demoralised by a shameless chit of a girl from the wilds of Donegal.'

I could hardly believe my ears. Here was I after wearing myself out trying to debauch my aunt's maid, being held up as a model of christian virtue and decorum, whilst Cassie—

'Aunt Mary' I said. 'You have got Cassie figured out all wrong.'

My speech seemed curiously thick. I tried to scrape away with my tongue the biscuit grit clogging my mouth.

'She is no piece of cake, believe you me—'

This was not what I meant to say at all. I started again:

'She is the sort of girl—'

How could I ever civilise the scurrilous language used at school to describe a tease who manages to remain an unrepentant virgin.

'She's . . . She's . . .'

I gave up.

Aunt Mary was watching me, her face gone all mushy and wet-eyed.

'You are a good boy, Jim,' she said. 'A loyal honourable boy.' She belched again—without apology. 'But I am afraid we may have to send Miss Cassie back to her native haunts if she does not mend her ways.'

'Listen, Aunt Mary. I'm trying to tell you—'

What was I trying to tell her anyway? That by a system of trial and error I had proved Cassie to be a modest virtuous girl, worthy of respect and capable of exercising the franchise in a manner befitting her station in life? That I was a clumsy, bungling operator, unlikely to bring to ruin the silliest, most susceptible pinhead of a kitchen maid? Or that—

'You could not do it!' I burst out. 'You could not possibly kick Cassie out just because the two of us were civil to each other?'

Aunt Mary's eyebrows rose.

'If I have to let Cassie go,' she said, 'it will be because I consider her unsuited for the job,

'Morally unsuited' she said.

This groundless accusation had to be rebutted.

'Aunt Mary,' I said. 'Cassie is a good girl, as straight as a die.'

I squirmed at the pompous words, so like a grudging testimonial. Surely I could do better.

'A finer girl you could not meet. Not if you were to scour the country from end to end.'

Insincerity oozed from this declaration. What could I say that would have the bite of truth?

'If you sack Cassie on my account, I'll not stay a day in the house after she goes.'

Unmoved at my ultimatum, Aunt Mary put her empty glass back on the tray and commenced picking biscuit crumbs from the sheet. Without looking up she said:

'You must, of course, do as you see fit, Jim. But I think you are carrying loyalty a little too far.'

She was now picking crumbs from inside the neck of her night-dress. She so resembled an industrious monkey, crouched in concentration in a corner of its cage that I could not help giggling. Glancing up she caught my eye. Immediately we were both gathered up in helpless laughter, though what Aunt Mary was laughing at, God alone knows. We hooted and shrieked and wheezed. We swayed to and fro with shaking shoulders. In a frenzy of delight we pointed at each other's face, twisted up and streaming with tears. Doubled up in pain we clutched our aching sides.

Each time I tried to stop, Aunt went rooting around after another crumb, starting me off again worse than ever.

A length Aunt Mary managed to gasp out, between fits of coughing:

'You'll be the death . . . of your poor old Auntie . . . with your crazy fooling.' She pointed to the tray. 'Take down those things and put them away. And don't forget to wash the glasses!'

I stood looking down at her, unable to muster the energy—

or perhaps the courage—to take up once more my defence of Cassie. I picked up the tray.

'You do not have to stay'cooped up in the house just because of me, darling,' my aunt said, as I moved to the door.

* * *

It was now late afternoon. When I went outside my eyes winced at the glare of the sun. The heat and clamour of the day seemed intensified, the high-pitched raucous sounds of summer drilling into my skull. I started to walk towards the paddock, dragging my sandals on the dusty ground, too uncaring to shake out the pebbles that gathered under toes and heels.

To my surprise Willie was working at an old sawn-off tree-stump that lay, smothered in rank grass and weeds in a corner of the paddock.

'You're back early,' I said.

He did not look up.

'So 'twould seem,' he said, the words sizzling like tobacco spits landing in the heart of a turf fire. 'Gimme a hand with this.'

He had wound one end of a long chain round the crutch of the V-shaped log. I strained against the timber arms whilst he tightened a running noose on the chain.

'That'll hold well enough now,' he said, still in the same sour tone. 'We'll try Sheba out hauling this old baulk of timber.'

He picked out the swingle-tree from the harness heaped nearby, hooked it up to the end of the chain and placed it carefully on the ground so that the chain was at full stretch.

'Now!' he said straightening up and putting his fingers to his mouth. At once Sheba, grazing in pretended indifference at the far end of the paddock, flung up her head.

Willie ignored her. Rooting among the harness, he lifted the bridle and shook it violently as though rattling a tambourine. At the jangling of the metal bit, the pony's ears pricked up. She pawed the ground with a fore-foot.

When the shrill whistle came at last, Willie was nearly knocked over by the butting, nuzzling, impatient animal. His face was wet with slobber but the sour look had gone from it. He rubbed his cheek against the pouting muzzle. I heard him mutter:

' A body would fare better sticking to his friends. Wouldn't he, girl?'

Without fuss or bother he slipped on the bridle, forced the bit into the pony's mouth, pulled the head-strap over her ears, tightened up the throat-band.

' How many rabbits did you get?' I asked.

' Hold her by the bridle now' he said, ' and don't let her stamp on my corns.'

With that surly voice, it was a walking certainty that the fox had beaten him to the snares.

' I saw a flight of mallard yesterday up at the wee lake,' I said. ' Did you see any sign of them?'

Gripping the bridle-strap, I steadied the pony's head while Willie fitted and strapped on collar and hames. He worked smoothly and swiftly.

' Did you rise any game at all?' I persisted.

He was now tying the rope reins.

' A brace,' he said.

' Pity you hadn't the gun with you. You might have got a shot at them.'

He broke off threading the rope-end through the metal ring on the hames. He looked at me over the mare's neck.

' They were sitting targets,' he said. ' It wouldn't have been right to shoot them.'

' Sitting targets?' I repeated.

'Aye,' he said. 'A brace of love-birds.' He spoke quite softly, in a voice loaded with bitterness.

'Where did you come on them?' I asked. Right well I knew what he was driving at.

'Bring over the back-band and the traces while I finish off this job,' he said.

When I came back, the reins were neatly coiled over the peak of the hames. I watched whilst he slipped the narrow leather back-band over the pony's back, working it to and fro till he was satisfied with its position.

'Where were they?' I demanded.

Sheba started stamping impatiently with a hind-hoof.

'Get up to the mare's head,' he said. 'D'you want her to make a shambles of my feet?'

I went back to holding the pony's bridle but my imagination was ranging the length and breadth of the district.

'Were they in the hunting lodge?' I whispered.

Willie had picked up the traces. Quickly he moved round the pony, clipping the chain-rings to the hooks on hames and back-band. He did not answer till he was back at the far side of the mare, with the traces hooked up in readiness for hauling. Once more he faced me over the neck of the horse.

'Where else but in yon derelict hut would they get cover for their dirty capers?' he said. He was staring at me blindly, his eyes busy on their work of reconstruction.

'I heard the noise and me passing the hut and I pushed back the shutter a piece to see what it was. There they were, as God is my judge, lying out full stretch with nothing between them and the floor-boards but a length of dirty old sail cloth. Not a stitch of clothes on the pair of them, no more than on the shameless heathen, coupling like animals in the jungles of Africa. I tell you . . .'

Willie's disclosure came like a blow in the stomach, leaving me breathless, sickened, numb. I broke in on his tirade:

'If you only got a glimpse of them passing the window, you might very easily be mistaken.'

'There was no mistake about it. Amn't I telling you I stood at the window looking in at them.'

'But sure they must have seen you?'

'They were too busy with their wicked antics to bother about me.'

I tried one last question. A forlorn hope.

'How are you so sure it was Cassie?'

'Wouldn't I know her yellow dress a mile away? And the policeman's tunic flung across the stern of the old duck-boat? Yon man's only half-human, that's what he is. With a mane of hair as thick as a badger's running down the small of his back. He would put you in mind of a stinking old conger squirming about in the bottom of the boat, trying to jook every belt you make at him with the butt of the tiller before you'd give him the sea-bed.'

The vision this evoked was too horrifying to credit. I let go of the bridle and stood back.

'Look here, Willie Nesbitt,' I said. 'It's a bloody shame telling this vicious pack of lies about Cassie. She's a stranger here with no one to stand up for her. You are only making up this lousy rotten story to get your own back on her because she would not go out with you.'

'I'm not saying a word against . . .' He scratched his head in agitation. He began again: 'You've had no truck with girls. You don't understand these things.'

He shook his head violently as though trying, like Sheba to dislodge the cloud of flies now swarming about us. The pony —ears gesticulating madly, mane and tail in constant furious motion, her flanks a crawling, twitching focus of activity— had now taken to stamping indignant hooves in her efforts to dispel her tormentors.

'The flies are driving her frantic,' I said. 'Would you not be better to wait till the cool of the evening?'

'The midgets will only be starting about proper then,' said Willie. 'Hold her steady till I yoke her to the swingle.'

He carried the traces back and harnessed them to either end of the swingle-tree making sure that each chain was of equal length. Moving up to the pony's head, he gathered up the reins.

'Get away back to the swingle,' he said. 'Start hauling on it and come with the mare as I ease her forward. Don't let go of the bar till the slack of the chain is taken up. That way there will be no jerk when she gets the pull of the log.'

I picked up the swingle-tree, moved back till the traces were clear of the ground and lay back on the dangling chains.

'Right you be!' I called.

Willie chirped.

'Get up, Sheba!' he coaxed. 'Get up, pony!'

The traces tautened. I began to shuffle forward, lying back on the wooden bar like a surf-rider. It was easy to imagine that I and not Willie was in charge of this sleek, unpredictable force.

'Give a shout when the chain leaves the ground,' Willie called back.

I watched the dwindling slack till the last loop uncoiled. When the chain straightened out and commenced to lift from the ground, I called:

'Easy now! Take it easy, Willie!'

As the log began to take the strain I released the bar and stood back. The pony jibbed at the extra pull of the lifting tree-stump.

'Quiet now, girl!' said Willie, patting her neck soothingly. 'I think we'll leave you standing a wee minute.'

We waited, Willie and I, while Sheba shifted about

uneasily, the chain dipping and rising with each movement, but never quite reaching the ground. Willie, the reins held slackly, was staring at the swaying chain, his brows drawn down in a frown of concentration. When he spoke, it was in a droning voice with as much meaning to it as the tiresome buzz of the flies still swarming around us.

'What would take you to the fair,' he said, ' is the way a decent modest girl could make such a disgrace of herself. To be found stretched out in your pelt on the floor of an old deserted hut and it littered with every class of slaughtering accoutrement from harpoon to punt-gun and an array of decoy ducks ringed round you like a squad of Peeping Toms and you in the company of a black-avised Judas the like of yon—' He shook his head slowly. ' It's beyond the beyonds.'

He brushed away a fly that had settled on his nose.

'Women are the rare oddities too,' he continued. ' In the midst of all the turmoil, hadn't she readied up her clothes and shoes. Laid out neatly they were—as if she were going to bed in her own room.'

He dug deeply into one ear with his finger.

'As if she was going to her bed,' he repeated in a puzzled voice. ' In her own room.'

I fixed my gaze on the chimney ledge of my aunt's house and tried to concentrate, to the exclusion of all else, on a crow waddling back and forth as if on patrol duty. It was a seedy bird with balding head and plumage dusty, frayed and ill-fitting. Its ungainly body was mounted on feet as large and flat as any station sergeant's. At each end of its beat it halted and twisted its beak rapidly to either side, the victim of a lifetime of suspicion.

When it had made certain the coast was clear, it hopped up on the centre chimney pot, its wings tucked tight to its sides, as though it had thumbs hooked in the breast pockets of a uniform. There it perched, gazing down the shaft, its head swivelling around so that each eye in turn could survey its depth.

The side-cocked head had a knowing look that told of a chimney worth investigating. Whose room, I wondered, did it lead down to? Perhaps to Cassie's bedroom. I remembered the shoes stowed away under the wash-stand. If there had been a fireplace in the room Cassie would certainly have her shoes neatly arranged along the bar of the fender. Just as her clothes would be folded away tidily, no matter what the circumstances.

The grotesque scene described by Willie unrolled itself before my eyes. The derelict hut, its hinged shutter ajar. A space in the centre of the floor cleared of litter and covered with sail cloth, round which squatted rows of wooden ducks, their painted plumage dull and faded, their round incurious eyes fixed on the neatly piled garments and on the two figures . . .

For the second time that day I was forced to squeeze my eyes tight shut on something I could not face.

It was at this moment we heard the footsteps coming up the road and the gay chatter, broken by bursts of laughter. We waited motionless, watching where the road curved inland and disappeared towards the village.

Round the corner they came; the tall rangy policeman stepping it out, uniform cap pushed back from his forehead, tunic slung over one shoulder, shirt sleeves rolled beyond the elbows; beside him Cassie, clinging with clasped hands to the crook of his arm, skipping and dancing like a schoolgirl. You had only to look at her as she snuggled against him, wriggling with happiness and staring up at him with admiring gaze to realise that Willie's story was true. It was easy to picture her, with swollen lips and eyes as black and glittering and sightless as they were that first night in the kitchen, yawning and stretching herself as she padded across the floor of the hut to the little heap of neatly folded clothes.

Squirming with disgust, I considered the full extent of my humiliation. Night after night I had cringed after her, grateful for the casual caress you would give without thought to a fawning nuisance of a dog. I had swallowed rebuff and ridicule that only gawky ignorance could have stomached. My projected epic of a debauch so sumptuous, so gross, as to merit narration in the school bogs, had shrunk, under Cassie's scorn, to the capers of an unfluffed kid from prep-school.

Cassie was the first to speak when they stopped at the paddock gate.

'Hullo, boys!' she called across. 'How's the work coming on?'

'Don't you see they are hard at it?' Constable Gibson said.

Willie ignored them. He beckoned me up, gave me the reins and went round methodically testing the straps on both collar and hames, checking on the traces where they hooked to hames and swingle-bar, tugging at the chain fastened to the tree-stump.

'We'll haul,' he said taking the reins back.

He chirped.

'Get up, Sheba! Get up there!' he said.

The pony moved forward till she felt the pull of the timber. She jibbed again.

'Easy now, Cassie! Easy, girl!' he said.

Gibson laughed, a piercing cackle that put Sheba's ears pricking.

'Did you hear that, Cassie?' he said. 'You never told me he calls the four-footed friend after you.'

'Behave yourself, Herbie!' she said.

Willie's face reddened. He rested Sheba for a few minutes before urging her on again.

'Get up, girl! That's a good lass,' he coaxed softly, chirping encouragement.

Still Sheba jibbed.

'Maybe a stick of dynamite would shift her,' Gibson jeered.

Willie flinched. And no wonder. The river had been dyna-
mited in the early spring and the police were said to be still
trying to pin the crime on some of the habitual poachers.

Ignoring Cassie's timid appeals, Gibson kept up his teasing
apparently intent on riling Willie:

'Crank her up, you boy you. Her battery's down.'

'You've left her standing too long. Will we give her a
push?'

'Och, sink her in a bog-hole and buy a tractor.'

Willie was getting flustered. His voice was louder—wheedling, urging, abusing. His hand was heavy on the reins,
jerking roughly where once the merest twitch had sufficed.
His movements—always slow, cautious, knowledgeable—had
become fussy and agitated.

Sheba, infected with his uneasiness, was turning sour—
sidling and backing to avoid the pull of the traces, jigging
peevishly from side to side, tossing her head violently in her
efforts to escape control. Nothing would persuade her to haul.
In fact Willie was put to the pin of his collar stopping her
from backing into and fouling traces, chain and swingle-
bar.

I was so immersed in the duel that the sudden shrill whistle
gave me the same jolt as it did Willie and the mare. Sheba
swung round, head up, ears cocked, gazing expectantly at the
grinning malicious face of Gibson, who was slouched over the
gate, fingers still dragging at his lower lip. Willie, pale with
rage, jerked on the reins, striving to pull the mare's unwilling
head around. Sheba resisted stubbornly.

I heard Cassie say:

'Stop it Herbie! You'll only frighten the mare.'

Gibson laughed.

'Hey there, Useless!' he called. And whistled again.

At Night All Cats Are Grey

Hesitantly Sheba moved towards the beckoning sound. At once Willie wrenched back her head. Shortening his grip on the reins, he hauled her forward till chain and traces were at full stretch again.

The pony stood trembling. A lather of foam fringed her mouth. Sweat darkened her neck and flanks. Her ears were laid back. Her eyes rolled in their sockets with terror and shock.

Willie was breathing heavily. He shook the reins.

'Get up there!' he shouted, his voice hoarse with fury.

Sheba did not move. Her ears were still flattened. Her eyes slanted back at the threatening figure with the unfamiliar voice.

Willie's free hand came up with the slack of the reins. He moved in closer to the mare.

'You stubborn bitch!' he whispered, staring across Sheba's back at the paddock gate. 'You silly, stubborn, betraying bitch!'

He brought the rope reins down smartly on her flank.

'Up—'

Sheba, plunging forward, seemed to pluck the word from his mouth at the same instant as she ripped the reins from his unwary hands.

What happened next had the remote ineluctable quality of a nightmare, where spectator and participant are one, and screams of warning are as soundless as the cotton wool that must be floundered through.

Helplessly I stood watching the pony gather speed. Willie ran a few crouching steps beside her, groping wildly for the whirling reins, regardless of the charging tree-stump behind him.

It was his undoing. The bouncing twisting timber caught up with him, dealing him a swinging blow on the legs that sent him staggering forward in a sprawled-out heap. The impact caused the pony to swerve: it did not check her panic-stricken flight.

There was a nightmare logic about Sheba's flight that absolved me from intervention. I should have shouted a warning to Willie. Perhaps I even did—a soundless nightmare scream, part of the cotton wool silence through which the bolting pony fled.

Gibson's hyena laugh unmuffled the sound of snorting breath, of thudding hoofs, of rattling trace-chains.

'Oh-Oh-Oh! Sweet suffering saviour, did you ever in all your born life see the beat of that?' He indicated, with wagging finger the sprawling form of Willie.

'Behold the decline and fall of Buffalo Bill, the wonder horseman of the Pony Express!'

'If you don't stir yourself, Nesbitt, your pony will be half-way back to the prairies of America,' he said.

By this time Sheba was stretched out in full gallop, mane and tail fanned out in splendour, a creature grown to twice her span by the speed of her going, flying hooves and threshing timber butt drumming the ground.

She was making straight for the paddock fence, a chest high construction, formed of three strands of rusty bull-wire, spliced and sundered and spliced again, attached to wooden paling posts so old and decrepit that some, freed by decay from their roots in the ground now hung between heaven and earth, like so many tethered souls condemned to the windy wastes of purgatory.

'She's going to tackle the fence!' Gibson shouted. 'Go on, you girl you! Nesbitt never reared a jibber! Becher's Brook itself would hardly daunt you!'

There was a sound of cracking timber, snapping wire, flailing hoofs.

Gibson said:

'Well, the curse of God on you for a thick, ignorant

cowardly Clydesdale. Baulking at a couple of feet of fencing.
Trying to barge through it like a bloody bullock. I tell you
if I was near you I'd rise you over it with a boot to your backside.'

Mashed against the wire by the tree stump, the pony
squealed with rage and fear, rearing itself up in its efforts to
free itself from the wire.

' You've made a right pig's diddy of that job, Nesbitt, Look
at the cut of that silly get wrapped up in bull-wire like a
Christmas parcel. The man that told you you could school
horses should get his head examined.'

Willie was squatted on the grass, arms clasping one leg,
his face—twisted in pain—pressed against the knees of his
blood-soaked pants.

A tearing, splintering clatter. Once more the sound of thudding hooves. The spliced wire of the fence had unravelled and
the mare was through, scattering wide a skein of twisted
fencing.

Off she galloped, dragging after her, besides the bouncing
tree-stump, a length of severed fencing that had somehow got
entangled in the tackle and now stretched out, writhing, jerking, flapping: a kite's tail of bull-wire and uprooted paling-
posts.

' Holy jumping Jeezus!' Gibson screeched. ' Give me a
mouthful of air before I choke myself!' He was wheezing and
coughing, one hand held over his mouth, the other smacking
his thigh.

' Do you know what it is, Nesbitt . . . You'd only want . . .
a band of yodelling Indians . . . a bloody stage-coach . . . and
that rusty old shotgun of yours . . . to make your bucking
fortune in the pictures . . .'

He drew in a deep whistling breath. Pointing a finger he
said:

' Would you take one look at yon careering creature and

admit like a man that she'll never stand between shafts.'

Willie was scrambling slowly to his feet, watching with dazed eyes the progress of the pony as it headed into the sand-hills, trailing after it the absurd string of leaping paling-posts.

Fouled by some obstacle, the timber hulk shot high in the air, snapping free the chain that linked it to the swingle-tree and carrying with it the length of fencing. By the time the last paling post had joined the confused twitching heap, the pony was gone—rid at last of her alarming burden.

Gibson let a great shout out of him, squeezing his hands to his sides.

' Oh, merciful God, have pity on my poor twisted guts.'

He moaned gently.

' Should I live to be as old as a cannibal pike I'll never see the like again.'

Willie was stooped down, holding back the torn trouser cloth and the torn bloodied underpants, examining the lacerated flesh of his injured leg.

The mocking voice kept rasping on:

' Did no one ever tell you that you never rise your hand to a spoiled slut the like of yon? Don't you know what old Spokeshave, the poet, said about beating dumb brutes?'

He cleared his throat and intoned:

> *" If I had a donkey and it wouldn't go,*
> *Would I belt hell out of it? No! No! No!"*

Cassie wailed:

' Herbie, didn't you promise me solemnly not to repeat—'

She broke off and faced around.

' Are you badly hurt, Willie?' she said. ' That was a sore toss you got.'

Gibson said:

' Saving your presence, girl, and not to put a tooth in it,

he must be shook to the core of his lily-white agricultural arse.'

He threw back his head and laughed, a long-drawn-out, seagull-screeching laugh.

A ball of anger rose in my throat. I looked at Willie straightening himself up painfully, at Cassie wretched with anxiety, at the torn fencing and the deserted sand-dunes. I looked at Gibson's swarthy face, alive with malice, grinning at his victims. Surely someone should give this vicious snapping brute a clout of the tiller to curb his flailing antics. Wildly I sought for words.

I said:

' Shag off, you big cackling jackass! You'll have little enough to laugh about if you have poled Cassie as you poled that poor silly ghomey from the Crooked Bridge.'

Willie spoke back over his shoulder, his cold indifferent gaze fixed on the two figures at the paddock gate.

' Are you coming, Jim?' he said.

Without waiting for an answer he started off, limping with surprising speed, making for the gap in the fence.

Crippling along, one shoulder up to his ear, fisted hands held stiffly to his sides, blood-soaked long-johns hanging from the torn trouser-leg, he should have looked ridiculous. Instead there was something tough and resolute in his bearing that made you forget he was balding, chinless, splay-footed: that lent inches to his puny stature and dignity to his limping gait: that sent me trotting proudly after him, deaf to Constable Gibson's bitter tirade of abuse and threats, heedless of Cassie's wailing curlew cries, unmindful even of the cool wind now fanning my cheek—a warning that the hot endless days of an endless summer were at last over.

Square Dance

'WE'LL stall here,' Duffy said, moving into the shelter of a
gateway. 'We'll be able to spot them passing under the street
lamp.'

Kinsella moved in beside him. He said:

'Let's hope you're not bringing me on a fool's errand.'

'You needn't worry. They'll turn up all right. I'll say one
thing for Mrs Kipoor, she never runs out on a date.'

'That's not telling me if I'm in for a wasted night.'

'If it is a wasted night, Kinsella, it will be your own bloody
fault.'

He pulled his hat still lower over his eyes, hunched up his
heavy shoulders and thrust his hands deep into his overcoat
pockets.

'They should be here any time,' he said.

Kinsella pulled down his own hat, sank his chin into his
turned-up collar and sprayed the deserted street with fore-
finger and cocked thumb. He said:

'Folk will be thinking we're a couple of hoods if we hang
around here like this for any length of time.'

Duffy grunted. He said:

'You'd maybe rather stand out under the street lamp where
every grinning get from hell to bedlam would have you taped.'

'What's so special about this trip anyway?' said Kinsella.
'Aren't we only on the prowl after a tender little slice of
dick?' With the edge of his right hand he carved laboriously
a wedge of left wrist, lifted it to his mouth and chewed with
grinding, grimacing, agonising effort.

'She's a respectable married woman, that is what's so
special about it. You're not long enough stationed here to
know her. Her husband runs a café.'

'Does he now? Is he a Chink or a Wop?' said Kinsella.
'Or would he be an Indian?' he added hopefully.

He shuffled around in a tight circle, the fingers of one hand fanned out at skull top, chanting softly:

> " *For I'm an Indian too,*
> *A red hot Indian stoo.* "

'He's a Derry man,' said Duffy.

'Mrs Kipoor's not so old either,' he said.

'She should be at home suckling her brood instead of roaming the roads looking for nookey,' said Kinsella.

'She must enjoy herself some way. The husband keeps her on short rations.'

At the sound of heels tapping the pavement, they turned towards the street lamp. As the two girls came under the light Duffy said: 'It's not them.'

In a high falsetto voice Kinsella said:

'Wrong number. Sorry you've been troubled.'

He commenced to whistle—high, clear, sweet—a hornpipe in time with the tapping heels, quickening and slowing the tempo so that the girls, caught in the melody, stumbled along, hopelessly out of step. Giggling and looking back over their shoulders, they disappeared into the darkness.

'A chancey enough looking pair,' said Kinsella. 'We'd maybe have been better off installed there, than mousing around here waiting for this Special Selection of yours.'

'Aren't you the right little rooster!' said Duffy.

'To get back to porridge,' Kinsella said. 'What's this lady friend of yours like anyway?'

'Mrs Kipoor? Oh, a choosey class of a dame. It's not everyone she will go with. Only bank fellows, shop boys, students. People like that.'

Kinsella cocked a bent dog-leg and broke wind noisily.

'A high class rocking-horse surely,' he said.

A flurry of people passed, mostly elderly men and women.
'Devotions must be over,' said Duffy.
'Pity there's not a Mission on,' Kinsella said. 'It's then the foolish virgins would be out in force.'
He pushed back his hat.
'I mind when I was stationed in the city,' said he. 'We used to wait outside the cathedral gates—'
He broke off.
'How are you so sure, Duffy, that this Kipper lady is a tandem job?'
'Oh, I'll have no trouble squaring her for you. Once she knows you're in the Bank, it will be all right.'
Kinsella laughed, a short mirthless bark.
'It will be alright, alright, alright—if you don't start playing Monopoly.'
The last trickle of worshippers had passed. Kinsella peered out from the gateway, listening intently.
'What's keeping the bitches?' he said.
'They always wait till the traffic has cleared,' said Duffy. 'I told you she's a respectable married woman. She doesn't want to get her name up.'
'What's the daughter like? Is she strong on the adipose tissue?' Kinsella's curved hands sketched out two formidable cupolas.
'A dead loss. When she's home on holidays, she takes to the road along with the mother. Like a class of a watch-dog. You'll be wasting your time if you bother with her.'
'Sure even a watch-dog must be in heat some time or other. I'll give her the once-over. Nil desperandum.'
He cocked his head aslant. Listening.
'Angels' footsteps,' he said.
'Here they come,' said Duffy.
As the two figures passed under the lamp, Kinsella pawed the ground with one foot, whinnying softly.

Duffy stepped out.

'Good-night, ladies,' he said, raising his hat.

Mrs Kipoor recoiled.

'Good gracious!' she said.

She craned forward cautiously.

'Oh, is it you, Mr Duffy? You quite frightened me.'

'Marina,' she said, turning to her daughter. 'You remember Mr Duffy, don't you?'

'Yes, Mummy.'

'Just taking your usual constitutional, I see?' said Duffy.

'Yes. I'm a great believer in a little stroll before bedtime,' said Mrs Kipoor. 'One sleeps the better for it.'

'Excuse me,' Duffy said.

He faced around.

'Kinsella!' he called.

Kinsella emerged, with bouncy confident step, from the shadows.

'I would like you to meet my friend, Mrs Kipoor,' said Duffy. 'Mrs Kipoor, Mr Kinsella.'

They shook hands.

'Pleased to meet you,' said Mrs Kipoor.

'And this is my daughter, Marina,' she said.

They eyed each other with cagey stare.

'A nice name,' said Kinsella.

'Yes,' said Mrs Kipoor. 'We called her after the Duchess of Kent.'

'A loyal gesture, I'm sure,' Kinsella said.

They stood in silent commemoration.

Duffy raised his head.

'This gentleman works with me in the Bank,' he said.

'How nice,' said Mrs Kipoor.

'I always think Bankers are the soul of politeness and consideration,' she said.

Kinsella coughed behind a deprecating hand.

'Wait till I get at you,' he whispered.

'I beg your pardon,' Mrs Kipoor said.

'I said, "You flatter us, don't you?" ' explained Kinsella.

'No flattery was intended. I have had the pleasure of meeting many of your colleagues. They were all most charming. But then, of course, they were all boys from nice refined families.'

'I'm afraid, Mrs Herring, we are known locally as the shiny-seated confraternity.'

'You are joking, Mr Kinsella. You are all most highly thought of in the community.'

'The name is Kipoor,' she added.

Kinsella's lips were moving silently. Before he could speak, Duffy said:

'Well, Marina. When do you go back to England again?'

The silence lengthened.

'Marina!' said Mrs Kipoor. 'The gentleman asked—'

'Sorry, Mummy. I'm afraid I wasn't listening.'

She gave a grudging look in Duffy's direction.

'In three weeks time,' she said.

They stood in a tight awkward group—Marina frowning at the pavement: Mrs Kipoor with a practised smile on her face: Duffy, open-mouthed and bulging-eyed, searching for words. Kinsella was whistling silently with puckered lips.

At length he said:

'It has been a most remarkable spell of weather, hasn't it?'

'It has indeed. One day better than the next,' said Mrs Kipoor.

'What do you think, Duffy? In your experience did you ever meet up with a better spell of weather?'

Duffy gave him a harassed look.

'Och, the weather's all right,' he said.

'The nights mild and balmy and in every respect seasonable?'

'Huh! Huh' said Duffy.

'Really delightful weather for this time of the year,' said Mrs Kipoor.

'Mummy!'

'Yes, dear.'

'I'm nearly certain that the cat has been locked in the sitting-room.'

'I see there is a heat wave in America,' said Mrs Kipoor.

'People dying by the thousand of sunstroke,' Kinsella said. 'Aren't we better off here? What d'you say, Duffy?'

'Aye.'

'You know what happened last time the cat was locked in, Mummy!'

'Yes, dear,' said Mrs Kipoor.

'You would wonder, Mr Kinsella,' she said, 'why people go abroad for their holidays. We have such nice weather at home.'

'That's right Mrs Kipoor. Thousands of them hiking around Europe when it is so much more pleasant walking the roads of their own country. Isn't that right, Duffy?'

'Eh?'

'Wouldn't you rather take a stroll in an Irish country lane than tramp a German autobahn? Provided you're in the right company, of course.'

Duffy nodded his head vigorously.

'Oh, I see,' he said.

He coughed.

'Mrs Kipoor,' he said.

'But Mummy, you can't have forgotten. We were for hours sponging the carpet. The smell has hardly left the room yet.'

'Don't be vulgar, Marina. You were saying, Mr Duffy?'

'I was just wondering, Mrs Kipoor, would you mind if we—'

'If we hurry home now, Mummy, we might get there before the damage is done.'

Kinsella pursed his lips.

'The symptoms point to feline enteritis,' he said gravely. 'In most cases incurable. It might be better to let nature take its course.'

'Marina, will you stop interrupting! Mr Duffy, you were asking?'

Duffy, confused and thwarted, blurted out:

'We'll go a piece of the road with you.'

'Of course, Mr Duffy. We would be glad of your company.'

As they moved off, Marina said:

'It's not too late to go back, Mummy.'

Kinsella fell into step beside her.

'I am sure the little creature will practise self-control,' he said. He squeezed her arm gently. 'Cheer up! You did your best for both of them.'

In a few steps their lengthening shadows were swallowed in the darkness. Ahead of them they could hear the footsteps of the other pair and an occasional word borne back by the wind.

Kinsella linked her arm and matched his bouncy stride to hers.

'Where are we heading for?' he said.

'The Creevenagh Road, at the foot of Campsie.'

'Oh, a fine and private place. None better.'

She pulled her arm away. They continued in silence until they caught up with the waiting couple.

Duffy stood, mute and embarrassed. Mrs Kipoor leaned forward.

'Mr Kinsella,' she said. 'Would you wait here with Marina for a few minutes? I want to consult Mr Duffy about a little private matter. I value his opinion very highly.'

She waved an airy hand.

'There is no need for me to explain. Financial affairs. You understand, Mr Kinsella.'

As she spoke, she began to edge towards the laneway leading to the shadowy bulk of a hay-barn.

'Are you coming, Mr Duffy?' she said.

He followed her, tripping and stumbling on the loose stones and gravel.

Kinsella laughed softly. He said: 'A very convincing performance. It's a pity Duffy fluffed his lines.'

Marina wheeled about.

'You are worse than him,' she said. 'He's is content to use her. You would abuse her as well.'

'Abuse her?'

'Yes. You would shame her with your scorn. All along you were laughing at her.'

'I was laughing at Duffy and yourself. And the cat.'

'You were mocking her. Because she is silly and flighty and weak-willed.'

'Look, Marina. The thought of Duffy giving advice on investment policy to a lady in a hay-barn at this time of night would make that wretched cat of yours laugh.'

'There you go again. Jeering at *me* now.'

'If you can't put up with your mother's friends you should not patrol the roads with her.'

'I try to moderate her. If she were out by herself there's no knowing how many men she would allow—'

She broke off.

'I suppose you mean to go with her when your friend comes back?' she said.

'Not if you are sufficiently nice to me.'

She gasped.

'How dare you?' she said.

He grabbed her, pulling her roughly towards him.

'Let me go!' she hissed. 'Let me go!'

Struggling, they reeled across the road into the ditch.

'I warn you,' she panted. 'If you don't . . . take your filthy
. . . groping hands . . . off me . . . I'll . . .'

'Eugh! ! ! Jeeeeeezus ! ! !'

Doubled up in agony on the ground, he glared up at her.

'I warned you,' she said. 'You can't say I didn't warn you.'

Grunting with pain, he levered himself into a sitting position.

'You will be all right in a few minutes,' she said.

He groaned.

'Try straightening out each leg separately. It helps with
cramp or muscle-lock. We were taught that at the convent.'

Through clenched teeth he ground out:

'A queer bloody convent that. Where they teach you rough-
house methods instead of manners and deportment.'

She giggled.

'I've had plenty of practice since I left school. There's no
lack of young blackguards like yourself around.'

Gingerly he got to his feet and walked a few cautious paces,
eyeing her sardonically as she circled him and sat on the
ditch.

'Tell me,' he said. 'Have you no sisters of a more gentle
disposition? Suitable material for chaperons?'

'Now you're laughing at us again.'

'I'm in poor shape for laughing. No, I was just wondering
at the set-up that drives you out at night on an errand like
this. A gooseberry that tries to maim the customers is a new
one on me.'

'I told you how it was. She needs someone to protect her.'

'Odd sort of protection, if you'll forgive me saying so.'

'Maybe I save her from humiliation. If I had not been with
her tonight, what way would you have treated her, d'you
think?'

She edged away as he sat down near her.

'Look, Marina,' he said. 'If your father had taken the stick many years ago to Mrs K., neither of us would be here tonight and I would be in better health.'

'It's not Daddy's fault. At least not now. Maybe in the early days . . .' Her voice trailed to silence.

Somewhere high in the hills a dog was barking steadily— a tiny irrelevant protest, muted by the ceaseless, hardly perceptible clamour of the night.

'Perhaps,' she said, 'if he had let her work in the café, it might have been different. But he claimed it would be too rough for her. Drummed into her all the time that it was no place for a woman of . . . of . . . of refinement.' She spat out the word defiantly.

When Kinsella did not speak, she continued:

'In the end she came to believe it. Now she is so full of notions she would be insulted if he suggested that she might do a spell behind the counter. Though God knows if she had something to do with herself at night, it would keep her from walking the roads.'

'Yes,' he said. 'It probably would.'

'Poor Daddy. Slaving away every night till long after midnight. So tired he is nearly sleeping on his feet. And then to find her cringing away from him at the vulgar smell of fish and chips. No wonder he raised no protest when he was banished to the spare room.'

'Fish and chips?'

'And why not?' she demanded. 'Did you think we ran a sea-food restaurant? Well, we don't. It's just an ordinary chip shop.'

She turned to face him.

'Now you can wrinkle up your nose and sniff,' she said. 'It will maybe make you keep your distance.'

'You are talking like a silly schoolgirl. This night watchman act is getting you down.'

'I suppose it is. But what am I to do? Mummy is getting more and more reckless. I don't know where it will all end!'

'Surely your father must have his suspicions by now?'

'I don't think so,' she said.

'Though God knows it's very hard to be certain,' she said. She shivered.

'He looks at her sometimes as if he hated her,' she said. 'It's frightening!'

Kinsella leaned over and patted her shoulder.

'Poor little watch-dog,' he said.

He jumped to his feet and commenced to prowl to and fro.

'Why don't you give a hand in the café yourself?' he said.

'I cleared off to England to get away from it all.'

'I could hardly blame you,' he said.

'What did you say you were doing in England?' he said.

'I didn't say.'

She relented.

'Physical Culture training.'

He swung round.

'Physical what?'

'I teach Physical Culture.'

He made a gesture of hair-tearing, scattering wild extravagant handfuls.

'Wouldn't it be just my luck,' he said. 'All the world to choose from and I pick on a P.T. instructor.'

He stopped in front of her. Hand to mouth. Brooding.

'Tell me, darling,' he said. 'Can you walk on your hands?'

She sprang up. With hands stretched forward she stood poised, rocking gently back and forth on springy feet.

'Come on,' he said. 'I dare you.'

She dropped her hands, walked slowly back to the ditch and sat down again.

'I might have known,' she said. 'You men can only think of one thing at a time.'

' And I was foolish enough to believe that you were sorry for me,' she said.

' What's eating you?' he said. ' Do you think it would shock me to see a P.T. instructor with the clothes over her head?'

She did not answer.

' If I do twenty press-ups will you walk on your hands?' he said.

Dropping down on the palms of his hands, he straightened out his body till it was balanced on his toe-caps. Grunting and puffing, he lowered himself till his chin touched the ground, then heaved up again.

' What about it?' he said.

Again he lowered and raised himself on straining biceps.

' Straighten out properly,' she said. ' There's a hollow in your back like a worn down door-step.'

She stood up.

' Keep your feet together! Straighten your knees!'

She was standing over him.

' Turn the palms of your hands inwards. That's better. Now splay out your fingers. Right out! Get a proper grip on the ground, man! Elbows out. More. More still.'

' Now,' she said.

' DOWN!'

' UP!'

' DOWN!'

' UP!'

' Would you for . . . Christ's sweet sake . . . count!' Kinsella gasped. ' I'm on five now.'

' Touch your cheek to the ground,' she said ' Not your chin.'

' DOWN! Right cheek to the ground.'

' UP!'

' DOWN! Left cheek to the ground.'

' UP!'

'That's better,' she said. 'Much better.'

Kinsella took up the count.

'Eight.'

'Oooooooough!'

'Nine.'

'Aaaaaaawgh!'

'Don't depress your seat,' she said. 'Keep it tucked out.'

'Tucked out?' he wheezed. 'You mean tucked in.'

'And breathe properly,' she said.

'DOWN! Breathe out.'

'UP! Breathe in.'

'I can't breathe . . . right . . . there's not enough . . . air hereabouts . . .'

'Stop stalling,' she said. 'DOWN!'

'Keep counting, will you!' he begged.

'Very well,' she said. 'Eleven.'

'DOWN! Down! Lower! Right down! Cheek to the ground. That's the way.'

'Now press up,' she said.

'UP! UP! UP! You're not trying. Press up! Straighten the back. Seat out. Don't let your knees sag. Press up!'

'See how easy it is,' she said.

'How many . . . have I . . . done?' he gasped.

'You're on your twelfth,' she said. 'No stealing rests. Get up off your knees.'

'On the hands . . . DOWN! DOWN! DOWN! That's the idea. Slow-ly—down!'

'Now what's wrong with you?' she said. 'You'll ruin your clothes lying there. Surely you're not giving up already?'

'Or are you trying to skulk?' she said.

'I'm whacked to the ropes,' he groaned. 'I couldn't lift myself off the ground to make way for a Council roller.'

'You're in very poor physical condition, Mr . . . what do they call you?'

' Kinsella l' The urgent whisper came from the end of the laneway. ' Kinsella l'

' What the hell do you want, Duffy?' he said. He rolled over on his side and spoke up to her. ' Not satisfied with trying to maim me, you would try to give me muscular paralysis. The name is Jim.'

' Kinsella l' The voice was nearer. ' Mrs Kipoor wants a few words with you. In private.'

' What are you doing rolling around on the road?' he said.

' What do you think I'm doing? Trying to ease the warbles on my back?'

He sat up rubbing his aching arms.

' Tell her I know nothing about the Stock market. I would only be wasting her time.'

' Didn't we arrange— '

' I have changed my mind.'

' But you said— '

' It doesn't matter what I said. It's *you* are the financial wizard.'

' But— '

' On your way, tycoon l'

Duffy shuffled off slowly. A few paces up the laneway he halted.

' Kinsella l' he called softly. ' You're the rare little banty cock l'

Kinsella stayed sitting on the roadway, hands nursing his bent knees.'

' Jim l' she whispered.

He looked up. She was standing beside him, so close he could see the puzzled expression on her face.

' Why did you change your mind?' she said.

With scuffling feet he tapped out the accompaniment to a soundless jigging measure.

'You were to go with her, weren't you? When your friend came back?'

He was whistling now, a gay bouncy bubbling tune, full of little runs and grace notes.

'Why didn't you go?' she insisted.

He looked up again.

'Maybe,' he said, 'like the Cork man, I have leave to speak twice.'

He took up the jigging rhythm where he had left off.

She stood looking down at him, one toe tapping in time with the melody.

'You're a terrible fellow,' she said. 'There's no sense to be made out of you, one way or the other.'

She made to go. Hesitated. Stooped and whispered:

'But you're a nice boy, all the same.'

This time she was gone. He heard her steps running lightly on the road. They ceased. A familiar rustling sound. The harsh scraping of a shoe on the ground. Then:

'Jim!' she called. There was something odd about her voice. It seemed to come from the wrong level. He swung round.

Lurching towards him was a fabulous insect. Long slender antennae waved palely in the darkness. A parti-coloured body curving with scorpion grace. Short clumsy limbs.

'Jim!' she called again. 'See!' Hand by hand she tottered forward. 'You've lost your dare.'

'Marina!' a shocked voice burst out. 'Have you gone out of your mind?'

The girl had barely time to spring back to her feet when Mrs Kipoor pounced on her. Shaking her by the shoulder, she said: 'You vulgar creature! Pull down your clothes at once and stop behaving like a street woman!'

Small, woe-begone, defenceless—Marina started fumbling with the skirt tucked into her knickers.

'Have you no shame at all?' Mrs Kipoor demanded. 'What must these gentlemen think of either of us after witnessing this display?'

Roughly she tugged out and slapped down the last fold of shameless skirt.

Kinsella scrambled to his feet. He said:

'Marina was only giving an exhibition—'

'You have no need to tell me that, Mr Kinsella,' said Mrs Kipoor. 'I have two eyes in my head and the wit to use them.'

She turned to Marina.

'You have cheapened yourself and your poor unfortunate mother with your brazen exhibition of indecency. Parading up and down on the public road in a state of undress—'

Kinsella interrupted:

'Mrs Kipoor, you are mistaken. Marina was only demonstrating—'

'Mr Kinsella, I am only too well aware what she was demonstrating. As for my being mistaken, I admit I mistook you for a gentleman. A person with some understanding of the respect due to a lady.'

'Mummy, please don't—'

'How dare you interrupt, Marina! Not satisfied with disgracing me, you would try to shield the young man who insulted your own flesh and blood.'

'Mummy, please!'

'Now, now, Mrs Kipoor! Don't agitate yourself.' Duffy's deep lubricating voice spoke soothingly. A large hand patted Mrs Kipoor's, by now, shaking shoulders. 'Leave it all to me. I'll take care of everything.'

Mrs Kipoor gulped back a sob.

'Oh, thank you, Mr Duffy. You are so kind.'

'And courteous.' She sniffed.

Duffy leaned over till his mouth was close to Kinsella's ear. He hissed:

'Dry up! D'you want to put the two bloody women at each other's throats.'

He drew back.

'Let the pair of you go on ahead,' he said. 'Mrs Kipoor and I will follow.'

As Kinsella turned to go, Duffy craned forward.

'You're an arch-hoormaster!' he said, in a hushed reverential voice. 'A bloody hedgehog wouldn't be safe in your company.'

At Night All Cats Are Grey

UNWILLINGLY he drifted up from sleep, burrowing deeper into the blankets, pulling around him the tattered fabric of his dream, clutching vainly at the urgent, embracing, anonymous arms that were slipping away into oblivion.

It was no use. The throbbing head, the parched and gritty palate drove him relentlessly awake. Soon nothing remained of the fierce demanding fingers tearing at his neck but an irritation below one ear.

He touched the spot. It was sore all right. Cautiously he explored elbows and knees. Nothing the matter there, thank God. Though it would be no surprise to find them bruised and cut. The whiskey that the publicans were dishing out these days was young enough to give you falling sickness. A few glasses and there you were—plunging around like a bee in a bottle. And, of course, the memory gone. Except for the inevitable glimpse of disaster. The close-up of a man's astonished face, streaked and frothed with porter. An uptilted shot of the underside of a lavatory cistern framed in what appeared to be the wooden seat of a w.c. The slow dissolve of a lower set of dentures grinning from a pool of puke. Just enough information to warn you of worse to come.

He rubbed his neck gently, trying to trace the outline of the injury. Barbed wire, perhaps? Or a thorn hedge? Could there have been a police raid on the last pub you were in? Maybe you were pushed out the back door, to stagger round blindly in the darkness, blundering against porter barrels, sheets of zinc, clothes-lines, empty bottles, in an effort to make a getaway? Were you caught? And questioned?

At this thought he squeezed his closed eyes tighter shut to dam up the flood of memories that might burst upon him.

It was all the fault of that wretched little mouse-about, Quigley—the curse of Christ on his hungry carcase. Serving up a bottle of stout that was no better than porter swill.

'Impossible to get the stout in condition this cold weather, Master James,' he whines, trying to rise a top on it by playing yo-yo with the bottle.

All because he's too mean to provide enough heat in his bar to condition the stout and warm his customers. By the time you've dealt with the flat, teeth-chattering brew you're just about ready to throw back a few whiskeys to warm your petrified stomach.

'A whiskey? I've a nice drop of Irish here. Ten year old. A large tumbler, as usual? And up to the top with aqua!'

When a publican elects to water your whiskey for you, it's time to watch out. But, of course, you know better. What matter if its smells like linoleum and tastes like first-run poteen. Drink enough of it and you don't notice. By closing time . . .

What time did you leave anyway? The last remembered sequence is of a foggy distorted Quigley mopping up the counter, from which all customers have, for some reason or other, retreated. Quigley is speaking but, due to faulty dubbing, the words do not synchronise with the movements of his mouth.

'That will be twelve shillings, Master James. And three shillings for the broken glasses.'

This scene, shot in blinding unforgettable Technicolor, ends abruptly with the sound of a heavy body falling.

After that, a jumble of vague impressions. A distant light, bobbing and swaying (a lantern?) in the darkness. A woman's voice (whose?) calling out: 'Who's there?' The loud ticking of a wag-o'-the-wall (in the name of God, where?). A hand (your own?) twisting the knob of a locked door.

What hell time did you get home last night? What shape

were you in? Only one person could answer that. He ran
a tongue round dry and tacky lips.

'Jeannie!' he called softly.

The shallow rapid breathing from the pillow beside him
never faltered.

He turned over on his back, eyes still closed.

'Jeannie!' he called again. 'Are you awake?'

He reached out an exploratory, an appeasing hand, to ruffle
gently the tangled mop of blonde silky hair. The breathing
changed to a steady purr. It was that bloody Siamese ruffian,
Wong!

Well, that was one mystery solved. The locked door. He
must have got home so late that the wife had taken avoiding
action. This must be the spare room he was in. Another spell
of banishment had commenced. And the ruddy cat had followed him into exile.

Obstinately he kept his eyes closed. What reason was there
to open them anyway? The window would be in the usual
place, looking out on the tiny cluttered yard. The birds had
hardly migrated from the absurd and lurid wallpaper. The
waxen-faced Christ, with scooped-out incandescent heart,
would still stare down on him morosely from the far wall. On
the mantelpiece the framed photograph of old Uncle Money-
bags, singular vessel of devotion and long-awaited comforter
of the afflicted, would still occupy the place of honour, though
the old bastard will probably leave all his money to the
Foreign Missions.

Did it really matter what time he was home last night?
Or what time it was now? Or even what day, for that matter?
There was no chance of change, even for the worse, in the
monotony of his days. His life stretched out ahead of him—
undeviating—settling deeper and ever deeper into the contented rut of happily married constancy. Gone for ever the
hope of the unexpected, the certainty that round the very

next corner lurks the fate that awaits you. Let it bring fear, delight, misery, enchantment—it is all one. The stimulus of change is what really matters.

Wong's purring had become intermittent. It was now laced with tiny sighs and moans. Shudders and twitchings racked his body as he sank back into sleep and, in shallow dream, stalked and killed, fought and rutted.

There was the life of Reilly! Owing no allegiance to anyone. Irresponsible. Receiving only gentle chidance for its sexual gluttony. Above all—discontented and disreputable.

The fog of second-rate contentment that fills this house . . . Ugh! You can hardly see out of the windows for the happiness clouding the glass. Like a bloody byre on a frosty night. Gum-chewing cows misting the air with their placid breath. Sweet-smelling, dung-fragrant contentment! Small wonder a fellow would tear the coupon occasionally. Like yourself. Eh, Wong!

He reached out from under the clothes and stroked the unseen furry warmth. A burst of purring broke out. Sensuous claws were flexed on crinkling eiderdown.

Ha-ha, you blackguard! Are you getting notions? Pampering doesn't keep you at home either, does it?

At the sound of her step on the stairs, he pulled the clothes over his head and commenced breathing loudly and deeply. The door opened.

'Oh!' she said. 'Are you there too, Wong? Were you out on the tiles with His Lordship? You lucky males have all the fun.'

He heard her uncork the bottle.

'Two spoonfuls?' she asked.

He tried to breathe as sluggishly as possible.

'You're codding no one, you big baboon,' she said. 'Come out of hiding and take your liver salts.'

Spoon tinkled on glass. Fizzing sounds. He groaned.

'Sit up now, home-wrecker, before it goes flat.'

She tugged at the bedclothes.

Heaving himself up, he reached blindly for the glass. Why open his eyes? She would be standing there, a fond and stricken Madonna, oozing love and pity and anxiety. And soapy good health and sanity and main drainage and all the other Christian virtues. He heeled up the last of the salts and, gasping, sank back on the pillow, his nostrils still stinging with the spray.

'Hey, wait a minute!' she said, as he wriggled back under the clothes. 'Do I see lipstick?'

He groaned. Surely she didn't think he'd fall for *that* lure.

Throatily she growled:

'Who's been eating out of my bowl?'

Her breath fanned his cheek as she stooped to look. A moistened finger rubbed his neck.

'It's blood, you poor lamb! Were you in the wars again?'

He focused bleary eyes on her. Tall, slender, fair-skinned, blonde hair tucked into a scarf, she stood nervously twisting round her fingers the sash of her dressing-gown. Twisting the blade of remorse into his soul. It was so bloody unfair. She should have married a plaster saint and reared a plaster family somewhere in the Holy Land.

'Go away, Jeannie,' he said, 'and stop teasing me.'

'I'm not teasing you, Jim. I'm just trying to pretend I'm not worried.'

She soaked her handkerchief from the water carafe.

'I'll clean away the blood and see what it looks like,' she said.

Gently she dabbed at his injured neck.

'You know, darling, you frightened the life out of me last night. Kicking and battering the bedroom door. I thought you were going to burst it in. And the dreadful language. You were never like that before.'

He winced.

'Sorry, darling,' she said. 'The blood's badly caked.'

'It couldn't possibly have been as bad as you make out,' he said. 'I wasn't all that drunk.'

'And why do you lock the bedroom door anyway?' he said.

'It was and you were,' she said. 'And you know perfectly well I hate sleeping in an empty house. That's why I lock the door.'

'You should . . .'

'It was Wong!' she said triumphantly. 'Didn't I always tell you it was dangerous to have him in the bed?'

Bewildered, he rubbed his throbbing temples. He said:

'What on earth are you talking about, Jeannie?'

'The cat. Some time during the night you rolled over on Wong. And he scratched your neck. You're just lucky he didn't injure one of your eyes.'

As if he understood the conversation, the Siamese got up and, yawning, arched his back, stretching upwards on stiff bunched-together legs like the tentacles of a swimming jellyfish. With tail erect and delicate grace he stalked, shaking the sleep from each paw as he went. At the bottom of the bed he stretched out, staring at them with disinterest from bleak blue eyes.

'Look at him!' she said. 'The picture of guilt.'

'The cat's not to blame, Jeannie. It was the floor of Quigley's bar. It reared up and bit me on the side of the head.'

She laughed.

'Poor lamb. Always the victim of circumstance.'

She pinched his cheek.

'You're a brute,' she said. 'A callous, cantankerous, guzzling brute. But you're the only brute I've got. So I must put up with you.'

Stooping, she kissed him and whispered against his closed lips:

'Get well, honey. Try to snap out of it.'

Desperately he floundered in the treacly flood that threatened to engulf him. His breathing quickened. The throbbing in his head took on a new, an urgent note. Weakly he pushed her away.

'I must smell like a sewer,' he said.

She pulled away, sniffing.

'Phew! Not exactly Chanel 5. Still, a hot bath and a good scrubbing out of your poor stomach-lining with Cascara and you'll be my sweet little baa-lamb again.'

He groaned.

'Beat it, will you?' he said.

She straightened up, grinning.

'Well, if it wasn't Wong scratched you, it was the claws of my hated rival.'

'Here!' she said, picking up a hand-mirror from the dressing-table. 'Look for yourself!' She threw it on the bed.

At the door, she turned. He was gazing into the mirror, a look of incredulity on his face.

She intoned softly:

> '*Mirror, Mirror, on the wall,*
> *Who is the fairest of them all?*'

Through the chink of the closing door she called:

'Don't go to sleep again, lazybones. I'm bringing up your breakfast directly.'

He heard nothing. He was staring at his scored neck. At the three parallel furrows reaching back from jaw-bone to God knows where on his neck. He screwed his head sideways but could not see where the scratches began.

These were never the claw-marks of a cat. They were much too far apart.

Painfully he tried to piece together the fragmented memories of last night. Had he really fallen in Quigley's? Could he have been in some sort of tussle? Did he stagger against anything on the way home? A fight or a fall would have left a permanent impression on his memory. Of that he was sure. Besides there would be tell-tale bruises.

No! It was something else.

Did he go straight home after leaving Quigley's? (He should have wormed out of Jeannie what time he had come home). Could he have knocked up some other pub for more drink? Not impossible, but it rang no bell. What about a private house? Could he have staggered in somewhere on the way home and made a bloody nuisance of himself? Been flung out on his ear perhaps? Still no alarm bell.

Wait a moment! What was this nagging memory of a wag-o'-the-wall? Ticking away remorselessly. Where had he run into one of those antediluvian yokes? There weren't many of them around any more. But hold on now! Someone had spoken of one. With a bottle of water used as a driving weight. Regulated by the pouring out or in of a few drops of water. A real leery effort!

He put down the hand-mirror, closed his eyes and tried to concentrate.

Where in the village was there a bottle-driven clock? Patiently he put the question to the blob of colour floating across his eyelids. Like a pendulum it swung, d-awn back and forth by his quivering jittery eyeballs. As the clock face began to take shape above the pendulum, he remembered.

Caroline, Jeannie's friend, had bought a wag-o'-the-wall recently at an auction.

Caroline Wentworth! Oh, God stone the crows! No matter how filthy rotten stinking drunk you were, you surely never burst in on the Wentworths—that pair of strait-laced, intolerant, sterilised snobs—to bore them with one of your open-confession-is-good-for-the-soul acts? Wallowing in your own filth so that Michael the Mealymouthed could punctuate your disclosures with dry censorious coughs and Caroline be given the opportunity of gazing at you with an expression of irony on her well-bred flawless features.

The images, flickering in vague merciful outline, sprang into focus. A long deserted street, in darkness but for a ground-floor light too many stumbling steps away. Towards this beacon you are making your way, groping along housewalls, doorways, windows, gateways. Bewildered when an entry or laneway sends you lurching into hollow darkness. Watching the solitary light grow nearer and brighter. Beckoning. It promises company. Talk, friendship, warmth, are at the core of its beam.

Then abreast of the window—halted. Listening. The wind, the river, the pounding blood, drowning out the murmuring voices. The finger-nail tapping the glass—gently at first —but persisting until a woman's voice calls out: 'Who's there?'

Mewing impatiently, Wong prowled around the bed, padding across his motionless body, eventually coiling up once more on the pillow beside him. Abstractedly he stroked the bubbling throat, his thoughts swinging to the warm, lighted kitchen, the kettle purring on the range.

Caroline is making coffee. Very graceful in an ivory dressing-gown, dark hair gleaming, cheeks fire-flushed. As she moves around, telling in lowered voice of children lightly sleeping overhead: of Michael not yet back from the city: of the need to wait up for his return: of how glad she is to have company to shorten the night: of the sobering properties of coffee when taken piping hot: of Jeannie's kindness to her which could never, never be repaid.

The soft voice murmurs on, settling into the steady drone of the Siamese who was now sprawled out, in abandon, across his chest. He lay on his belly, hind paws outstretched, a front paw shielding his eyes. Like a beckoning finger, the tip of his tail kept twitching spasmodically. At last it ceased and the purring dribbled into silence.

It is a silence with explosive qualities. Caroline is gazing at you oddly. As though something startling has been said. Her parted lips have surely this moment questioned: 'Why?' Or: 'Who?' Or even: 'Me?' Something must be done to shatter this perilous hush.

The halting tick of the wall-clock gives you your clue. Up with you on your feet. Finger pointing dramatically at the poor old wag that is just doing a job of work and minding its own business. 'There's the enemy! That bloody one-legged trickster! Ticking away like an arthritic old tortoise. But God help the hare that gets in its path. It'll get short shrift. It's no use, I tell you. It's too late.' Then, gripping the pendulum in one hand and the bottle-weight in the other: 'I've a right to tear its guts out!'

All a lot of old hat. Angling for sympathy.

The next thing Caroline has jumped up. She is beside you whispering: 'Maybe it's not too late, Jim!' You stand facing each other with the clock ticking away goodoh, until someone (who?) sways forward.

A sight for sore eyes, surely. The pair of you, locked in each other's arms, bolt upright in the middle of the kitchen floor, the lights full on, the children probably earwigging overhead, a scandalised Michael due to open the door any moment and Caroline . . .

Caroline clutching at you as if you were the last tattered fragment of a dream, slipping inexorably into oblivion. Caroline pleading: 'Don't, Jim, please! Please don't!' as if she really meant it. Caroline shivering as you slide a tentative hand along her smooth flanks. Caroline grinding her body against you and moaning: 'Darling! Darling! Darling!' Caroline's fingernails raking your neck before you manage to untangle yourself, soothing her with a promise . . .

'Did you go to sleep again, you loafer?'

Jeannie's voice, from the open door, startled him.

'And, good heavens, look at Wong! Get away, you treacherous brute!'

She pushed the Siamese roughly aside with the rim of the breakfast tray.

'He shouldn't be allowed up on the bed. Sit up straighter, Jim, or you'll dribble tea on the bedclothes. It's a bad habit to give a cat.'

Wong, sprawled where he had fetched up, watched with cold, feral, unblinking eyes, as she settled the tray in place.

'That cat gives me the creeps. He looks at me as if I'm a mouse or a bird.'

She sat on the edge of the bed.

'How's your poor stomach, darling? I didn't do a fry. I thought tea and toast might be better. Don't take too long over it. You've only got an hour to go before Mass time. And you know how sharp Father John is. He hates people coming in late . . .'

Gingerly he swallowed a mouthful of orange juice and battled with his quaking stomach to keep it down. He closed his eyes. Jeannie's voice rippled on—soft, drowsy, meaningless.

'Beautiful day . . . sun splitting the trees . . . quick lunch . . . away early . . . golf date . . . Caroline . . .'

'Wha'sat?' he asked sharply, opening his eyes.

'You dozed off, you wretch. You didn't hear a word I said!'

'Sorry, Jeannie. I'm spun out about proper. More sleep's the only cure. What were you saying about golf?'

'Caroline and I are playing golf after lunch. Instead of wallowing in your bed, you should root out your clubs and come along.'

Racked by a violent fit of coughing, he put down his teacup. With streaming eyes and wheezing breath, he coughed and spluttered into his handkerchief.

'We shouldn't have too much trouble gathering up another male for a foursome. The bit of exercise would make a man of you. Was the tea too hot, dear?'

'I . . . I . . . I . . ,' He broke out coughing again.

'It's the same old excuse, I suppose. You're in bad form. Couldn't swing a club without your head bursting. But that's not the real reason. I know perfectly well what's wrong.'

Over the masking handkerchief his startled eyes queried her.

'You don't like Caroline. You think she's a snob. Well, she's not. She's just shy and quiet. Why don't you try to be nice to her? After all, she's my friend.'

Slowly he diced and buttered the fingers of toast. Without looking up, he said:

'I never thought I was anything else but nice to her.'

'You treat her as if she were some sort of a . . . what do you call that thing . . . that insect . . . that eats its husband?'

'The mantis,' he prompted. 'The praying mantis.'

'That's it. Like a praying mantis. That's how nice you are to her. And take that superior smile off your face, Mister Superman. You're going to treat her different from now on, or you'll have *me* to contend with.'

She glanced at her wrist and jumped up.

'Look at the time. We'll be late if we don't hurry.'

She rushed off, slamming the door. He heard her call from the head of the stairs:

'I'll run a bath for you and give a shout when it's ready.'

He pushed the breakfast tray to the side of the bed, grabbed up the Siamese and buried his face in the grassy fragrance of neck-fur.

'How's that for service, Wong?' he whispered.

He rolled the cat over on its back. Supine it lay, paws outstretched purring ecstatically while he tickled its belly.

'Things are beginning to pick up around here, Catty-puss. Eh?'

And indeed things were. The wallpaper was gay with flamingoes, pink and white absurdities, sleeping one-legged with heads wing-tucked: grazing in shallow water, spare sections of their hosepipe necks buckled inward: flying, neck and legs outstretched, like exotic coat-hangers. From the wall, Christ smiled down on him indulgently. Uncle Moneybag's photograph seemed to promise the certainty of honourable mention in his last will and testament. The sunlit window opened up on a new world—a world of excitement, anxiety, intrigue, enchantment. A world of tip-and-run delight. Where desire prowls its path with breath sucked in and pounding heart. Where sleep is an enemy and daybreak disaster. A world of blanket-smothered coughs: of creaking bedsprings: of faces lit by pulsing cigarettes. A world of lies and cheating and fret and fear where love mushrooms up all-powerful only to creep away on stocking soles, parched and shivering.

Who would ever have thought that a few hours would have wrought such a change in his destiny? One moment faced with a lifetime of boring happiness: the next . . .

He stroked Wong's chops, flattening the cat's ears back, driving little squeaks of frenzy from its bared teeth.

'We'll have to make plans, Wong. Cunning, cat-like stratagems. What would you suggest, my friend?'

The first item on the agenda was to fill in last night's blank patches—where his mind had blacked out. Only Caroline could do that. It would require skilful probing indeed to draw out significant memories without revealing that, for him, they had passed into oblivion. But it would have to be done. Without knowing where he had broken off, he would not know where to recommence.

But how to go about it? One false move and the delicate dream-like fabric of seduction would be ripped to tatters.

'Jim!' The call came faintly.

The Siamese was gnawing noisily at the pads of a hind-paw. He pulled its head around gently by one ear.

'Did you hear that, Whiskers?' he said. 'There's the answer to our prayers!'

Jeannie! Of course! She was the solvent that would loosen Caroline's tongue. An evening spent in their company could well be a profitable one. After Jeannie's insistence on his being pleasant to her friend, she was hardly likely to suspect his sudden interest in Caroline and the innocent-seeming questions he would ply her with. And what woman, in the presence of the betrayed one, could resist the temptation of answering with the sly, ambiguous prattle of betrayal?

From the staircase well the call came again, louder:

'Jim!'

The cat cocked its ears, faced towards the door and made to rise.

'Stand your ground, gutless!' he said, flattening the struggling body against the counterpane. 'A little moral support, if you don't mind. We can pretend we're asleep. See!'

She was talking as she mounted the stairs:

'There's a poor way on a man when he's forced to talk to himself for lack of company. Though, of course, if he's getting hard of hearing he mightn't know he's speaking out loud,' and opened the door:

'Don't tell me you didn't hear me. I called you often enough,' and stood by the bed:

'Is that wretched creature still here?' and tossed what felt like his dressing-gown across his length:

'Come on now, my old hunker-slider! Don't pretend you're sleeping. You tried that already this morning. Up you get! Your bath's drawn,' and lifted away the breakfast tray:

'If there's no harm in a lady asking, what's the significance of the smirk that's cracking your face in half,' and blew on his closed eyes until he was forced to open them:

'Out with it!' she said, grinning down at him. 'Whose saucer of milk did you lap up?'

She looked so vulnerable, so young and giddy and innocent, that the thought of betraying her was inconceivable. He said:

'I was just thinking I might make a few shillings of beer money by taking on yourself and Caroline. A three ball. Dollar a hole. And a dollar for dykes.'

'Would you concede a stroke a hole?'

'What do you think, Wong?' he said, running a finger gently up and down the cat's spine. 'Could we do it?'

The Siamese stretched out a paw and laid it delicately on his bare forearm. It was a gesture of trust and he was curiously moved by the pressure of the sponge-rubber pads. He continued to tickle the cat's spine whilst it squeaked and cried in slit-eyed ecstasy.

'We may take it that Wong thinks a stroke a hole reasonable,' he said.

'Perhaps we might have a meal somewhere afterwards. And a few drinks. Just the three of us,' he said.

She ruffled his hair.

'There are times, Jim, when you become almost human. Promise me only one thing and I'll sponsor you for husband of the year.'

'We know what she's after, don't we, pal?' he said, quickening the stroking pulse. 'We're not to guzzle more than two bottles of whiskey and a case of stout. Nor will we.'

Her hands fluttered in a small gesture of dismay.

'It's not that at all, darling. You can drink as much as you like. You know I never object. All I want you to do is to be nice to Caroline.'

His heart missed a beat. The stroking hand bore down convulsively on the cat's back.

Wong squealed. The velvet paw resting so innocently on his bare arm fanned out, claws exposed. With a swift movement it raked his arm from elbow to wrist.

'Jeeeesus!' he exclaimed, shoving the cat away roughly.

Still squealing and purring fervently, Wong retreated to the bottom of the bed where, with stiff legs and arched back, it danced ceremoniously on the bedclothes.

He stared at his scored arm in dismay. The three furrows, parallel and widely spaced, were just beginning to sprout blood. He watched as it spread, trickling through the hairs on his arm with little spurts like the zigzagging course of raindrops on a window pane.

'Oh, Jim, I told you so!' she wailed, grabbing up his handkerchief to staunch the blood. 'I warned you not to allow him in the bed. You know I did!'

He looked at her with eyes cold, implacable, sick with hatred.

'I told you so! I told you so!' he mimicked, in a cracked high-pitched voice.

He brushed her hand away. Wearily, bitterly, emphasising each word with upturned shaking head he told the stricken tallow-faced Christ:

'God almighty, how I loathe people who say: "I told you so!"'

Suburban Idyll

MR CHARLES KILLINGLEY HUNTER had no intimations of mortality when he woke for the last time in the front bedroom of 18, Sycamore Avenue (Sem.-det. 3 beds., 2 recs., kitch., sep. lav.) on the Harrington Estate.

At the first elbow-jog in the small of the back he gave a little mew of annoyance, at the second he muttered: 'All right! All right!' and snuggled down lower in the bed. The third was no more painful than usual.

He dragged himself reluctantly from the bed and stood, one foot rubbing the other, moodily eyeing the eiderdowned hummock that was his wife, Amy.

Mr Hunter did not love his wife. He admired her. He respected her. He was even, in an odd stealthy fashion, fond of her. But no emotion, however strong and enduring, could survive twenty years of constant well-intentioned nagging. Bent on swaddling him in safe middle-class respectability, she had patiently moulded him throughout the years, rooting out a dangerous originality here, damping down an awkward indignation there, ever on the alert for the monstrous heresy of vulgarity. At the same time she sought to fill his leisure hours with harmless, and possibly useful, activities. In fact the book he was now studying, with such a puzzled expression, *Yoga—A Way Of Life*, was another of her projects for his betterment. With mounting apprehension he read for the third time the opening of Chapter 3, '*Breath is Life.*'

'Squat down on haunches, legs crossed tailorwise, back erect with hollowed spine, chin raised and eyes fixed on cornice of far wall, hands placed in lotus gesture palm upwards on knees, as in Plate 18—" Brooding Buddha ".'

Gingerly he lowered himself until he was perched painfully on crossed ankles, his body jerking madly around in his efforts to keep from falling. The rest of the instructions—the hollow back, the lifted head, the upturned petitioning palms—were beyond his powers but he compromised by adopting a crouching position with the aid of his fingers outstretched on the floor, looking, with his pink puffy cheeks, bulging eyes and querulous expression, like a squirrel in the throes of cacation.

Placing the open book on the floor, he prepared to follow the injunctions commencing—'*Relax and breathe deeply.*' Diligently he widened his nostrils, moved his lower ribs sideways, impelled the bony structure of his chest outwards and upwards in a fan-like motion but instead of the promised soundless respiration with its resultant sensation of '*oneness with the great rhythm of life and the universe,*' the breath snored in and out through his gaping nostrils with a deplorable whistle and wheeze—a depressing reminder that, in spite of his wife's many warnings, he had not yet seen a nose specialist. By opening his mouth to its fullest extent and breathing very slowly and cautiously, he managed to eliminate much of the nasal whine, but there was still a snoring quality to his breathing that made him glance anxiously at the hunched-up figure in the bed.

At length, his Yoga exercises completed, he should have been safely started on a routine working day. But the Laws of Physics ordained otherwise. It is laid down that a body in motion cannot come into contact with a body at rest without producing a tangible result. In Mr Hunter's case, the skidding of the hearth-rug as he straightened up and the consequent collision of gravity-stricken rump and stationary floorboards produced two results—one constant, one variable—a searing pain at the point of impact, spreading rapidly to the whole lumbar region, and a reduction, by an indeterminate number of years, of his expectation of life.

At Night All Cats Are Grey

He staggered to his feet, clutching the end of the bed for support.

'Blast it!' he squealed. 'Hell rip and roast it!'

'Charles!' A shocked voice came from the bed.

Even in moments of crisis Mrs Hunter never forgot the conduct proper to a lady of breeding and refinement. So now, though sitting bolt upright, tangled hair streeling around her face, peering at him with blinking sleep-gummed eyes, she contrived, by hugging the eiderdown modestly to her bosom, the impression of dignity and decorum, as surely—he thought —on the Day of Judgment she would manage to gather together a tattered decency of burial rags before facing the teeming nakedness of eternity.

'There is no need to be coarse, Charles,' she said. There was only mild reproach in her voice, the tone of an indulgent parent to a badly-spoiled child.

Without a word he whisked out of the room and slammed the door viciously behind him.

Now, just because a creature—a squirrel, for example—is small, weak and inoffensive, it does not follow that its emotions are any the less intense. Its anger may seem to us a scolding grimacing futility, too puny to merit better than derision. But in squirreldom the impotence of the weak is their most dangerous weapon. So it would be foolish to laugh at Mr Hunter as he shaved with wild swooping strokes of his cut-throat razor, chattering furiously at his reflection in the bathroom mirror. True, he may not have been capable of gutting a struggling wife into the hand-basin, but then there are many more ways of choking a dog than stuffing it with butter. The bathroom floor can be splashed, the guest towel used for wiping off a razor, the mirror blobbed with lather. Mr Hunter did all these things, methodically and with a nice regard to detail.

At the door he turned round to survey his handiwork.

'Very tasty,' he muttered.

Suddenly he grabbed up the end of his dressing-gown and commenced to polish the mirror with a scrupulosity that would have gladdened Mrs Hunter's heart. Then with the shaving brush freshly lathered he placed a large creamy blob on the spot where her startled face should be mirrored. He stepped back, head cocked to one side.

'That's better,' he said. 'She'll appreciate that.'

He dressed leisurely and by the time he came down Mrs Hunter had already finished her breakfast.

'What kept you?' she asked. 'It's getting late.'

She was drumming on the table with impatient fingers. Her eyes were still hazy with sleep and there were sleep blotches on her cheeks and forehead. The old-fashioned quilted wrapper, buttoned up, as usual, to her throat, swathed her tiny body in thick clumsy folds from which her tortoise head emerged with uneasy questing distrust.

He looked away.

'Razor pulling badly,' he growled.

She glanced at him sharply as she got to her feet.

'I want you to change some library books for me,' she said, on her way to the door. 'Don't go till I come down with them.'

In Mr Hunter's disturbed state, this remark was fatal, serving only to stoke up the fires of revolt. In consequence, when she returned ten minutes later it was to find that her husband had left without finishing his breakfast and, worse still, without closing the hall door after him.

By this time, Mr Hunter, in the front seat of a city-bound bus, was contemplating the events of the morning with considerable relish. The ease with which he had emerged from the snug cocoon of habit gave him an intoxicating sense of gaiety and irresponsibility. He sat whistling softly through his teeth, occasionally wriggling his shoulders gleefully as if he felt the urge to try out the brilliant wings already stirring under his woollen undervest. Nevertheless he got through his day's work at the office without committing any overt act of mutiny.

Dozing fitfully on his journey back to the Harrington estate, he was jolted awake when the bus braked suddenly and watched, without interest, a herd of cattle go milling past, urged on by the frantic cries of the drovers and the monotonous thud of flailing ash-plants. As the bus was gathering speed once more, he saw the poster. It proclaimed in large, black capitals: ' MILLIONS NOW LIVING WILL NEVER DIE.'

This notion appealed to Mr. Hunter. An earthful of people spared the indignity of dying. Free passes for all. Positively the last performance. Closing down for much-needed repairs. Hardly fair to the paying patrons, though, this issue of complimentary tickets to the Life Everlasting. A much better job to make them all pass through the turnstiles. But, of course, the dead-heads would never know their good fortune until the box-office opened. A nice bit of irony there from the Management Regrets. Poor unfortunates working up an everlasting blood-pressure over the state of their eternal kidneys and immortal gall-bladders. A queer old how-do-you-do if they found out. Letters from irate clergymen, indignant G.P.'s and numerous shocked citizens. Threat to the very foundation of the state. Menace to our youth. Violation of the Natural Law. Government promises early legislation. Mortality tests visualised. Probably finish up belting hell out of each other to find out which of them was immortal. Still it would not be a bad way to quit, a mass migration into secula seculorum. Like the lemmings. Millions of little bobbing muzzles swimming close together for company. Just drop out when you are tired. Muzzle behind moves up one.

These speculations occupied him till he reached home and, even there, continued to distract him. During tea he hardly

spoke a word, contenting himself with an occasional grunt
from behind his propped-up newspaper. Whilst his wife was
washing up, he sat in an armchair at the fire, an open book on
his lap, considering the endless possibilities of an orthodox
Doomsday. Soon he was fast asleep.

Returned from the kitchen, Mrs Hunter had still much to
say. But she was prepared to wait. She was one of those who
believe in timing, with exquisite precision, the most insignifi-
cant disclosure, the better to inject its dry bones with the
potency of revelation. All the same, she was annoyed. She
had a feeling that he had gone to sleep deliberately, guessing
that there was something important she wished to tell him.
It was all of a piece with his childish behaviour of the morning. Perched primly on the edge of the chair, she waited,
glancing up occasionally from her knitting with an exasper-
ated frown.

He woke with a startled gurgling cry, sending the book flying to the floor with his jerking limbs.

'Did you have a nice sleep, darling?' she asked.

He squinted up at the clock.

'Surely it's not that time?' He knuckled his eyes. 'I must
have dozed off.'

'I didn't like to waken you. You must be very tired. After
last night, I mean. Though I slept through it all myself.'

He stared at her, stupidly.

'Mrs Grant of 23 told me she did not sleep a wink. She
said it was disgraceful. Really, Charles, something should be
done about it.'

'I—I—I beg your pardon,' he said.

She waited, savouring to the full the delicious apocalyptic
moment. She leaned forward.

'That creature gave another of her parties last night!' She
spoke in capital letters.

Oh God, he thought, here we go again.

' Who?' he asked.

' Don't be difficult, Charles. You know perfectly well who I mean. That dreadful woman from Number 62.'

' Mrs—Mrs—the lady with the foreign name?'

' Yes. It lasted till nearly daybreak. A regular drunken orgy. Singing and shouting at the top of their voices. Mrs Grant said they seemed to be throwing glasses at each other.'

' But, Amy— '

' She recognised some of the voices, too. You would be surprised to know who they were. It is abominable the way she is allowed to carry on. A woman like that...'

Mr Hunter settled back in his seat and tried to concentrate on a moth that was cruising round the shade of the standard lamp, letting the familiar biographical torrent flow over him.

A vulgar hussy. Posing as a married woman. No more in wedlock than the Queen of Sheba. Her house a scandal to a respectable neighbourhood. Strange men calling at all hours of the day and night. Even married men from the estate.

The moth was now whirling madly around inside the lamp shade, shuttling back and forth between the scorching bulb-glass and the taut plastic.

Silly little fool, he thought. Getting wrought up over nothing.

' What can we do?' he asked.

' Complain to the Authorities. Have her flung out on the street. Mrs Grant says— '

' Never mind that venomous old witch. She'll only get you into trouble.'

' And what do you propose, pray?'

' If you feel compelled to protest, why not ask the lady to call and thrash the whole thing out over a friendly cup of tea?'

She stared at him, open-mouthed.

' Do you realise what you are saying?' she demanded.

'Invite that creature here? To a respectable God-fearing house? I can assure you, Charles, she'll never set foot in this house. Never.'

'A common article from the back streets of some foreign city,' she said.

'The very idea of it,' she said.

Mr Hunter got to his feet. This situation required firm handling.

'Look here, Amy,' he said. 'I don't give a damn if she came all the way from Sodam or Gomorrah. You've no right to blacken the poor woman's character just because she's a giddy young tit of a foreigner. No wonder there are married men visiting her if their wives go on the way you do. Talk like that would put notions into any man's head.'

He allowed his voice to rise.

'It would fit you better to be preparing for the next world instead of retailing the gossip of this one.'

Her attention was caught at once.

'I don't understand, Charles.'

'There are some very disturbing rumours circulating in the city,' he said, in a grave pompous voice.

'What about?'

'Oh! There's probably no truth in it. Just another ball of smoke. Still, I got it from a reliable source. A senior official in the Department.'

'Will you stop dithering, Charles, and come to the point?'

You're well and truly hooked, darling, he congratulated himself. I'll just give you a wee race up and down the pool before I land you out on the bank.

'Apparently during the past few weeks there has been a wild scramble on the Stock Exchange and on the property market. It has been kept out of the newspapers, of course. For fear it might start a run on the Banks.'

He paused to see how she was taking it.

'Good gracious!' she exclaimed.

'People have been selling their stocks and shares, their houses, their land. Even their motor cars and furniture. Turning everything they can lay hands on into cash. Where buyers could not be found, they have borrowed from the Banks.'

He noted her awestruck expression with satisfaction. Now for the facts. There can never be enough facts. Tall, thick, creamy facts.

'I know one man, a car salesman, who surrendered his children's life policies and pawned his wife's jewellery. It's common knowledge—'

'But why?' she interrupted. 'Why, Charles?'

'To give away, of course. To the poor and the afflicted.'

'To . . . the poor . . .'

'Yes. Some madman or other has prophesied that a great calamity is about to happen. Perhaps an explosion of some sort. Or another Deluge. At any rate the fly boys in the city are making sure they will be on the right side if Gabriel blows the long whistle for full time. You know what it says in the Bible about giving away all your worldly gear?'

The puzzled frown on her face deepened.

'Is this your idea of a joke?' she demanded.

'One of the wealthiest men in the city has given away everything he possesses. Down to his very clothes. He goes around in an old boiler-suit. Probably thinks he can peel it off quicker on the Day of Judgment.'

'How perfectly ridiculous! Giving away clothes! Wearing dungarees! You can't be serious, Charles?'

'Amy, dear,' he said, trying to make his voice sound as reasonable as possible. 'You surely don't mean to present yourself at the Seat of Judgment all dressed up in your Sunday best. I'm afraid that would never do at all. Such a vulgar display of modesty would look terribly out-of-place with the neighbours all running around in their pelts. No, darling.

Naked you came into the world and out you must go the same way.'

'Charles—'

He went on remorselessly:

'I really believe, Amy, that if the Trumpet did sound you would make me put on fresh socks, vest and longjohns before allowing me to face my Maker.'

He gave a great shout of laughter.

Mrs Hunter glared at him, the expression on her face a mixture of fury, shock and bewilderment.

'There is no need for this display of rudeness and vulgarity. Surely, after all these years you could show more sense of responsibility. Making me the butt of your stupid jokes. Jeering at your religion and the very God that made you.'

'I am sorry, Amy,' he said gently. 'I only meant to tease you. I thought it would be a relief for all hands if I changed the subject from the Scarlet Woman of Sycamore Avenue.'

He gave her a friendly pat on the head before he moved away. At the door he turned round:

'If it is any consolation to you, darling, every day is a Last Day for some poor devil.'

'Where are you going, Charles?' she called after him.

'Out for a walk,' he shouted back from the hall.

'But surely not at this time of night. It's long after your usual—'

He closed the door firmly on the rest of the sentence.

It was a clear starry night with a bite of frost in the air. Already a thin skin of ice was beginning to form on the rain-soaked road. Mr Hunter stepped out briskly. He was feeling pleased with himself. Every few steps he chuckled softly at the memory of his wife's puzzled face. It must have seemed to her that the worm, not satisfied with turning, had reared up and sunk its fangs in her. Taken by and large it was an occasion for a quiet celebration.

At Night All Cats Are Grey

In the saloon bar just outside the entrance to the estate he sat contentedly on his own, slowly drinking his three bottles of stout whilst he listened idly to the meaningless roar of conversation. He was not to know that the loud voice proceeding from the neighbouring snug—a drunken, aggressive, sports-car-owning-voice belonged to one whose chief mission in life was the destruction of Mr Hunter himself, for which purpose Providence—as fond of a joke as the next one—was even now tempering its chosen instrument with balls of malt and chasers of beer.

Mr Hunter left the pub before closing time. The road back through the estate, much used as a short cut by drunks returning to the city, was at this hour deserted, and he strolled along, lulled to a pleasant stupor by the few drinks and the peaceful quiet of the night. Turning into Sycamore Avenue, he started across the roadway, his feet mechanically taking the long diagonal approach to No. 18. He paid no attention to the approaching whine of a car and was half-way across when the beam of the headlights swung round the corner, mowing down a great swathe of darkness.

It was all over in a few seconds. Trapped in the glare of light he hesitated for a fatal second, then made a wild plunge for the pavement at the last moment. But for the icy road he would have made it. As it was, his slipping feet, working with the lunatic fury of a circus clown, carried him as far as the gutter.

The skidding car, as it roared past, only struck him a glancing blow. But it was enough. Mr Hunter was sent hurtling into eternity, badly denting a front mudguard, smashing through a pair of unlatched wooden entrance gates, ploughing up a newly-scuffed garden path and coming finally to rest in a bed of dwarf dahlias, during the course of which he sustained what are euphemistically called 'multiple injuries.'

*　*　*

Though Mrs Hunter's forebodings of a bad ending to a nasty day were merely confirmed by the shuffling footsteps on the gravel path and the loud whispering in the porch, she was unprepared for the squalid spectacle that confronted her when she opened the front door. The four dreadful characters, shabby, ill-favoured men, all far gone in drink if she was any judge, standing cap to mouth in a grotesque attitude of sorrow, their free hands gripping the supports of what looked like a camp-bed: the little throng of loafers watching curiously at the gate: the shapeless figure covered by a tattered army blanket, with a muddy, dented and madly-incongruous soft hat placed like a plumed helmet on a slain warrior's bier —this sight was not the high tragedy that Mrs Hunter would have wished.

The opening lines of a poem she had learnt at school came echoing back to her with hateful irony:

> *' Home they brought her warrior dead:*
> *She not swooned, nor uttered cry—'*

She had often pictured the tragic scene. The torches blazing in the courtyard. The sombre circle of defeated soldiery and loud-wailing women. The four tall bare-headed stalwarts, slowly mounting the castle steps, bearing aloft with awful dignity the body of their dead chieftain. At the top of the steps she stood, a tiny waiting figure, framed in the light from the open doorway, her chin defiantly upraised, her eyes tearless, the only signs of her anguish the clenching white-knuckled hands gripping her skirt.

The wretched reality appalled her. Overwhelmed by the magnitude of this social and personal disaster, she remained standing speechless at the door, until one of the bearers, as if in answer to an unspoken question, said in a deep slurred voice:

' He's in very poor shape, ma'am.'

Someone at the gate gave a suppressed titter. She pulled herself together and stepped back.

Only when they commenced to ease their burden into the narrow hall, did she realise how drunk they were. They shuffled forward, taking the hall mats with them, their movements as unco-ordinated as jerking puppets. One man staggered against the grandfather clock, setting weights, pendulum and striker clanging and for a couple of heart-beats Mrs Hunter feared that the tall swaying mass would come crashing down, bringing living and dead in dreadful confusion to the floor.

'Easy does it, chum!' said the deep voice. 'Keep your end level or you'll spill him.'

At length they came to a halt, gazing at her with red-eyed enquiry.

'Where will we leave him, Missus?' someone enquired.

As if he was a piano, she thought bitterly. She glanced quickly around. Not the sitting-room. Nor the dining-room. And certainly they were not tramping upstairs with their great dirty hob-nailed boots.

'Until the bedroom is made ready, perhaps you had better put—'

She broke off in confusion. Should she say 'the corpse'? Or perhaps 'the body' would be better. It was too soon yet to speak of him as 'Mr Hunter'. And to use the word 'it' might sound callous and unfeeling. Though, goodness knows, it would be justified. Making a public spectacle of her. She would not be one bit surprised if it was all done on purpose.

In desperation she pointed to the kitchen.

'In there', she said.

When the camp-bed, with its shrouded occupant, was placed with drunken exactitude against one wall, the men stood around, cap in hand, waiting patiently.

What was she to do now? Tip them? There was only small

silver and coppers in her handbag. There would surely be change in the trouser pocket. But that was out of the question. Offer them a drink? Most certainly not. They had far too much taken already.

'How did it happen?' she asked.

They all started to explain at once.

'A terrible business, Ma'am—'

'Another few steps and he was right as the mail—'

'Shocking altogether—'

'The poor man hadn't a chance—'

'It's a terror to the world—'

The deep-voiced man leaned towards her confidentially:

'It's my belief, Missus, that the bowsie in that car was rightly scuttered. In the horrors of drink, I'd swear.' His warm beery breath fanned her cheek. She tried not to flinch from the earnest birsey red face. 'He followed your husband right up onto the pavement. He must have thought he was coursing a hare.'

She gave a polite excuse-me nod and moved away—a glossy magazine hostess dealing tactfully with her fractious guests.

But in the small kitchen there was little room for man-oeuvre and she found herself standing beside the improvised stretcher, looking down at the blanketed form of her late husband.

The men were now talking together, ignoring her completely. This abominable rudeness, this brutal flouting of the quiet decencies of convention was an outrage beyond all sense or reason.

You planned all this, Charles Hunter, she whispered. You did it deliberately. Just to humiliate me.

Behind her the voices had become raised, as if an argument had broken out. They seemed to have become much drunker all of a sudden. Perhaps it was the heat of the kitchen. They were weaving around, grabbing each other by elbow or lapel, shouting into each other's faces, gesticulating in wild abandon.

A hoarse voice dominated the rest.

'He was stepping off the pavement when he was struck. Doesn't it stand to common sense?'

A shrill reedy voice piped up:

'I tell you you're wrong. He was struck going in.'

The deep voice joined in:

'That's right. Didn't the bloody car try to follow him in the gate?'

'What gate?' Mrs Hunter demanded.

Hoarse voice continued:

'He was lying on his back, wasn't he? If he was hit going in the gate he'd have been sent ass over tip on his mouth and nose. There's no two ways about it, he was hit leaving the house.'

'What house?' she asked.

Reedy voice was still unconvinced.

'Wouldn't they have to roll him over on his back to see who was in it?'

'No need of that. Wouldn't she know him at once and he only after leaving?'

'Who would?' Mrs Hunter faltered.

Deep voice was speaking in her ear again.

'It was an awful shock for her, too, Ma'am. She was carrying on like one demented. You could hardly make out a word she was saying.'

A hand plucked her sleeve.

'Excuse me, lady. D'you want to have a dekko at him? He's as peaceful-looking as a new-born babby.'

Without waiting for a reply, hoarse voice pulled down the blanket and spoke back over his shoulder.

'Judge for yourselves, lads. Not a bloody scratch. And the back of his poll like a butcher's shop. D'you still want to make out he was struck going in?'

Mrs Hunter gazed horror-stricken at the changeling she had cherished these twenty years. The grey austere face, the lips curled to a thin sneer of contempt, the wide-open eyes fixed in an implacable stare, the eyebrow twisted up by the brutal fury of death into a gesture of mocking irony—these were the features of a stranger.

Deep voice was still talking.

' Sure you'd nearly have thought it was her own man was slaughtered, the way she took on. Crying and screeching and wringing her hands. And then insisting on coming over here to help you out when she got tidied up. She's a real lady, that one, Ma'am. Not a mean bone in her body. You'd know by the way she lashed the drink into us that the breeding was there. Though I'd say she was a class of a foreigner by the cut of her jib.'

' What lady?' she asked, not really expecting an answer.

She felt that a thick fog of confusion and misunderstanding and ignorance and downright wickedness was closing in around her so that she had difficulty in attaching any significance to the knot of pushing, staggering men or any meaning to their senseless outcry.

A painful nudge in the side brought her back to awareness. The deep voice hissed a warning:

' Here she is now, Ma'am!'

For a moment she panicked, but the years of self-discipline stood her in good stead.

Straightening herself up, her chin held high, she faced the open door—a lonely figure, small and appealing in the amber glow of the spot light, waiting in the castle porch, dry-eyed, unvanquished, ever preserving the dignified restraint that was the hall-mark of a lady of breeding and refinement. Beyond in the torch-lit courtyard the clamour of defeat arose in a wild tumult of intemperate shouts and fierce troopers' oaths. A struggle seemed to be going on—there was the sound of blows, grunts of pain and the crash of sprawling bodies. A voice bellowed, ' Give over, for Jazuz sake! Can't yous behave like Christians in a bucking wake-house!'

She took a single step forward.

' It is good of you to call, Mademoiselle,' she said, in a loud affected voice. ' But there really was no need. These gentlemen have been most helpful.'

The Lake

(1)

'Well!' Mac says, 'This is the place!'

He sounds pleased with himself.

'What d'ye think of it Jim?' he asks.

We are standing on the edge of a huge crater hollowed out of the mountain ridge we have just climbed. Below us, a thousand feet or more, is a dark rock-strewn valley walled in by towering slopes. Massive boulders are scattered around higgledy-piggledy—a crazy pavement of grey rock that runs round a small lake, fans out and piles itself up in a jagged barrier choking the gap that is the only entrance. The crater has a raw lacerated look as though some great beast had flung itself on the mountain slashing and tearing gobbets of rock from its flanks in savage fury. The tiny pin-points of white that are grazing sheep might be maggots crawling on an open wound: the lake, brown and still, a smear of clotted blood. Gigantic shadows roll across the valley, dashing themselves in a smother of sunlight against the slopes facing us.

'You certainly picked a choice spot,' I say.

'Bloody apt I did. Yer man'll stay roosting down there till the crack of doom and damn the one'll be a bit the wiser.'

He grins delightedly.

I try to place the bare-gummed smile. A glass-tank. The green-glow of scummy water. A long grey shadow, dull-eyed jutty-lipped, nuzzling at the glass.

'And what's the lay-out like?' I ask.

He squats down, rummages round in his pockets and flings across a packet of fags.

'It's like this. There's an old sheep-track runs up from the

road and in at the butt of yon pass. A bare mile of easy going.
We could be in and out of here with the job done in under
two hours. And mark ye, not a sinner lives within five solid
miles of where ye stand. Sure, man alive, it was created for
the job.'

A pike, that's what he is. An amiable dull-witted black-
murdering pike.

There's forty foot of water if there's an inch in yon lake.
Forty foot of ould bog-water that ye couldn't see a stymy
through. And I've got tucked away under a heap of stones a
ten foot length of anchor chain and a bloody great iron bar
as thick as yer arm. Enough to sink an elephant, let alone a
Christian. Man, he'll never rise till the Day of Judgment,
that's certain sure. Now what d'ye think, Jim?"

' I think you're a cold-blooded sod,' I say.

He gapes up at me.

' What's bitin' ye anyway?' he asks.

I drop down beside him on the broad of my back, hands
locked behind my head. I have to close my eyes against the
glare of the sun.

' I don't like this job,' I say. ' It's a dirty business.'

' It stinks,' I say.

He lets out a great neigh of a laugh.

' Oh, lovely jazus,' he says. ' Would ye for Christ's sake look
what's talkin'? The hard man himself. Listen to this, will
yez . . .'

I hear him clear his throat.

' It stinks! It stinks!' he says in a high nasal voice.

He whinnies again. I feel his hand grip my knee.

' Is it coddin' me ye are? Puttin' on a bloody act or
what?'

' It's a dirty business,' I say. ' Riddling a man and sinking
his body underwater as though it were the carcase of a mangy
dog. One of our own crowd, too.'

'But what would ye have us do? Give him a blank wall and a firing squad?'

'It might not be a bad idea.'

'Well, I like that. Of all the girning, contrary . . .'

He spits noisily.

'Listen here, Jim. It's the bloody Government makes the rules of this game. Not us. Aren't the jails of this country stuffed with prisoners whose only crime is being good honest Republicans? Aren't they tryin' to smash the Movement with every kind of blackguardism? Couldn't ye hunger-strike till the walls of yer belly met other and not a one know ye were even in jail? I tell ye we're bloody outlaws—that's what we are. This is the only way the fight can go on.'

The sun beats down on my face and seeps through my eyelids. I feel too lazy and contented to reply. What is there to say anyhow? Mac has all the answers—match force against force, cunning against cunning, secrecy against secrecy. No use telling him that it is merely evil vindicated by evil. And that it will go on and on until nothing is left but a hard core of bitter hatred.

A cloud passes across the sun, stroking my face with a cold hand. Perhaps we have already reached the stage where growth ceases and all chance of broadening out into something massive and urgent has gone for ever.

I fling away my cigarette and sniff at my fingers savouring the rich tang of smoke-scorched flesh.

'You're wrong, Mac,' I say. 'As well might you piss against the wind and start calling down Heaven to witness the spatters.'

'So ye'd have us sit down on our backsides and never so much as stir a hip to stop an ould skin-the-goat from rattin' on us? Oh, there's only the one cure for them boys—the bloody lead. That's the medicine for them.'

'But are you sure he *is* an informer?'

'Wasn't the hoor court-martialled? Isn't that a fair enough crack of the whip for any man?'

I open my eyes. A gull floats belly up on the surface of the sky. I wait till it glides past the sun with only the tip of a wing scorched. I say:

'Can't you for once in your life form an opinion of your own? You know the man's record as well as I do. Through the whole racket from '16 on. Not a labour dispute or a bit of land agitation but he'd have to be in it up to the neck. In and out of jail as often as fingers and toes. And when he wasn't in the Joy or the Glass-House or in Arbour Hill he was being kicked out of one job after another because of his activities. This is the man you're so sure is an informer. Why, if they couldn't batter information out of him each time he was arrested, is it likely he'll slobber up anything now for a few lousy bob?'

'But the court-martial . . .'

'It be damned. Sitting in smug judgment with us to do its dirty work.'

'What's the use of talkin' that way, Jim? Aren't we only doin' our duty as soldiers of the Republic? You're not meanin' to forsake yer principles because the goin' gets rough. Sure a man's life is a small thing when . . .'

'Bullshit,' I say.

I roll over on to my stomach and wriggle forward to the lip of the crater.

The gun in my pocket presses against my groin.

Queer how much the lake seems to resembled an eye—a grotesque disembodied eye like the Cyclopean all-seeing eye of God that used to stare down at me from a holy picture in my bedroom—at night cold and antagonistic; in the morning with a knowing, malicious, I-told-you-so sneer.

I say to myself:

Hump you, I'll bloody soon wipe that look off your dial.

And I raise myself on my elbows, slip out the gun and let drive. The bullet drills a neat hole in the smooth water, the delayed sound of the impact coming up to me with a startled phut. Like a grunt of annoyance. I'll swear on the Book that the sleek tawny surface gave a startled blink.

Mac jumps up.

' God blast yer maggoty sowl, are ye gone mad?" he shouts. ' D'ye want to have the whole countryside in on top of us?'

' What d'ye think ye're doin', anyway?' he asks.

' Oh, just a bit of target practice for tonight,' I say.

And I let fly again. I don't let up until I've emptied the revolver into the lake. Each time I fire I seem to reach down effortlessly and tease the water with a flicking fingertip. A feeling of power and immensity grips me. The giant shadow sprawled out across the crater is my own. I have but to crouch down for sunlight to come foaming back, or stand erect for my shadow to darken the land.

I get to my feet.

' Would you believe it, Mac,' I say. ' I've got an arm as long as ever reached down out of the sky.'

' We'll go,' I say.

Mac scratches his head.

' Christ, ye're the odd bloody fowl,' he says.

(2)

We trudge along in silence—the prisoner in front, Mac and I a few paces behind. At first we walked abreast but when the path commenced to narrow, winding in and out amongst the rocks, the two of us dropped back. There was no danger of the prisoner getting away—a full moon and a clear sky took care of that—but to be certain I knotted one end of a length of rope to his bound wrists, holding the other end myself in

my left hand, the other gripping the gun in my pocket. It was
a mistake. If the rope goes slack for an instant he pulls up,
frozen into the tense attitude of a pointer. He remains like that,
his whole body clenched in expectation, until I give a chuck
at the rope and shout:

'Get going, blast you.'

Then he throws back his shoulders defiantly and moves off
again.

I try keeping the rope taut. Immediately he quickens his
stride. It is as though the steady drag of the rope, twisting
his bound arms back from his shoulders, is at once a menace
urging him forward and a temporary guarantee of safety. He
steps it out bravely with an insolent swagger to his shoulders.

Everything assumes the fantastic logic of a dream. One
moment I am trying to check a wild Gadarene rush towards
destruction: the next it is myself who is being dragged along
bewildered and protesting.

I try to concentrate. I tell myself:

'You've got to plug this bowzie. A .45 bullet in the back of
the poll and the job is done. Quick and clean. That's all there
is to it.'

But my thoughts keep coming back to the rope. It sets up
a curious intimacy between myself and the man I am to kill.
It is an umbilical cord linking us together, fusing our separate
thoughts and feelings into a single consciousness.

I feel my blood pounding through his veins. There is a
gnawing pain at the back of my skull as though the casing
of bone is stripped away exposing a palpitating web of shrink-
ing tissue. My arms are tearing at their sockets; my wrists
numb; my neck stiff from the effort of not looking back. I keep
my gaze fixed on the path ahead but I cannot escape the casual
beauty of the night—a star swinging below the moon, the
sweep of the mountain black against the sky, the delicate
moon-shadow of a leafless tree. Alert for the click of a cocked

hammer, I catch the furtive scamperings and rustlings, the tiny comings and goings of the mountain. I am intensely aware of my own body. It brushes against my clothes like a kitten, neglected and importunate. I should like to press my cheek against the warm skin of my shoulder or run the palms of my hands down my flanks or grip a scruff of plump belly-flesh and feel the taut muscles beneath.

A snipe gets up with a screech and a rush of wings. I jerk back on the rope.

' Sorry,' I say.

Then:

' Come on! Keep going!'

We move off again towards the gap, the prisoner striding along with the same jaunty swagger.

I find myself keeping in step. Even placing my foot down where he has just trodden.

I shorten my stride and half-close my eyes, allowing myself to be led along like a blind man. I count a hundred paces and look up. I am back in step again.

I pick out a rock a long way ahead and guess the distance. Now, I decide, I shall not look up until I am level with it. I commence to count. Before I reach five hundred my gaze drifts up. The barrier of rock is only a few minutes distant.

The muscles of my legs go slack and the increasing tension settles in a warm lump in the pit of my stomach. I wonder if he feels the same way. Probably does. Kidneys loosening up too. Probably wetting himself by now.

At this I become aware of my own urgent physical need. The gnawing discomfort helps to steady me. There is even something funny in the thought of the three of us, lined up, shoulder to shoulder, as we pumpship against a rock. You could hardly shoot a man after that.

A hundred yards more.

A dark cloud slides across the moon. Mac flashes on his

torch, cutting down the beam with a cupped hand. It lights up the shabby coat, the frayed trouser-ends, the patched shoes. A hole gapes in one sock. At every step the ill-fitting shoe slides up and down emphasising the stained unlovely flesh.

I won't do it, I swear. So help me God, I won't do it.

The torch flicks off. Ahead lies the lake—a smooth sheet of polished steel rimmed with moon-bleached rock.

An elbow is dug into my ribs. I can barely hear the whisper:

'Now!'

At the same moment the man swings round and faces me, whipping the rope out of my hand.

'Ye cowardly bastard,' he says.

I don't even know that I've drawn the gun till I feel it leap in my hand. The bullet must have grazed a bone, for it whines away across the lake with the sound of ripping calico.

He remains facing me, standing stiffly erect, feet sprawled apart, his face white and featureless against the dark background of the mountain, the lake draped across his shoulders like a billowing silver cloak.

'Ye cowardly little rat,' he says.

I let him have it. The bullet goes home with a crunching kind of thump—like you drove your boot into a bag of meal. His mouth gapes open in a black soundless scream. His arms and shoulders jerk violently. You would swear for all the world that he is a great bird flapping pinioned wings in an effort to get off the ground.

All at once the knees buckle under him and he slithers to the ground. He starts to scream—a thin wisp of sound like the whining of a peevish child. He drums his heels in the ground.

Mac is shouting:

'Do something! For Christ's sake do something!'

I see and hear all this, but it means nothing to me. Inside

me is a cool, spacious emptiness. I am strong and light and spare—gutted clean of emotion. I am only aware of one thing —the limp, yielding beauty of the lake. It stirs up something inside me that I cannot control. I want to strip off my clothes and wade in, very, very slowly, letting it creep up my thighs, my belly, my chest. Up over my closed mouth and wide-open eyes until I am silvered over from head to feet. I want to slip down into the womb of the lake where there exists no impulse to feel or think or act; where there is nothing but a dim swaying silence.

The twisting grotesque is still screaming: the other is down on his benders. Praying.

Home - airy - mur - gaw - pray - frus - inner - noun - tower - death - men.

Gabble and whimper become one unbearable irrelevancy.

I go over to the writhing figure, I pour shot after shot into it. I keep jerking the trigger even after the revolver is empty. And all the time I keep shouting:

'Shut up, you bloody slob!'

Not knowing which of the two I mean until at last there is nothing left but the night and the black jaws of the mounain—and the lake. The kneeling man looks up at me. In the moonlight I can see his eyes flickering rapidly from side to side as though they are loose in their sockets.

I fling down the gun and start running towards the lake.

I run as in a dream—flying with gigantic strides on sluggish leaden feet. Drawn irresistibly forward and just as powerfully held back. Dreamways the ground keeps pace with me. I seem to make no headway. As well might I be ploughing through a snow-drift or a bank of cloud.

I feel tired. All the strength and certainty has left me.

I lean against a boulder, my head whirling dizzily.

My left arm is numb. Aching abominably. I stare down stupidly. It is held out stiffly in front of me, the fist clenched, the thumb still pressing down on a non-existent rope.

The emptiness fills up inside me with a sickening rush. I press my forehead against the cool surface of the rock, teeth gritted, eyes squeezed tight, fighting down the choking waves of loathing and nausea. I hate myself and every living creature. I hate the loyalties and prejudices that bring us buzzing together like dung-flies. I hate the night and the mountain and the pale-faced bitch of a lake. All that has happened tonight will mean no more to her than a splash and a few fugitive ripples—the merest shadow of a frown of disgust on the lovely ageless face.

My knees are shaking, my eyes scalded, I keep gulping down mouthfuls of bile.

Mac is beside me. He says:

' Ye're a hard man all right, Jim. Ye made a proper butcher's shop of him.'

' Well,' he says. ' We'd better be startin' in if we're to have his nibs dumped before mornin'.'

My stomach gives a final heave and I retch up the griping bitterness inside me.

I feel his arm firm across my shoulders. I hear him murmuring to himself.

' Ho-ly God! Oh, Ho-ly God!'

He starts slapping my back vigorously.

' Spit it up, lad. It's better out than chokin' ye.'

He stops. His fingers drum a tattoo on the back of my neck.

' Bejazus, ye're an odd duck surely,' he says.